His breath was warm and his breathing rapid as he rested his face between her breasts. Sliding her fingers through his hair, she pressed his face into the soft valley, loving the shudder of heightened intimacy that passed through him.

Drew's heart was pounding deafeningly in her ears. She had never asked a man to make love to her before. In fact she had spent her first marriage avoiding the prospect with all of her energies. And now she was at a loss of what to do.

"Rolf? I don't want you to go."

"Do you want me to sleep here?" He sounded doubtful. "I can't spend the night here beside you just sleeping. I'm no saint, Drew."

"I don't want you to be a saint, Rolf."

Dear Reader,

It is our pleasure to bring you a new experience in reading that goes beyond category writing. The settings of **Harlequin American Romance** give a sense of place and culture that is uniquely American, and the characters are warm and believable. The stories are of "today" and have been chosen to give variety within the vast scope of romance fiction.

Renee Roszel clearly defines what the word freedom means in both passion and physical presence on two continents. Drew McKenna and Rolf Erhardt will lead you on a journey of unsuspecting attraction and strange devotion that will leave you breathless and surprisingly satisfied.

From the early days of Harlequin, our primary concern has been to bring you novels of the highest quality. **Harlequin American Romance** is no exception. Enjoy!

Vivian Stephens

Vivian Stephens
Editorial Director
Harlequin American Romance
919 Third Avenue,
New York, N.Y. 10022

Hostage Heart

RENEE ROSZEL

Harlequin Books

TORONTO • NEW YORK • LOS ANGELES • LONDON
AMSTERDAM • PARIS • SYDNEY • HAMBURG
STOCKHOLM • ATHENS • TOKYO • MILAN

To the two that gave me life,
and to the many that fill it.

Published June 1983

First printing April 1983

ISBN 0-373-16010-0

Prologue

"You've played your little game. Now I'm coming to get you," the letter ended. Drew sat for a long moment without moving, staring at the brief note until the familiar heavy-handed script blurred before her. Then, with a sudden unreasoning need to be rid of the written threat, she tore the page in half and let it drop to her desk.

Jim was coming! After all this time of silence, he was coming! Heaving a ragged sigh, she brought the heels of her hands up to her eyes. As she did, she realized that her head was moving slowly from side to side, unconsciously negating, rejecting the very idea. He couldn't really mean to come here, to Los Alamos, and drag her back to San Francisco.

"No!" she breathed, a cloying unease shrouding her like a damp wool blanket.

"No?"

Drew jerked her head around to her office door, surprised to see Gladys Sims, her boss, peering in, the ever-present grin splitting her round face. "I never figured you for a yes-man, Drew, but you really *should* have the decency to wait for the questions before you say no." Her wink was as quick as her wit.

Drew smiled a bit weakly at the older woman and tried to make her greeting sound light-hearted. "Hi, Glad, come in." Her success was minimal. She could see that clearly in the concern that suddenly clouded her superior's eyes.

Gladys's grin faded slightly as she stepped into the small, but comfortably furnished office. Cocking her graying coiffure toward the torn letter lying in front of

Drew, she asked, "I know it isn't my business, Drew, but is that bad news?"

Shaking her head, Drew picked up the torn page and dropped it into the wicker basket beside her desk. "It's nothing." She worked on her smile. No matter how inwardly shaken she was by Jim's threat, she couldn't bear to talk about it to anyone. Sitting back, she crossed her arms, hoping that she would appear at ease before querying, "What can I do for you?"

The statuesque woman moved toward the desk with characteristic briskness, "Well, since you asked... " Holding out a folder filled with yellow, legal size pages, she explained, "Dr. Mott's paper on his magnetic fusion research is ready for editing, you lucky gal." She grinned and dropped the clutter of rumpled pages in front of Drew.

Gladys's theatrics always managed to take Drew off guard, and she felt a bit of her tenseness ease. Pulling a wry face, Drew made a real effort to join in the fun. "Has the good doctor discovered the joys of punctuation since his last paper?"

Gladys's laugh was almost masculine in its depth, and she waved a braceleted hand negatively. "Heavens no! What you have there, Drew, is *one* seventeen-page sentence."

Gladys's lively personality was infectious, and Drew's smile was now almost genuine. She lifted her shoulders in an exaggerated shrug. "Well, I suppose if Dr. Mott is willing to try to solve the world's energy problems, I can at least attempt to correct his punctuation crisis."

"And you'll be a lead-pipe cinch for the Nobel Punctuation Prize." She flicked the folder with her index finger. "What a grandiose mess that thing is." Almost as an afterthought, she added, "Say, with *your* Nobel, you and your father will be a two-Nobel family!"

Drew laughed in spite of her dour mood. "I'll try to be as humble when I accept mine as Dad was."

Gladys shook her head doubtfully. "Nope, I'm afraid

your daddy pretty much invented humility. Besides''— she swept Drew with an appraising look—''beautiful redheads never do as well with humility as bashful doctors of physics.''

Drew felt her cheeks grow warm with the light compliment. Deciding a subject change was in order, she opened the folder and began to thumb through the questionable scrawl. ''This is written in Greek, no doubt.''

Gladys leaned over her shoulder and her chuckle gurgled near Drew's ear. ''My guess was ancient Babylonian.'' She patted Drew's shoulder. ''Remember, you are my only physicist-journalist on staff.'' She straightened. ''If you didn't want to deal with eccentric professor types, you shouldn't have wasted all that time in school getting a masters in journalism and physics.''

''Now she tells me.'' Drew shook her head, grinning. ''You live and learn. And one thing I've learned,'' she added with a sigh, ''is that I should have taken some courses in the handwriting *reading* of doctors. Look at this''—she pointed—''it either says, 'tomahawk reunion planned,' or 'tokamak reactor plasma.' ''

Without a moment's pause, Gladys tossed back easily, ''Go with either. I like them both.''

Drew smiled, but didn't look up. As associate editor for the *Los Alamos Scientific Monthly*, a sleek magazine highly regarded in the scientific community, she was accustomed to rewriting the ungrammatical articles compiled by scientists at this New Mexico government installation. This latest project was no more of a problem than most. And though she was prepared for Gladys's seemingly offhanded attitude, she knew from experience that this easygoing manner was not to be confused with disinterest or lack of expertise. With a doctorate in both chemistry and journalism, Gladys Sims, managing editor of the *Scientific Monthly*, was not a woman to be taken lightly in either field.

Drew could hear her boss's heels click toward the door, and realized that she was leaving as she tossed the

last of her instructions over her shoulder. "I'm assign-
ing Beverly to do the color illustrations. After you
translate that gobbledygook into readable prose, tell her
what drawings you'll need."

"Right." Drew closed the folder as the office door
clicked shut. Sitting forward, she put her elbows on the
desk and allowed herself a deep sigh. The letter from
Jim had been a shock, and pretending calm before her
boss had been draining. She drummed nervous fingers
on the folder, clenching and unclenching her teeth in
agitation. The last sentence of Jim's letter ran, once
again, through her mind: *"I'm coming to get you."*
With suddenly trembling fingers, she flipped her desk
calendar from Monday, March 2 to Friday, March 6,
when Jim had said he would arrive—only four days
away. *Four days!* The reality clutched at her like piercing talons of a hawk. Why couldn't he accept the fact
that it was over between them? She'd thought, hoped,
she was finally free. Obviously she had been wrong.
Wincing at the buildup of emotions within her, she
slammed a fist on Dr. Mott's helpless folder, crying out
with a seething hatred, "Why, Jim? Why must you tor-
ture me?"

Her body was taut with angry frustration. She wanted
to scream, to cry, to run. She was not only furious with
Jim, but also with herself. Why did she allow him to
upset her so? Why did a few words scrawled on a piece
of paper and sent a thousand miles frighten her? She
swallowed hard, knowing, remembering well what Jim
could do if he had her within reach.

A knock at the office door broke through her black
reverie like a bullet piercing thin glass, making her
jump. "Yes"—the word was high pitched and breathless.

"Hi-ho," sang Beverly Atkins, one of the three
magazine illustrators, and Drew's closest friend in Los
Alamos. Oblivious to Drew's stress, she strolled casually in, looking very arty in her paint-splotched smock.

"Sorry, kiddo, but I can't give you a ride home tonight. Tom's asked me to stay for a cup of coffee."

Drew slipped the Mott folder into her desk. The movement was a poor substitute for the active flight she craved. Concentrating hard on sounding conversational, she asked, "Tom? Things must be looking up in the Art and Design department if you've got the director asking you out." Looking up into Beverly's pixie face, Drew noticed that it had pinkened.

"Well, it's not really *out*, not yet." She paused, lifting her thin shoulders. "Do you mind about the ride?" Walking closer, she leaned against the metal desk. "Say, I like that black sweater with the gold threads."

"Thanks." Drew smiled at her friend. "And I don't mind about the ride. Dad can drop me. He won't mind." She pulled the long sleeve of her sweater away from her watch, noting the lateness of the hour for the first time, and began clearing papers from her desk. "Never let it be said that Drew McKenna stood in the way of romance."

Flipping the desk calendar pages back to the proper date, she finished, "Besides, I know that look. Good luck."

Beverly's cheeks were now a classic shade of red. "Does it show so much?" It was asked with uncharacteristic shyness.

"So much," Drew repeated with a sympathetic curl of her lips, "but it is lovely on you."

"And I thought I was becoming so sophisticated." Beverly shook her short dark curls. "I guess sophistication and weak knees are incompatible, huh?" Lowering her eyes to the desk, she picked up a partially covered pink envelope. Without waiting for an answer to her previous question, she eyed it curiously. "What's this cute little thing?"

Drew followed Beverly's gaze to the small envelope, a frown of puzzlement replacing her forced expression of placidness. "I don't know. It must have come in with my other mail." She paused, realizing that after seeing Jim's letter she had completely forgotten that there had been anything else. "I—I guess I didn't notice it."

Beverly grinned playfully. "Well, since it's pink, it can't be from a man. Junk mail, no doubt."

Drew stifled the desire to say that she had had all the letters from men that she cared to receive for one day, but forced herself to laugh. "You're incorrigible, Bev." Taking the envelope from her friend's fingers, she went on, "I hope you never have to find out that a man and happiness are not necessarily synonymous."

Beverly crossed her arms across a modest chest, eyeing Drew narrowly. "Someday you'll have to tell me what male animal soured you on love, honey. Why, with your looks, you could have every single guy around here going after you in no time if you'd just—" Noting Drew's squelching look, she held up a halting hand. "Okay. I won't pry. Besides, I think I'd rather have Tom all to myself." She dropped the envelope in Drew's lap. "Gotta go."

"Bye," Drew tossed absently after Beverly as she made a hasty exit; her interest was now centered on the little envelope with the return address from Berlin, Germany. A silver letter opener made quick work of opening the letter that Drew knew to be from her college roommate, Megan Roman, now married to Army Captain Curt Cutler. They had been living in Berlin now for nearly a year.

The announcement was short: "Drew Marie Cutler, 7 lbs. and 8 ozs., was born to Megan and Curt Cutler on February 17." On the back of the card was a brief note in Megan's feathery hand. It read:

Question: Where should a godmother be on the date of March 8, when her namesake is being christened in Berlin?
Answer: Holding the diaper bag, of course. See you soon, love.

Drew rolled her eyes heavenward. It was just like Meg to drop a note like this, assuming that she would drop everything and go to Berlin within the week! She hadn't changed in the five years since they had graduated from college. It was not Meg's way to ask if Drew would come—she would just expect her to be there. That was how close they were. Meg knew that Drew would come if she possibly could. But Meg also knew that Drew's father's position would make her decision very difficult.

She sat back resting her chin thoughtfully on her knuckles. Of course, she wanted to go. And had it been anywhere else—*March 8!* A sudden thought struck: *Jim!* She sat erect, breathing excitedly. *Perfect.* Providence had stepped in and solved her problem for her. Biting her lip, she reached for the phone. She knew that she was acting rashly. But she had made her decision. Within minutes she had sent a cable to Megan, accepting the invitation. Jim could just come to Los Alamos. He could waste his time. She would be gone, a half a world away—just about far enough! That should show him once and for all just how it was between them— absolutely finished!

DREW pulled the collar of her down jacket up to cover her ears in an attempt to block the icy March wind. Leaning into it, she trudged toward the multistoried lab where her father, Dr. Drew McKenna, Tokamak Program Manager, supervised eighty-two scientists and technicians. Nearly six o'clock now; dusk was rapidly deepening into darkness. Drew quickened her step, concerned that, for once, her father might have decided to leave work at a reasonable hour, and she would miss her ride home. Pressing her hands deeper into the flannel-lined pockets, she felt her determined expression soften into a melancholy smile. Dr. McKenna, a Nobel Prize winner in physics for his advances in the field of fusion, was basically a good man. But as a parent, Drew had to admit, he had been minimally supportive, at least in the emotional sense. Oh, Drew knew that he cared for her. But the affection she received from him had always been more appropriate to a professor's interest in a favorite student, rather than a father's love for his only child. Dr. McKenna's work was his life, his family, and his passion. And Drew had reconciled herself to that fact years ago. That was why, when she returned to Los Alamos nearly a year before, she had decided to rent a small A-frame house on Los Alamos's outskirts rather than move back in with her father. A widower for some years, Dr. McKenna lived alone, preferring it that way.

As she pushed open the fusion lab door, she found her mind wandering to thoughts of her mother, Lenore McKenna. Dead in a car crash when Drew was five, her memory of her mother was vague but pleasant. She recalled an attractive blond woman, always happy, always laughing. This vision she carried with her of her mother made Drew feel sure that it had been her mother who had served as the catalyst that made the McKennas a close, contented threesome. Drew reasoned that her mother must have been a very special woman to have captured the attention and affection of a man so totally engrossed in scientific research. And she surmised that her mother must have had a great deal of strength to have lived and blossomed in the shadow of her father's all-consuming work. But, of course, these were things that Drew had decided for herself, for her father was painfully noncommunicative in areas outside his scientific specialty. He never spoke of Drew's mother. And when she asked questions about her mother, he would merely smile softly and say, "Your mother was a woman of quality, Drew. Strive to be like her, not like your plain old father."

She sighed and shrugged. This was the sum and substance of what she knew about her mother. And in her earlier years, it had been a point of frustration for Drew to be told to be like a person she knew so little about. Even now, she doubted that she would see the day when her father would tell her she had come particularly close. She had no idea if she was much like her mother or not. Actually, she was fairly sure that she lacked the sparkle that had set her mother apart, made her the "woman of quality" that her father remembered so fondly.

Yet in dusty family albums Drew had seen pictures of her mother. And it was obvious from them that there was a striking physical resemblance between mother and daughter. Except for the fact that Drew's hair was not blond, but more the color of fire-lit brandy, they were very alike. Both had gray eyes framed by curling dark lashes. A rather poetic maiden aunt had impressed Drew with the comment years before, that "Lenore's eyes changed with her moods from smoky gray when happy to the sparking color of lightning when angry." Drew had clung to that glimpse of her mother like a starving man to a scrap of bread.

Drew knew one other thing about her mother. She had been tall and willowy, and Drew had inherited her mother's beautiful figure. Drew knew this because she had worn her mother's wedding dress.... Pleasant thoughts faded with the memory of ideals gone sour, and she felt her jaw tighten in rekindled anger.

"Hi, Drew." The distant voice of a young male technician echoed in the nearly empty building, cutting into her mental ramblings. She looked up to see a rather bookish young man hurrying toward her. He was dressed in the casual blue-jeans style of a lab technician, his flannel shirt sleeves pushed up to just below his elbows. An ever-present clipboard was tucked under one arm.

"Hi, Pete." Squinting, she let her eyes wander for the first time since entering the building. Powerful lights from fifty feet up blazed in the cavernous room, illuminating the huge embodiment of the essential systems of the Tokamak reactor. To outsiders the towering metal housing that rose to meet the ceiling appeared to be a rather unstreamlined spacecraft. But in reality it was an experimental fusion reactor. Drew's father agreed with most authorities that when perfected, the Tokamak would be a far superior energy source than present-day nuclear fission reactors because it would be fueled by easily accessible and safe hydrogen, rather than the rare and difficult to handle uranium and plutonium. In addition, and most importantly, fusion reactors would not hold either the hazards of devastating nuclear accidents or radioactive wastes. Making this dream of fusion energy a reality for the United States was Drew's father's lifework.

"You sure brighten up this barn."

She turned her attention to the smiling young man, matching his pleasant expression. "Sure, me and a half million watts of electricity. But, thanks." Unbuttoning her coat she asked, "Say, Pete, have you seen Dad? He didn't answer his phone when I called a while ago."

He cocked his head to the side. "I just walked him to his office."

"Great, thanks, Pete." Shrugging off the coat, she turned in the direction he had indicated, her low-heeled pumps echoing loudly across the tile floor as she circled the massive Tokamak toward her father's office, or "sanctuary," as she thought of it—his place of safety against the emotional onslaught of the outside world.

Pushing the slightly ajar door wide, she breezed in. "Hi, Dad." It was her plan to overwhelm him with her happy anticipation of the trip, of seeing Megan, and of being made godmother to the baby.

He sat back in his leather chair, peering up at her from behind half-spectacles. "Why, Drew, I didn't expect to see you today." His gaunt, hawkish features clouded in a puzzled frown. "Am I late for something?"

She laughed, shaking her head, "No, Daddy, I just need a ride home. Will you be leaving soon?"

He heaved a long sigh, sliding his glasses up to his

carrot-red hair. "No, dear, I'll be here until at least six o'clock."

Biting the inside of her cheeks to hold back a smile she hung her coat on the rack by the door. Accustomed to her father's single-minded concentration, she answered offhandedly, "Okay, I can wait." Then, looking pointedly up at the round wall clock above the office door, she went on, "Since it's nearly a quarter after that now."

His frown deepened as his eyes followed her gaze up. "You don't mean it." He pulled the wire-framed glasses carefully from his ears. "Why just a minute ago—"

She took his overcoat from the rack and held it out, interrupting him. "I know, just a minute ago it was 1967." She walked around his desk. "Now, let's go. I'll even fix your dinner."

Obediently, he pushed himself up. Dropping his glasses into his shirt pocket, he asked, "Dinner?"

As he slipped his arms into the coat sleeves, she teased, "Yes, Daddy, you remember dinner. It's the last time you have to be interrupted from your work to take in fuel."

He turned, smiling at her for the first time since she'd entered his office. "You're a pushy woman, Drew. Why, just then you reminded me a great deal of Lenore."

She stopped short. "Mother? Why, Dad"—her voice went very soft—"was she pushy? You never said that before."

His smile faded and he turned away in what appeared to be embarrassment. "I didn't mean it as a slight, Drew. Your mother was—"

"I know, Daddy." She slid her hand into his. A lump formed in her throat making words difficult. "Mother was a woman of quality." It came out in a whisper. Knowing her father as she did, Drew realized that this comparison of her with her mother was the closest Dr. McKenna could come to praising her. Struggling to keep emotion out of her voice, she tugged at his hand. "Let's go."

She was too preoccupied with how to break the Drew-McKenna-is-going-to-Berlin bomb to her father to worry with polite chatter on the ride home. And since he rarely spoke unless spoken to, the ride to Drew's house was very quiet. As they drove, she looked up over the small business section of the town to enjoy the final flames of sunset framing peaks of the distant Sangre de Cristo mountains to the west.

Ironically, Los Alamos was situated peacefully on a picturesque mesa within native piñon pines and scrub cedars and had once been known as the "Capital of the Atomic Age." Originally, in 1942, what is now Los Alamos was a boys' school, secluded in the New Mexican mountains. The school was taken over by the United States Government and turned into a facility for highly classified atomic bomb research, and the country's most brilliant scientists were recruited to work there. On July 16, 1945, the laboratory scientists exploded the first atomic bomb at White Sands, New Mexico. Drew closed her eyes to the beautiful sunset, seeing in her mind's eye the awful mushroom cloud, the violent product of the bomb, which had been necessarily nurtured at Los Alamos to help end the last world war. Though the installation there was still classified, and researchers still did some defense work, most of the areas of concentration now ranged over a broad spectrum of scientific and medical interest, such as fusion reactor energy research, her father's area of expertise.

She opened her eyes as the sunset flickered and died. Turning her gaze back down to look into the lighted shop windows along the main street of the intellectually oriented town of 17,000, she caught a muffled call and cheery greeting from the owner of Los Alamos's bookstore as he closed up shop. Waving back Drew registered that it must be exactly six thirty. Bracing herself as Dr. McKenna turned off onto Arizona street toward the town's outskirts, her thoughts returned to finding a way to tell him something that he would not want to hear.

AFTER dinner, Drew cleared her mother's Haviland from the oak table. "Go on into the living room, Dad. I'll be right with you." Pushing the ladder-back chairs into their places, she moved to the antique dry sink that stood before a wall that she had recently painted yellow beneath the wainscoting, having added a cheery, pink and yellow floral wallpaper above.

Removing from the sink a large wooden planter made from an oak burl, she replaced her yellow dancing-lady orchid plant in its position as the table's centerpiece.

As she turned toward the kitchen with the last of the dishes, she noted that her father had gone into the living room and was now seated on the white cotton-duck couch, apparently oblivious to the fact that the walls had been freshly painted a pale buttercup yellow, and there were fluttery, feminine Priscillas at the windows. Previous renters had chosen a gray-blue brocade window covering and an equally drab color for the walls. She had lived with the unfortunate combination for as long as she could, while accumulating some nice pieces of furniture. But last week she had worked like a drudge painting and papering the small A-frame to make it seem more like a home.

Smiling to herself, Drew shook her head. She should know by now that her father would not have reacted to the change in his surroundings, even if she had blown a gaping hole in the wall! She pushed through the louvered swinging doors into the kitchen. Hurriedly, she took two of her mother's Haviland demitasse cups from one of the glossy white cabinets and placed them on the green tiled countertop. After filling the delicate cups with coffee, she sugared one for her father, and carefully pushed her way back through the doors into the living room. It was definitely time to broach the Berlin sub-

ject. She could put if off no longer. Determined not to
bring Jim up as a reason for leaving, she began, "By the
way, Dad, you remember Megan Roman."

He accepted the tiny gold-rimmed cup with a blank
expression. "No."

She exhaled helplessly as she took a seat beside him
on the couch and leaned heavily into the softness of a
pink velvet throw pillow. Laying the cup on the glass-
covered wicker chest that served as her coffee table,
she tried again. "Megan Roman—my roommate in college."

The blank look remained unchanged, but he nodded.
"Well, I'm sure you are right, dear."

Drew bit the inside of her lip and twisted uncomfortably. "Well, uh...yes." As she forged ahead, she tried
to seem nonchalant by making slight rearrangements of
the three brass planters on her coffee table that contained her prized collection of lavender moth orchids.
"I received a letter from her today. She's had a baby
and named her Drew. She wants me to go to the chris-
tening." Pausing, she tried to judge his reaction. There
didn't seem to be one. "It's this weekend."

He took a sip of the coffee, then looked down at the
cup. "This is coffee." Drew was accustomed to this
type of remark, out of the blue. It hadn't been a question, nor an exclamation of excitement over the superb
brewing of the dark liquid. He had merely taken verbal
note of the fact that there was a cup of coffee in his
hand. She sat quietly as he turned his eyes back up to
hers. "Actually, Drew, I really don't have time for a
cup. I must get back to the lab. We're closing in on entering the reaction regime. Today we came very close to
exceeding the necessary temperature for fusion."

His mind was on work, as usual. Drew knew that she
would have to make this fast. "Okay, Dad. I'll let you
get back. It's just that I'm planning to go to Berlin on
Wednesday to see Megan and Curt and their new baby,
my godchild." She rushed on, seeing his expression

finally register some interest, however horror-stricken. "I know your opinion on the subject, Dad. But I'm going. So there's no use discussing it. I just thought you ought to know."

There. She had said it. Her heart pounded anxiously against her ribs as she watched her father's complexion go purple. Biting her lip, she pulled slightly back. She had never seen him become angry. For that matter, she could probably count on the fingers of one hand the times she had seen him become even mildly animated.

His mouth worked for a long moment before he spoke. When he did, his voice was oddly quiet. "Well, Drew, since you already know the foolhardiness of that decision, I will not reiterate it."

She gulped. He appeared to be through. Setting his cup down with hardly a sound, he stood up slowly.

"Dad?" She squeaked, darting to her feet. "It's not that bad, honestly. Nine hundred and ninety-nine chances out of one thousand. . ."

His head, moving slowly, maddeningly, from side to side, quieted her. "Don't quote numbers to a physicist, Drew. Too many scientific breakthroughs have come regardless of the fact that their chances of happening were equally remote." As he continued, the only betrayal of his emotion was the plunging of his hands deep into the pockets of his tweed trousers. "You are my child, Drew. In some areas of the world that fact alone would place you in a very precarious position." He stopped, his eyes directed at hers. "Don't delude yourself about that fact with vague discussions of probabilities."

"But, Dad, you don't understand." She put a pleading hand on his arm. "I'll be flying over the East. It's the *safest* possible way."

"*Safest*, Drew, is a very unsatisfactory word." There was a sadness in his dull eyes that hurt her badly. But she couldn't tell him the truth. She couldn't tell him that Jim was coming here to get her in four days. She had never told him what Jim had done to her, and she couldn't stand the idea of dredging it up now.

Swallowing hard, she stiffened her resolve. Perhaps he saw the spark of determination in her eyes, for he finished abruptly, "I have never told you what to do. I won't begin now." Pulling away from her grasp, he walked with a rather awkward gait toward the entry hall. "I will see myself out." Drew was heartsick to note that he did not turn to look back as he spoke.

Chapter One

The Lufthansa flight 807, Berlin to Frankfurt, lurched violently, throwing Drew forward against the confining restraint of her seat belt. Her queasy stomach turned menacingly and she pulled one white-knuckled hand from her chair to cup her mouth until the nausea subsided.

The "Fasten Seat Belt" sign flashed above their heads in German, French, and English, accompanied by a continual "ding, ding, ding." Within the cabin there was little else to be heard but for an occasional groan or muffled crying.

Drew tried to turn her attention away from the distress of her fellow passengers and found herself looking out of the window at her side.

The double-glassed porthole was being heavily pelted with ice crystals from the angry storm. Yet it was a soundless anger, making this eruption of nature seem like a voiceless beast, incensed by his muteness, determined to rip the hapless plane apart in his effort to be heard.

Drew peered at her watch. It was 10:10 now. Only eight minutes had passed. But eight minutes, when each minute is spit violently out as though it were the last grain of sand in life's hourglass, can seem to last an aeon. She knew that the storm that raged about them must have been very sudden and intense to have hung about the jet so long. Suddenly, her frayed nerves grasped at the fact that the abusive buffeting had slackened. The minister on her right mirrored her thoughts as he said, "Well, praise the Lord! I believe we have come through the tempest."

Drew turned to look into his ruddy face. He was smiling weakly over at her.

"It appears you fared the weather's impulsiveness better than most, Mrs. Pollard."

Drew winced inwardly at the clergyman's use of her married name, but matched his smile wearily and shook her head. "Not really, Rev—"

Her words were interrupted by the crackle of the intercom announcing the "all clear" in three languages. Drew turned to the window to look outside at a sky showing promise of sun once again. Her thoughts turned inward. *Mrs. Pollard*. That name brought bitter memories crowding painfully to her mind, constricting her throat. It had been over a year since she had considered herself to be Mrs. Pollard, over a year since she had left Jim, ending their two-year marriage. And since the final decree, she did not consider herself to be Mrs. Pollard anymore. Now, at twenty-six, she was, in essence, starting over, choosing to use her maiden name—except for this trip, since her passport was still in her married name.

She was drawn from her sober reverie by a light tap on her arm, "Mrs. Pollard?"

She started, realizing that the pastor was speaking. "Dear me!" His voice had taken on an urgent tone, and Drew turned to look into his sober face, noting that his eyes were intent on something outside the porthole. "That small jet appears to be dangerously close to us."

Drew followed his gaze and squinted out into the brightness of a much-recovered sky. "Yes," she breathed as she took in what looked like a fighter plane. She quickly scanned the blue expanse outside. "I see two more, one above and one below. They're staying very close—almost like an escort."

The scratchy sound of the intercom interrupted her words as the voice of the captain began in clipped German that neither Drew nor the pastor could understand. As the captain spoke, the minister craned his neck toward the porthole for a better view of the planes. A buzz of alarm began to grow among the German-speaking passengers, prompting an odd feeling of apprehension to slither up Drew's spine.

The captain began again, repeating in heavily accented English: "Ladies and gentlemen, there is no cause for concern. However, it appears that during the turbulence, our directional instruments were affected, and we were thrown out of the required travel corridor for foreign aircraft. We are now over Soviet-controlled East Germany, and we have been intercepted by Soviet jet fighters for violating their air space. We have been ordered to accompany them to land for an investigation."

Drew and the minister exchanged nervous glances as the captain continued, "I regret the inconvenience. However, I repeat, there is no real cause for concern. This is merely a frontier formality of the Soviet military machine."

The big jet banked and Drew once again looked out at the smaller planes maneuvering about them. She realized that their altitude was now much lower as she watched their plane's shadow pass over an expansive forested area of rolling hills. White crystalline snow covered the ground and lay like a punctured blanket across the thickly branched pines of the chaste, frozen landscape.

"I don't understand," breathed Drew. "The East Germans have to make allowances for planes flying to and from Berlin."

"Of course they do," remarked the reverend thoughtfully. "However, I have heard of an 'air tunnel' that foreign planes have to fly through over East Germany when approaching or leaving Berlin." The elderly gentleman was speaking more to himself than to Drew. But she turned her attention to his words as he continued, "I believe the required area is between thirty-five hundred and ten thousand feet of altitude and within a width of only twenty miles—a corridor in the sky, so to speak." He was gesturing with his hands, shaping a square in the air above him.

Drew interjected, turning her eyes back to the window, "And because we were forced to remain in this—this air tunnel, we couldn't avoid that sudden storm? And now we've been literally thrown into the hands of the East German Communists?"

The reverend nodded. "I would imagine we're a goodly distance away from the required air space by the Soviet's radical reaction, making us land and all."

She rubbed a fist nervously across her tightly closed lips, an unquenchable panic raising her voice to a squeaky breathlessness. "I wonder if the captain told us the truth—if it really is only a formality?"

The pastor shook his graying head and sighed heavily. "We can only hope so, Mrs. Pollard, and put our trust in a higher power than that of small-minded men."

Once again the "Fasten Seat Belt" sign flashed on and began its insistent dinging. Drew pulled her eyes from the frozen scene below and automatically reached for her belt, only to realize that she was still strapped in securely from the earlier turbulence.

The pastor spoke wearily as he closed the harness over his large stomach. "Well, that certainly didn't take long. I do hope that we can be off again with a minimum of fuss."

Drew could only nod. Her words caught behind the lump of fear wedged in her throat. Her mind tumbled to the argument that she had had with her father before she left. That had been the last time she had seen him before her trip. And with the visit almost successfully completed, she had relaxed with the knowledge that her father's forgiveness would be automatic with her safe return. But, now, his final words stalked her memory: "*Safest,* Drew, is a very unsatisfactory word." This simply must be a distressing coincidence. They couldn't be diverting the plane to get her! Circling her dry lips with her tongue, Drew hooked her fingers mechanically around the buckle of her belt, squeezing her hands into tense fists as the intercom clicked back on. After a brief announcement in German, the captain spoke in the now familiar accented English, "I repeat. Do not be concerned in any way over our forced landing. However, I have been informed that the plane will be vacated so that it may be searched for photographic and other unauthorized equipment. Also, all luggage will be checked, and all camera film will be confiscated." Her feeling of regret over the loss of precious baby pictures was short-lived as the captain continued, "This type of forced diversion is rare, but not unheard-of. We will, no doubt, be on our way—soon."

Somehow, the brief gap of time before the final word was less than reassuring, and Drew found herself chewing painfully at the inside of her cheek.

A short time later their commercial jetliner was touching down on a long, snow-cleared runway. The little jet fighters, which several of the passengers had referred to as "MiGs," zipped overhead in close formation. Drew had been sitting in a numbed silence until touchdown brought her back to the present. She cocked her head to the side to get one last glimpse of the hornet-like MiGs as they sped away, sparkling silver specks in the wide blue of an East German sky.

THE sixty-one passengers and seven crew members were moved quickly off the plane into a cement-block building by a dozen or so armed, grim-faced soldiers in gray. Upon entering, one rather stout officer demanded in German and then in halting English that they hand over their passports and be seated on long, pewlike benches that stood in rows within the large room.

Hours dragged by. The room, heated by steam, was growing warm with the press of humanity. Earlier Drew had removed her white karakul lamb jacket. And now her soft gray cashmere sweater and slacks were becoming uncomfortable.

She looked at her watch again, her only pastime for what had seemed like an eternity. Nearly 5:00 P.M., she noted with a heavy exhalation of breath, her nerves wound taut. Feeling the need to do something, anything, she stood and stretched.

Glancing around the crowded room, she noticed the minister, her seatmate on the plane, sitting alone near a frost-covered window. With a sudden urgent need to talk to someone, she crossed to stand before him. "Reverend?"

"My dear"—he seemed to want to talk too—"call me Norman...Norman Peabody. Join me, please." He patted the rough bench beside him.

"My Margaret and Sarah are being questioned now. They wouldn't take us all together, but Mama wouldn't allow them to take her baby alone. She's got spunk, my Margaret." He smiled weakly. "I know this is only a formality, but these Communists see treachery behind every stone."

Drew felt a surge of compassion for the man and sat down, putting her hand over his. "They seem to be taking us in alphabetical order." She leaned back against the rough wall. It felt cool through her sweater. "Six hours to get to the P's. Well," she sighed, "it'll be my turn soon. Would you mind telling me what they ask?"

He lifted his hand from hers and began to count off on his short fingers: "First, your name...where you're going, where you've been...if the trip is business or pleasure..." He stopped and looked up at her as his face crinkled into a half-hearted grin at a sudden thought. "You know, I'm surprised they didn't just come right out and ask if I'm a spy and if I conjured up that storm to..." His words fell away in midsentence as the heavy door opened and a guard entered with his wife and daughter. They looked like plump bookends, both bundled up in heavy dark serge coats, the younger woman a chubby copy of her mother.

Reverend Peabody stood abruptly and hurried to his family. Drew's thoughts turned inward. *Only a few questions. I can handle that. Just keep calm, Drew, keep calm.*

She stiffened at the sound of her name being called.
"*Frau* Pollard!" repeated the officer in charge, more
loudly this time.

Drew felt a brief weakness in her knees as she stood
and moved to retrieve her jacket. Donning it, she pulled
the white-furred hood up over her auburn hair and
walked with feet of lead to the guard at the door.

The blunt-nosed soldier jerked his head toward the
exit in a gesture for her to precede him. After tugging
the door wide, Drew plunged bare hands into her
pockets and stepped out into the frigid, late afternoon.
Clouds had moved in, obscuring the sun and giving the
daylight a gray shroud of doom. Drew picked her way
cautiously across twenty-five yards of crunchy, trampled snow ahead of the sullen guard to a second cement-
block building. Mounting five ice-sheeted steps, they
entered heavy double doors and turned down a dimly lit
corridor, their footsteps echoing hollowly on the worn
floor. The guard stopped abruptly before a door and
knocked. Shortly, a brusque reply admitted them both.
Closing the portal, the soldier posted himself and
gestured for Drew to go forward. The room was unusually dark for early evening. But Drew guessed that this
was purposeful and psychological. She bit her lip tentatively, desperately wanting this interview to be over.
Her heart thudded in her temples and she gritted her
teeth. *Keep calm!* her mind ordered. Steeling herself to
remain rational, and in an effort to keep a sense of pro-
portion, she glanced around, taking mental notes. There
was a metal desk behind which sat a spectacled man in
uniform, an officer, Drew guessed. And to her far left
stood another man, his arms folded casually before
him. Whether by design or by accident this quiet
stranger had positioned himself before the room's only
window, almost filling it with his wide shoulders. The
light from the nearly sunless sky illuminated the crystalline frost on the panes at his back, leaving his
darkened face featureless. Something about the silent

alertness of this silhouetted figure sent an intense shiver of apprehension up Drew's spine.

The officer sitting behind the desk barked in heavily accented English, "You are American?"

Drew blinked her eyes back to him. A single lamp burned low on the desk, its light directed down on the passport in his hand, her passport. "Yes," she whispered and gulped to ease the dryness in her throat.

He adjusted his dark-rimmed glasses and spoke, his voice acid-filled, "Sit down!"

The words were a nasal order. Startled by the abruptness of his shouted demand, she moved quickly to the only vacant chair in the room, directly across the desk from the questioning officer.

"Your name?" came the officer's brusque query.

"Drew McKenna," was her automatic response, not having used her married name in nearly a year.

The seated man looked pointedly up, his brows drawn down in a frowning V. "That is not what is written here." He picked up a pen and began to make a note on a pad at his elbow.

"Pollard! Drew—Mrs. James Pollard," Drew stuttered, shaken by her fright-induced witlessness. "You see, McKenna is my mai—middle name."

A deep voice from the silhouetted figure by the window cut across Drew's explanation as he spoke in clipped German to the officer at the desk. Drew turned toward the man cloaked in darkness. He appeared to be the one in actual command here and she was puzzled by their tactics.

"*Ja, mein Herr,*" replied the officer as he returned the pen to the desk top, abandoning his note-taking. Turning back to Drew, the subdued officer went on with the required questions. "Mrs. Pollard, you were in Berlin for business?"

Breathing a slow sigh of relief that her slip had seemingly been ignored, she answered, "No, to visit a close friend and her husband, and to see their new baby."

So it went, the routine questions were ground out. Drew, without hesitation, answered them all, for there was nothing for Mrs. James Pollard to hide.

"That will be all, *Frau* Pollard. You will now be returned to the others." He looked down at her passport, slapped the covers together and laid it aside. Having been so completely dismissed, Drew rose to go. As she did, the shadowed figure before the window walked silently forward, addressing the seated officer.

"Ja, Herr Erhardt." The spectacled officer rose to rigid attention and gave a curt nod as the man from the shadows strode to the door where Drew and the bulky guard waited. He stood aside as the guard opened the door and preceded them both out of the small office.

Once in the hall, the tall man spoke in English, his low, gravel-edged voice held a slight but pleasing accent, "Your husband is not traveling with you, Mrs. Pollard?"

Startled by the odd query, Drew turned to face the questioning man. For the first time she realized how very tall he was, much taller than most of the men she knew—six foot five, maybe six six. Drew, five seven herself, found very few men whom she considered to be really tall. But this man—she looked up into his face. Lit by one stark bulb above their heads, his features appeared ruggedly angular. The hollows of his lean face were black beneath the high wide bones along his cheeks. Thick lashes framed deep-set eyes, leaving Drew to wonder if he was scowling down at her or at some point beyond her head. She stiffened. "I really see no valid reason for your asking that question."

The tall man's expression did not change, but Drew thought she could see a flicker somewhere in the darkness that held his eyes. "Mrs. Pollard, any questions that we care to ask must be considered valid. I suggest that you remember that. You are not in your precious United States now."

Drew swallowed hard, remembering that her situation

was perhaps more precarious than most. "My husband and I are divorced." She let the statement fall flat for she had no taste for discussing it, or even remembering.

There was an almost imperceptible tensing across the broad shoulders. The stranger at her side issued a command to the guard standing quietly at Drew's back. She heard a click of heels and turned to see her guard disappear out of the double doors through which they had entered earlier.

She turned back to the tall man at her side, puzzled. Why had he sent her guard away? Drew searched the darkness that held his eyes. Though she could not see them, she was very aware of his close observation of her. What did he want with her, this tall enigmatic stranger? He was no soldier as suggested by the civilian clothes he wore. A red plaid shirt-jacket fit snugly over wide shoulders, tapering to a narrow, flat-bellied waist. She was surprised to see that he wore a pair of snug-fitting blue jeans that molded themselves closely to his muscular thighs.

Jeans, Drew knew, were very difficult for East Germans to get. And even when they were able to acquire them, they were usually prohibitively expensive. Yet this man, even behind the Iron Curtain, was dressed like a casual American. Ironically, he was anything but that, this German. For Drew had seen the way these Communist soldiers snapped to at his command. Yes. Though it was not clear to Drew what it was, this. . .*Herr Erhardt* obviously held an exalted position of command here.

"Come!" His low growl interrupted her thoughts. He grasped her arm roughly, pulling her along the darkened corridor, back in the opposite direction from which Drew had entered.

"Where—" she began, but his "Quiet!" whispered under his breath, held a dangerous undercurrent.

Keeping her silence, she walked, almost ran, being dragged along at his long-legged pace until they reached a set of narrow stairs. Descending, they moved through

a nondescript metal door. Once outside, Drew could see
an iron gate, guarded by an armed soldier in gray.

The red-jacketed man exchanged a few low-pitched
words with the guard who smiled and nodded, eyeing
Drew with interest as he readily opened the gate, allowing them both to leave the compound area.

She was briskly deposited in the front seat of a jeep-
like automobile. The tall man took the wheel, ignited
the motor, and they sped away.

"I demand that you tell me where I'm being taken!
You have no—"

He interrupted her shrill demand curtly. "Once
again, Mrs. Pollard, I must remind you that you have
no rights at all."

He flicked on a set of windshield wipers, clearing a
wide V across the front window as snow began to fall.

Drew turned to look at his rigid profile. His face was
set in a dark mask. A muscle twitching near his jaw was
the only sign that he was not carved from granite.

He seemed agitated, angry—intent, but on what?
Was it only the ice-sheeted winding road that they
skimmed over in the growing dusk that demanded his
rigid attention? Or was it something more?

A nagging fear squeezed Drew's stomach. She
grasped the dark vinyl of the seat unconsciously and
turned her eyes away from his face.

Her mind whirled with fearsome thoughts as she
stared ahead, watching the hypnotic to-and-fro movement of the wipers as they worked in a futile attempt to
rid the window of the falling snow.

Suddenly, he braked the jeep to a skidding stop and
jumped out with the natural grace of a jungle cat.

Drew had braced her hands against the dashboard at
the sudden stop and was more than a little surprised to
see that they were parked before a rustic stone cottage
set back from the road among towering pines.

A light scattering of flakes filtered listlessly down
among the thickly needled branches, settling across the

tall man's shoulders and in the brown curls of his hair as he turned to face her. "Well, get out, Mrs. Pollard!"

Drew jumped at his growl and pushed open her door, climbing out into the ankle-deep snow. She shuffled as quickly as she could to catch up to his receding back, not trusting him, yet unable to disobey his order. Once inside, Drew discarded her coat absently on a chair by the door. She looked about her noting that they had entered a well- kept, masculine den. At the far end of the room stood a brown stone hearth, a fire glowing low in its depths. An antique clock sat on the mantel, its pendulum ticking out the seconds with singular importance.

On either side of the old oaken clock stood a collection of fine beer steins. Some, Drew guessed, must have dated back over one hundred years.

Before the fire a snowy sheepskin rug covered an age-darkened pine floor. It separated the fireplace from a low heavy table and a rust-colored couch and chair.

"Sit down, Mrs. Pollard." Drew moved her eyes quickly to the origin of the command. He stood before a door near the hearth. Opening it, he stepped out, closing the door at his back.

Drew stood, her eyes remaining where the man had been. She did not move. She was unwilling to sit, yet unsure whether to attempt to escape.

Before she made up her mind which route to take, the door opened, carrying with it a burst of icy wind, a flutter of new snow, and...*Herr Erhardt*. In his arms he carried a stack of snow-covered wood.

Drew found her voice. "What is all this? Why have you brought me here?"

He stopped at the sound of her questions and looked her up and down with a disconcerting masculine thoroughness. Then with a nudge of one broad shoulder, he pushed the pine door closed at his back.

Without acknowledging her, he fed the dying fire, filling the room with the angry hiss of melting snow. When fire had won over ice and it was pleasantly blazing, he straightened and turned back to face her, leaning casually against the hearth's stone mantel.

"Sit down." His voice held the tone of command that demanded obedience.

Drew stiffened and set her jaw stubbornly. "No! Not until I know why you brought me here."

She remained standing, willing herself not to show this man her gnawing fear.

A spark flickered to life in his brown eyes, oddly golden in the room's semi-darkness. Those glowing eyes somehow frightened Drew more than his menacing frown.

"If you are unwilling, or unable to seat yourself, Mrs. Pollard, I am sure that I can find a way to lower you to the couch," he stated curtly. Then more quietly, as if reasoning with a witless child, "Or is your safe release, and that of your fellow passengers, of no importance to you?"

Drew ground her teeth in an effort to find a stinging retort to his condescending question. But she could not.

"Yes. . . of course it is."

Feeling at a loss, she relinquished her determined stance and sat down dejectedly on the sofa. When seated, she laced her fingers together in her lap to keep them from trembling and turned her face up to his, waiting.

He appeared to be studying his captive passively. Then, after a moment, in a verbal surprise attack, he dropped the revelation like a hand grenade.

"I know who your father is."

The world bottomed out for Drew. "Father!" She gulped at the sudden raspy dryness in her mouth. "I—I don't know what you mean."

His lips opened in a humorless smile. "Very good, Mrs. Pollard. But, your slip in the interrogation room gave you away."

Drew could feel the blood drain from her face. She couldn't speak. Wide gray eyes faced hard brown ones for a moment of heart-thudding silence. The pressure-cooker quiet became too much for Drew. "But how? How did you pick up on the name so quickly?"

"It doesn't require a *genius* to connect the name of 'Drew McKenna Pollard' to that of 'Dr. Drew McKenna,' now does it?"

Drew was not convinced. She shook her head in confusion, russet wisps of fire-lit hair dancing along her cheeks.

"His name is not that well known, except in the scientific community. How would you know of him unless"—she had a sudden thought—"unless—" Her eyes flew back up to his face. He did not speak, but merely watched her as realization struck. "Erhardt," she breathed quietly. "*Erhardt*—Dr. Rolf Erhardt! So that's it? That's how you knew." Her voice trailed away at the magnitude of her new knowledge.

He nodded crisply at her mention of his name. "I'm gratified to know that my work has been recognized in the United States."

Recognized! Drew's mind whirled as she remembered her father speaking with obvious respect for his Communist counterpart. The young East German genius Rolf Erhardt and his amazing strides forward in the field of fusion reactors. Drew put it all together—why their plane had been diverted and forced to land, why the jet was being searched for photographic equipment, and why their film was being confiscated. Dr. Rolf Erhardt, though only thirty-five, was director of the *DDR—Institute of Plastics Research* located on a secret base in East Germany. Their jet, Drew was now sure, had inadvertently breached the security of that highly classified research installation. She felt herself shudder as the full impact of what was happening to her struck like a heavy blow.

"Your presence here will be considered an act of espionage." Though he had spoken quietly, Drew again felt as though she had been hit. She felt a fist tighten in her chest, squeezing. With great effort, she said, "But—but that's crazy. It was a random chance thing...a storm!"

He raised a sarcastic brow. "That is your story, Mrs. Pollard. But the fact remains that you are *here*. That, alone, will prove your guilt."

Breaking eye contact, he allowed his gaze to wander over her body as he continued, "What could appear more innocent. An attractive young woman, who by profession must be a physicist, a woman whose father is the foremost authority on fusion—and finally, a woman traveling under false papers. And you would have me believe, Mrs. Pollard, that this whole thing was not carefully planned?"

She blurted, "But you're twisting everything—"

He held up a halting hand. "But I believe you now see how easily your guilt could be proved."

The answer to that was too obvious to ignore. She turned her eyes from his, hypnotic, iridescent—like a wild animal's at night—and gazed into the comparative peace of the fire instead. She had little faith that she would regain her freedom now. But desperation urged her to speak. "I—I really know nothing of importance. My job is only to do the final drafting of scientific papers to be published." Her voice was low and without hope. "I never see anything really secret."

Rolf shrugged indifferently mirroring her fears with his words. "It really doesn't matter whether you, personally, have classified knowledge or not. It is your relationship to Dr. McKenna that is important."

His eyes narrowed slightly. "With you as a hostage, Dr. McKenna could, perhaps, be persuaded to give us information in exchange for the safe return of his daughter." He paused, giving Drew a moment to absorb his words. "Do you not see the benefit to us, Mrs. Pollard, of keeping you as a hostage?"

Drew inhaled sharply at the mental image of her father, torn between national loyalty and concern for his child's life. She turned her eyes back to his, her heart pounding savagely in her breast.

Unable to restrain her horror and frustration she shot back, "I'm no fool, Dr. Erhardt! I know all the benefits to your government for holding me as a political pawn."

She pulled her hand through brandy-wine curls in a nervous gesture.

"But what I can't understand is why you feel you must torment me with vivid pictures of it...unless you get some sort of sadistic pleasure out of watching people quail before you in fear."

He viewed her narrowly from beneath half-closed lids. "Believe me, Mrs. Pollard, My motives are much more important than a perverted effort to seek pleasure."

He crossed to the chair that sat at an angle to the couch and lowered himself into it. "No, you have been brought here for another reason...another reason entirely."

Drew felt a wariness prick at her mind. "Then why? What other reason?" Her words were high-pitched and thready. She inhaled slowly, dreading what worse fate this man might have in mind for Dr. Drew McKenna's daughter.

Dr. Erhardt took his time to answer. He seemed to be casually evaluating the woman before him.

Drew felt his gold-flecked eyes penetrating deep into her gray ones, grasping hold of her whole consciousness so that her senses were forced to remain centered on this powerful, silent man.

His words, when they came, broke the quiet between them like a sledgehammer smashing the glasslike tenseness of her brain: "I brought you here, Mrs. Pollard, to discuss our marriage."

Chapter Two

The statement was so matter-of-fact that it took a moment before the meaning penetrated.

Drew's mouth dropped open. She sat stunned, unable to believe this offhand statement.

"Marriage..." came the weak response. "You can't be serious."

He sat slightly forward, watching her closely.

"Dead serious, Mrs. Pollard."

Drew's eyes grew round and she pushed herself up from the couch, feeling the need to put distance between them. She crossed to the hearth and paced back and forth across the helpless sheepskin, her thoughts in turmoil.

Marriage...No! Once was enough. The first time was a bad experience... one she did not want to repeat.

Jim Pollard had proved to be a womanizer, always on the lookout for a new conquest. Yet if another man so much as smiled at Drew, Jim became violently jealous. This, coupled with his drinking, was a dangerous combination, destined to spark disaster.

And one night, it nearly did. Jim came home filled with rage, believing that Drew had had a clandestine lunch with another man, when what he had actually seen was his wife in conference with a graduate student who had asked Drew to help him by proofreading and making suggestions on improving his master's thesis in physics.

But Jim had been drunk and beyond listening to explanations. He had made up his mind that she was a cheat and needed to be taught a lesson. He struck out at her, knocking her down. Drew shuddered at the memory, still fearful of what might have happened if Jim had not passed out. With his superior strength, he could have beaten her badly—or even killed her. Stunned with the reality of Jim's dangerous, unbalanced jealous rages, Drew had stumbled to her feet, packed a bag and walked out, returning to Los Alamos to resume her work as associate editor for *Scientific Monthly*. There she quietly filed for divorce, refusing to answer Jim's letters or calls.

That experience with marriage had soured her on the whole institution, and she had vowed not to become involved again. But now, this man, this Communist stranger was suggesting that she marry him! She whirled to face her captor. "No, Dr. Erhardt. You don't know what you're asking of me!"

Rolf rose from his chair and closed the space between them with two brisk strides, blocking her path. "I am not asking, Mrs. Pollard."

His stonelike grip encompassed her shoulders, eyes blazing like molten ore, bore down into hers. The radiant nearness of his body competed violently with the heat of the fire, making Drew uncomfortably warm.

She pressed her hands against his wool-clad chest to ward off his gruff presence. "This is all insane...I won't...I can't marry you!"

"I fear you have no choice in the matter, Mrs. Pollard."

Drew stopped her struggling and looked up incredulously into his solemn face. "No choice? What do you mean, no choice?" she managed falteringly.

He shrugged, his handsome features unperturbed by her total rejection of the proposition. "Must I remind you that you are totally without rights here"—he tightened his grip on her shoulders—"while I have total unquestioned power."

Drew's heart hammered deafeningly in her ears with the truth of his words. She controlled her voice with great effort. "What is your purpose in all this, Doctor?"

He relaxed his grip measurably. "You have said that you care for your fellow passengers' safe release, have you not?"

She nodded blankly at his pause.

"And you prefer to be returned to the security of your own country?"

Drew inhaled rapidly. "Of course, but—"

He jerked his head toward the sofa. "Then, I strongly suggest you take your seat and hear me out."

Drew's confidence in fair play was badly shaken. She returned wordlessly to the couch, realizing that she had no choice but to listen to what her captor had to say.

This time, Rolf took a seat beside her, placing his arm across the sofa's padded back, allowing him a better view of the girl sitting stiff and pale in the wavering firelight.

"You see, Mrs. Pollard," he began, "because your passport is in your married name, no significance, or note, has yet been made of your slip of tongue at your interrogation an hour ago," he remarked dryly. "I am the only person, so far, to know that your father is Dr. Drew McKenna."

Her heart caught in her throat with this unexpected turn. At his pause, she ventured, "But why? Why have you kept it a secret?" She searched his dark features expectantly, "And what does it have to do with marriage?"

Rolf stood and moved to a narrow table before the window. Lifting a decanter, he poured an amethyst liquid into two goblets. A heavy pelting of wind-gusted snow caught Drew's attention in the room's quiet, and she became aware of a building storm beyond the cottage walls. She mused that its restless rage was no more turbulent than the emotions that were being buffeted about in her own mind.

Carrying the twin glasses back to his place on the couch, Rolf repeated her question, "What does all this have to do with our marriage?"

He handed her one of the delicate glasses.

"Everything."

Drew accepted the glass absently as he spoke. "It is this, Mrs. Pollard." He sat back. "Your only means of escape from the East rests with our marriage."

His eyes were hooded by darkly lashed lids, half-closed and unreadable. Drew held her breath.

"Conversely, with one word from me, the possibility of your rejoining your father can be permanently ended."

She ran her tongue around dry lips and took a sip of the wine to ease the dryness in her throat.

His deep voice burned her consciousness as he continued. "For a price, you may buy my silence...insuring your eventual freedom, as well as guaranteeing the safe return of your fellow passengers."

Drew's hands began to tremble uncontrollably and she lowered her glass to the table. "And my marriage to you would assure all that?" she breathed the question. "But, why?"

Pursing his lips, Rolf gave a slight shrug. "I am a scientist, not a man of politics." He raised one booted foot to rest against the corner of the heavy table. "You must know that a scientist requires a great deal of liberty to pursue his experiments to their fullest potential."

He turned his face toward the dancing flames, the flicker illuminating the craggy maleness of his profile. "It is my desire to go to the United States and work with men I feel to be the most brilliant nuclear physicists in the world." Turning back to her, he added, "In particular, your father. This is why your appearance here was too much of an opportunity for me to let slip away."

Drew pulled her lips together in a thin line as she realized his intent. "So! You want to defect. That's it." She shot to her feet and faced the seated man. "Well then, why don't you just do that. You don't need to be married to defect, not a scientist of your caliber."

Rolf reached for his glass and fingered it. "You are wrong, Mrs. Pollard." He returned his eyes to her and pushed the glass away. His words were measured. "I had planned to defect in April at the Oberammergau conference. But, because of several recent top-level defections by Communist scientists, all travel permits have been restricted to Communist Bloc countries. It is now unlawful"—he paused, a humorless smile revealing strong white teeth—"for a scientist of my caliber to leave the country to make good my escape." The words held a bitter edge.

"But," he went on, "if I marry an American, the United States government can initiate extraordinary measures to gain my release because of my acquired American citizenship."

Drew absorbed his daring plan for a moment before venturing, "Then, really, all you need is an American willing to marry you." She spread her arms in a pleading gesture. "Since I don't want to, surely there is someone else from the plane you could approach."

Rolf lifted a brow quizzically at her desperation. "Would you have preferred that I chose the American minister's sixteen-year-old daughter?" He eyed her evenly. "No, Mrs. Pollard, you were the only logical choice."

Slowly he unfolded his muscular frame to face her, eyes intent, glistening. "You can see that, can't you?"

She stared blankly. It was true. Except for Sarah Peabody, Drew was the only single American woman on the plane.

A sardonic smile parted his lips. "I owe your husband a great deal for divorcing you." There was a trace of amusement in his voice as he continued, "We *socialists* have a saying"—he reached out and touched her chin with a long finger—"a cow, gone dry and barren, may be useless to the poor farmer, but highly prized by the butcher."

Drew's mind thundered, and her stormy eyes flashed

sparks of lightning as she jerked her face away from his touch. "How—how dare you!" she choked out, wanting to inflict pain, the same kind of pain he had just inflicted on her with his cruel assumption that Jim had tossed her aside like—he had put it so crudely—a barren cow! But appropriately cutting words would not come.

Flinging out an arm blindly in her distress, she struck a rock-hard bicep with her fist and cringed at the hurt she caused herself. Tears blurred her vision and she spun sharply from him. Her only thought was to escape, to get away from this cruel tormentor who was determined to force her into the horrible trap of marriage that she couldn't bear to face. Not again. Instinctively, she darted toward the back door. Throwing it wide, she dashed out into blowing snow. Large flakes lashed about her as she ran, stinging her face and hands. Unthinking, weaving through the dense pines, Drew stumbled on, plunging deeper and deeper into the frigid dusk-darkening wood. With each step she floundered almost knee deep in the accumulating snow. It pulled and sucked at her shoes, making progress agonizingly slow. The kid high heels that had seemed so stylish in the old-world elegance of Megan's West Berlin townhouse were hopelessly out of place here. Useless as protection against the elements, the high heels fought her every step as she struggled to get away—away from Rolf Erhardt who, with so little effort, had reopened the tender, slow-healing wound in her pride.

"Marriage. No!" she sobbed. "I won't be used like that ever again, no matter what the reason!"

Lungs aching with cold, Drew's breath now came in rasping, pain-filled gasps as the subzero temperature took its toll. A protruding stone caught her heel, sending her sprawling headlong into the frigid softness. The fall left her breathless and she rolled from her face in an attempt to clear the fiery snow from her eyes and mouth, sputtering and coughing for air, further abusing her raw lungs.

Life-sustaining body heat was swept away by the howling wind as it pushed through the soggy wetness of the cashmere sweater and slacks. Drew tightly clamped her teeth to stop a violent bout of chattering as the dampness seeped deeper. She shuddered spasmodically, her fingers burned as she burrowed in the snow for solid support, trying to prop herself up. Another shiver convulsed her slender frame, and she hugged herself in a weak attempt to ward off the encompassing glacial storm. The windstrewn snow stung her eyes and she blinked repeatedly to clear her vision, rubbing stiffened fingers over closed lids to ease the nettling pain. Another tremor shook her body violently. She tried to push herself to her feet, but her cold-weakened limbs would not respond.

"God! Is it all to end here? Am I to freeze to death in an East German blizzard?"

She rubbed her numbed hands along her legs, trying to restore circulation as hot tears burned down her cheeks.

The world turned red as something large and warm enveloped her like an answered prayer. She found herself being lifted effortlessly from the paralyzing cold, within the circle of a revitalizing heat. She could feel the slow thud of a heart beating near her shoulder and pulled the scratchy fabric away from her face to stare into the grim countenance of Dr. Erhardt. His voice held a flintlike edge as he shouted over the gale-force winds, "Mrs. Pollard, it is a child's ploy to run away rather than face a problem. I did not expect this of you."

His jaw twitched in his anger as he silently trudged back toward the cottage with his trembling burden.

Drew noticed that he had removed his coat to help protect her from the elements, leaving him with only the limited covering of a beige turtleneck shirt.

Yet he seemed not to feel the knife-sharp wind that whipped the snow about them in random, frenzied gusts.

Kicking the door wide, he strode back into the cottage's tranquil interior. An instant later, after he pushed the door closed at his back, Drew found herself deposited on the couch. A curt order brought her large gray eyes to his resolute face; snow sparkled in his tousled hair and across his expansive shoulders.

"You'd better remove those wet clothes or be prepared to suffer pneumonia tomorrow." Turning on his heel, he stalked out of the den, leaving Drew in a confused, huddled lump before the fire.

After a moment, he returned with a white bath sheet. "Here." He tossed it to her. "After you remove those clothes, wrap up in this."

Drew shrank back against the confines of the couch. "You don't mean that I am to strip down and be left with nothing but this puny towel!" She lifted one corner of the terry fabric tentatively, her fingers tense and cold. "Don't you have a—a robe, or something more substantial that I could borrow?"

"No." His voice was flat. "Perhaps you should have asked that question before you decided to run out into a blizzard."

Sarcasm laced his words as he continued, "Be grateful I chose to loan you the...puny towel, Mrs. Pollard."

He moved toward the hall, calling back over his shoulder, "We need to talk. Be quick about changing."

Drew sat stunned for a moment after Rolf left her alone in the den. She looked around, unsure of her next move. A new convulsive shiver shook her to the core and set her teeth to chattering.

Clamping her jaws tight, she realized that he was right, at least, in the fact that she would have to get out of her soaked clothes...and soon.

Pushing his jacket away, she kicked off the ruined shoes. Crouching in the limited shelter of the sofa, she tugged the clinging sweater over her head and wriggled out of her soaking slacks. Reluctantly, she had to admit that just getting out of the cold damp wool was an improvement, for she could now feel the fire's radiant warmth caressing her chilled skin.

Drew took a deep breath, knowing that she would be warmer still without the damp bra and panties that clung transparently to her skin. Quickly removing them, she stood, wrapped herself sarong-style in the towel, tucking the loose end between her breasts.

She looked critically down at herself and shook a dejected head of damp reddish hair. The towel, though large and thick, hung just to her mid-thigh, leaving much of her long slim legs exposed. She shrugged and heaved a heavy sigh as she bent to retrieve the discarded clothes.

"I will take those," came a deep voice at her back.

She straightened abruptly, dropping the rumpled cashmere to the floor in her haste.

Turning, she saw Rolf leaning casually in the door, his arms folded loosely across his ample chest. Something in his eyes made Drew's heart pound erratically and she quickly bent to retrieve her garments, clutching them protectively before her.

He closed the space between them, moving with an easy grace. Drew caught her lips between her teeth and pushed the soggy bundle at him. His quiet closeness made her nervous. She abruptly turned away. Immediately she knew this had been a mistake, for she could almost feel his forceful gaze penetrating the soft white toweling at her back. A spasm of apprehension shot up her spine, making her shiver.

The sound of his solid booted footsteps retreating from the room caused a surprised sigh of relief to escape her lips. But that relief was short-lived, for he returned within a minute, his booming voice startling her.

"I'm afraid you will not be able to return to the compound in that condition, Mrs. Pollard." He moved to face her as he spoke.

Drew stiffened at his matter-of-fact statement.

"Afraid? I sincerely doubt that, Doctor, when you have all the chips stacked on your side of the table."

His voice was low and instructive. "I don't play the game to lose." As he spoke, Drew lifted her eyes to his. "It will be easier if you stay the night."

She bristled defensively and moved her hands to her hips in irritation. "How so? Or do you plan to...compromise me and force the issue of marriage that way?"

"Compromise?" A crooked half-smile softened his rugged features as his eyes moved over the rapid rise and fall of Drew's partially exposed breasts, rosy in the firelight, "What makes you think that I require as much as a compromise to have my way in this?"

Seeing his eyes drop from her face, Drew abruptly moved her hands to her arms, hugging herself in an effort to better mask her body from his view.

"All right," she flared, "let's not mince words. Do you intend to use *rape* to terrorize me into suffering through this marriage?"

A golden flicker sparked to life in his brown eyes. "Perhaps your opinion of your charm is a bit...inflated." He moved away from her and leaned casually against the stone hearth. "I have never forced myself on a woman. And I don't intend to start now."

He rubbed fisted knuckles across his deeply cleft chin. "I mean only that it will be expedient to have you here so that in the morning the American minister can perform the ceremony for us here."

Drew gasped, "Reverend Peabody? He'd never be a party to such an—an unholy union!"

Rolf lifted an arched brow casually. "I believe he will, once you convince him of our desire to be married."

Drew stiffened, dropping her arms to her side in disbelief. "You must be joking!" Her voice was a whispered gasp. "Just tell him what you told me...that none of us will get out of here unless he marries us. I think that will take care of any objections he might have, no matter how valid!"

Rolf slowly shook his curly head, his eyes remaining intently upon Drew. "No, Mrs. Pollard, I must insist that this charade be played out my way."

Drew's mouth dropped open. "But, I can't...I won't be blackmailed into pretending some starry-eyed infatuation for you!"

"*You can,* Mrs. Pollard," he barked harshly. "And you will, or the entire bargain will be null and void."

His eyes surveyed her thoroughly for a moment before he continued, "Or would you rather resign yourself and your fellow passengers to a much longer, less comfortable stay in East Germany?"

Drew shook her head, fighting back an hysterical sob. "Do you mean that unless I tell Reverend Peabody that you and I are madly in love...so much so that you are willing to leave your 'beloved' country for me..." She stopped, nearly choking on the bitterness of that lie. "Unless I say all *that,* you won't let us go?"

He placed his hands calmly at his back. "Correct."

"But that's not fair! This marriage bargain is bad enough without the added humiliation of playacting that I love you...when in reality—"

His lips curved up without humor. "I know, Mrs. Pollard, you loathe me."

"Yes," she hissed, tossing her head defiantly. "Yes, I do...I *loathe* you."

He appeared completely unperturbed by her heated confirmation. "Be logical, Mrs. Pollard. Would it be more humiliating to have the reverend believe that we spent the night together drawn by love...or merely by animal lust?"

Drew moaned. "You'd allow him to think that we...?"

She pulled a shaky hand across her forehead, sweeping a strand of damp chestnut hair behind her ear. "How low are you willing to stoop to get to the United States, Doctor?"

His eyes shot golden sparks. "I'll do what I must,

Mrs. Pollard. And keeping your reputation untarnished is one of the least of my concerns right now." A deep wave of color blushed Drew's cheeks as he continued, "At this point, I can't afford to have the minister martyring himself because of his moral principles."

Drew felt drained both mentally and physically. She had lost. There was no way out. There never had been. Now, though, her exhausted mind finally had to admit to it.

Tomorrow she would marry this stranger... this East German genius. And like an avalanche having begun its plunge down the mountainside, there was no stopping it. Hopelessly, she slumped down onto the couch, dropping her head into her hands. A moment of taut silence dragged by between them before Drew heard him comment bluntly, "Your marriage must have been a poor one to make you abhor the idea of repeating it."

She raised hostile eyes to meet his in stunned disbelief. Her own father had never had the audacity to burden her with useless questions or hurtful recriminations about her divorce. What right did Rolf Erhardt have to pry into her past?

"That's none of your business!"

Her face grew hot as he stood there, unruffled, eyeing her coolly. She shot out at him in her frustration, "But you are right about one thing. I wholeheartedly detest the idea of *this* marriage."

She had a sudden overpowering urge to rake her nails across his arrogant face and she pushed herself up from the couch, moving toward him as she spoke, "I am not a bride. I am your prisoner without a choice in the matter." They were nose to nose now and Drew's anger nudged her recklessly on, "At least with Jim, I was involved in the decisions."

"Poor though they must have been," he countered.

Livid with rage, Drew raised her hand to slap his face. Anticipating her move, Rolf caught her wrist in a hard grip. Turning ner arm to her back, ne pressed her towel-wrapped breasts into his solid chest.

Drew cried out, "Let me go! What do you know about any of it...about me!"

She struggled to free herself from his grasp, unaware that as she did so the precarious hold the corner of the towel had between her breasts was giving away.

"You may be able to force me into this counterfeit marriage, but don't delude yourself into thinking that we could ever be...close..."

She was breathless with his tight hold on her.

His voice had taken on a husky quality. "If you despise being close to me, Mrs. Pollard, then why did you come into my arms?"

He loosened his grip slightly allowing gravity to pull the loosened towel from her body to the floor.

Drew caught her breath in an inhaled cry of alarm as she tried to retrieve it. But Rolf pulled her back to his chest, a dark shadow passing across his rigid face. Deliberately, he leaned toward her until hard brown eyes stared into shimmering gray from little more than a hand's width away.

"From what I have seen so far, Mrs. Pollard, you are not the woman I would have chosen to be *close* to...if given *my* choice."

They stood there, motionless for a long moment, locked in voiceless combat as Drew seethed inside. *Had his choice!* She trembled with indignant fury. Yet even in her all-consuming anger, she was more than vaguely aware of his disturbingly intimate hold on her body. Though he held her fast, his touch was unexpectedly gentle, caressing, and she relaxed slightly in his arms, surprised at her sudden lack of fear. She could feel the slow warmth of his breath titillate her throat, and the heavy, regular thudding of his heart beating against the hummingbird flutter of her own as he held her molded to him.

His large hands moved along her back, one dropping

slowly down from her slim waist over the soft curve of her bare hip. His boldness shocked Drew back to alertness, and she inhaled sharply, suddenly very aware that her nakedness was affecting him in nature's most primitive way.

A twitch had begun in his rock jaw, and a dangerous, feral gleam lit his eyes, making Drew feel like a rabbit caught in the teeth of a hungry wolf. He was the animal—man—and she was just one tempting morsel among the many to be devoured and then forgotten.

She steeled herself to fight him with the only weapon she had at her disposal. . . words. "If I am so repulsive to you, Doctor, then kindly get your hands *off* of me!" The last was a hiss that Drew barely recognized to be her own voice.

Instantly she found herself free of his confining hold and she hurried to retrieve the towel. Fumbling, she wrapped it around herself with trembling fingers, her voice breaking with emotion. "Must you stand there gawking?"

Rolf fought for mastery over a smile, pretending surprise. "Gawking, Mrs. Pollard?" He turned away and bent to coax the flames with a metal poker, sending sparks and revived flames up the chimney before he added, laughter rippling in his voice, "Let us be accurate, at least. Schoolboys gawk. As a scientist, I was merely investigating."

Drew's moan was guttural, and she spun away from him and hurried to the safety of the couch.

With her retreat, Rolf straightened and turned back toward her, his face now serious. "There is really no reason for us to be enemies, Mrs. Pollard." He replaced the poker in its bracket. "This marriage will require of you very little suffering. Once the ceremony is over, I will release your plane."

Drew fought to avoid his eyes, but lost, turning her face back to his as he spoke. "And you, along with the proof of our marriage, will be flown back to the safety of West Germany '' He crossed his arms in front of his chest. "I don't see any reason that we'd ever require any further involvement with each other beyond this." He paused, watching her flushed face absorb this new thought before he continued. "As to having no choices, I will give you one now." He lifted a foot casually behind him, bracing it against the stone of the hearth. "You may remain and join me for dinner—if you can be civil—or you may retire to my room for the night. It is your decision."

"Your room?" It was a weak, fearful question.

He gestured tiredly toward the couch. "I will sleep here." His voice was patronizing. "Your honor is perfectly safe with me."

Drew's cheeks burned. He was treating her like a child, or worse yet, a brainless, totally uninteresting woman. And for some reason, in Drew's mind, that was the most unforgivable sin he had committed since he'd kidnapped her outside the interrogation room. She spat back, "I would rather starve than sit across a table from you!"

One corner of his mouth curved up, but there was no laughter in his eyes as he shrugged disinterestedly. "All right. But don't say that you had no choice in the matter."

Clamping her jaw shut, lips drawn down in a tight line, she whirled from him and retreated down the dark hall to his proffered room, not sure if her pride had won her a victory or merely lost her a meal.

Chapter Three

Drew's eyes fluttered open at a slight sound and she stirred in the large bed. Pulling the thick down comforter up to her chin, she called sleepily, "Who—who's there?"

"You are finally awake," Rolf's deep voice reverberated in the room's quiet.

Drew gasped in a shocked breath. Coming full awake, she raised up on one elbow nearly uncovering her breasts in her haste.

"How dare you! What do you want?"

He stood leaning easily on the closed door, his lips curled in amusement.

"Reverend Peabody is here. I told the guard that 'questioning' would require an hour, so we don't have much time."

"And what possible excuse could you have had for questioning a minister?" Drew frowned irritably.

Rolf's amused expression remained unchanged, "People are not necessarily what they appear to be, Mrs. Pollard. I do not need *excuses* for my actions. I thought I had fully explained that to you."

Realizing that there was no future in that argument, Drew tried again, "But I can't face him...I have no clothes!"

Rolf gestured toward a ladder-back chair that stood by the bed. On it, neatly folded were her gray slacks and sweater, plus a pair of gray wool socks. "Where did my clothes—"

He cut across her question brusquely. "I brought them earlier—"

"Earlier?" Drew's eyes grew round. "You?"

He shrugged. "This is my room, Mrs. Pollard. I came in here to dress for our wedding."

The smile that broke across the rugged sun-bronzed face was wicked and Drew was suddenly struck by an animal magnetism that radiated from this man. He had indeed changed clothes, and they suited him well. The suede sports jacket was of a soft golden tan, blending with the earthiness of his complexion and bringing out the shimmering flicker of his eyes.

He wore no tie, and the starkly white dress shirt was unbuttoned at his throat, revealing the rich brown mat of hair on his chest. The golden glint of a chain sparkled next to his tanned skin and fell away from view beneath the white fabric.

Drew self-consciously pulled her eyes away from his chest, moving her gaze down to note his expertly tailored charcoal-gray slacks and matching shoes.

Her perusal was interrupted as Rolf continued more softly, "You sleep soundly, Mrs. Pollard."

She stiffened, looking up at his self-satisfied face, and frowned, not knowing what he meant by the offhand statement.

"I was quite tired. Now, please go. What will the pastor think?"

"Probably exactly what I want him to think. . . ." He placed one hand inside a coat pocket, hooking the thumb on the outside.

Drew came up to a sitting position holding the comforter before her.

"OOOOHHHH! Will you get out of here?" It was an angry groan.

Unperturbed by her outburst, his eyes moved lingeringly over the woman in his bed. Her color was high, nostrils flared in outrage as the back-lit hair glowed fiery red in wild disarray about her face.

Rolf pursed his lips and lifted his hand, pistollike, toward her. "There is a storm in your eyes, Mrs. Pollard." He cupped the brass knob on the door. "You

had best get your temper under control. The freedom of
many depends on it.''

Drew hugged the comforter close, her knuckles paling
with their hard grip. His words had been spoken softly,
yet they held a warning undercurrent as he went on,
''The pastor and his family will expect to see a radiant
bride, momentarily. Do not disappoint them—or me.''

Drew expelled a gasp of astonishment. ''His *family*!
They're all here?''

''Witnesses.'' He shrugged. ''A necessity at any wedding.''

Drew frowned, regarding him resentfully. ''And at
any *execution*!''

Rolf's lips curved into a sardonic grin revealing white
teeth as he turned the knob. Opening the door, his final
words were spoken louder than necessary. ''Now, put
on some clothes, love, the minister is waiting.'' He
stepped out with a chuckle and closed the door quietly,
leaving Drew to sit, mouth gaping at the nerve of the
man.

A shiver rippled through her, a reminder of her state
of undress. A fact that was now no secret to anyone in
the house. She gritted her teeth. After yesterday's brush
with freezing to death, she knew it wouldn't do to
chance another chill. Quickly, she put on her clothes, as
well as the pair of soft wool socks that Rolf had included with her things, refusing to credit him with a
thoughtful gesture.

''He just doesn't want me to die of anything before
we're legally married!'' she fumed.

A dresser against the wall opposite the bed caught her
eye. Padding to it she saw what she was looking for, a
brush and comb. Standing before the wood-framed mirror she pulled the brush churlishly through her hair. The
night-tossed curls succumbed reluctantly, even with her
overheated ministrations, framing her oval face obediently. Parted naturally on the side, the long loose
waves fell in carefree, yet ordered grace to her shoul-

ders. She inspected the woman who stared back at her from behind the mirrored glass. Her large gray eyes were dark and stormy with anger and humiliation at Rolf's parting words. She hated him for using her to gain his freedom and for forcing her to agree to this bargain.

Bargain! That ordinary word had taken on a distasteful and sinister connotation. She ran a hand irritably through her hair and let out a heavy sigh. There was nothing to do but go through with it—and on his terms. Her reflection soured into a deep frown before she remembered his warning and altered her expression to a stiff, unconvincing smile. No good. She tried again. Better. Nodding, she spoke to herself, "I can get through this thing with my head held high." Squaring her shoulders, she bit out in a whisper, "It'll just be a matter of a few hours, at most, before we leave here. And, as he said, I'll never have to trouble myself with the company of that arrogant man again."

There was a heightened angry blush in her cheeks as her thoughts centered on her captor. "And once Rolf Erhardt is safely out of East Germany, I'll file an uncontested divorce, and that will be that. Simple." Giving a determined nod toward her reflection, she turned quickly away, and with long, purposeful strides, left the room.

Entering the den, Drew stopped short as Reverend Peabody, his wife and daughter turned in her direction. Both the pastor and Margaret were seated on the couch. Sarah stood quietly before the fire.

Rolf unfolded his long frame from the chair as she entered. "*Kindchen,* at last." His smile was dazzling and Drew couldn't help but be affected by it, though she knew it was only part of his act.

She wet her lips and tried out her smile. But she did not answer.

"My dear." The reverend pushed himself up from the couch and circled it to meet her, taking her hand. "We were quite concerned last night when you didn't return from the interrogation...."

There was a fracture in his voice. And Drew could feel the minister's tense embarrassment before he continued, "Doctor Erhardt has just informed us of your desire to be married." He squeezed her hand reassuringly. "Margaret and I were most astonished, I must say."

His wife turned further in her seat, smiling pleasantly. "Oh, Mrs. Pollard, it is so very romantic, isn't it?" She clasped her hands to her ample bosom, "Two young people finding true love...even under such dire circumstances as these!"

Drew nodded, gritting her teeth into a pseudo-smile. "Yes...very."

The pastor turned toward Rolf, who now stood behind Drew. "I must say, Doctor, I am not one to question the Lord's will. But I never expected to marry two people from such diverse backgrounds." He grimaced nervously. "You really haven't known each other... long." His eyes passed from Rolf to Drew, "Are you sure it is marriage you want?"

She gulped convulsively, unable to speak. An expectant hush cloaked the room.

A hand on her shoulder made Drew start. "Tell him, my love." Rolf's voice was as soft as velvet, but his fingers on her shoulders held a sterner message.

Drew found her voice, feeling the threat in his hand. "Yes, Reverend." She lifted her chin a notch. "This marriage is very important to me."

She finished with a carefully selected smile to match the carefully selected words.

The pastor nodded, satisfied.

"Reverend Peabody, I think we should proceed." Rolf spoke with casual authority. "There is little time."

"Of course, Doctor."

The minister relinquished hold of Drew's hand, passing her to Rolf's care.

As he guided Drew to stand before the nearth, his hand slid to her arm.

Sarah and her mother quietly took a place on either side of the young couple. Now, with all obstacles out of the way, the pastor faced Rolf and Drew in his official capacity, opening his leather-bound book to the proper page and clearing his throat importantly.

He began.

Drew stiffened, hearing, in the familiar ministerial monotone, the solemn words she had heard over three years ago. Then she had thought that the vows exchanged would last forever. . . .

She had been wrong, learning with Jim that there was no such thing as a true, unselfish love. Men did not have that tender capacity.

So she stood, now, numbly listening to the same words again, yet this time the man beside her had made no pretense of commitment. He made it clear that he did not even consider her much of a woman. She was to him nothing more than his ticket to freedom.

The reverend's words came to her as if through a long tunnel. . . . "And do you Rolf Erhardt, take this woman. . ."

She held her breath as his softly accented voice spoke the two words calmly: "I do."

"And do you, Drew McKenna Pollard, take this man. . ." Her mouth felt prickly dry and she could not swallow. A sudden weakness in her knees made her feel that without Rolf's strong grasp on her arm, her legs would relinquish their support of her body. "I—I do," she heard herself whisper.

"Will there be a ring, Doctor?" the pastor asked quietly.

Without a word, Rolf removed his supporting hand and withdrew the chain hanging from around his neck and placed it over Drew's head, the small charm that dangled from it falling over the cowl of her sweater.

She looked down at it in some surprise and fingered the beautifully crafted piece. It was a figure eight laid on its side.

Drew immediately recognized it as the scientific symbol of ''Infinity'' and was struck by the irony of Rolf's choice. Obviously, Drew decided, this was something of his own, a stage prop for the witnesses...a substitute for a wedding ring for a woman who would not have been his real choice had circumstances been different.

Infinity. It meant ''boundless, without limits.'' Drew thought darkly that the only infinity about their relationship was the boundlessness of their deceit.

She felt Rolf replace his hand on her arm as she lifted her eyes back to the minister's face.

''Fine,'' breathed Reverend Peabody as the charm was laid in place. He nodded. ''And now, with the power vested in me, I pronounce you husband and wife.''

Closing his book, he looked up. First to Drew he smiled reassuringly. Then turning to Dr. Erhardt he said, ''According to custom, Doctor, now would be the time to kiss the bride....''

Rolf lifted a hand halting the minister's explanation. ''A fine custom, Reverend, and practiced the world over.''

He turned to face Drew, his eyes dark, taunting, daring her without the need for words. Drew did not draw away, but faced his challenging look, unblinking.

His arms encircled her waist as he lowered his mouth to hers, his lips were hard and demanding, devoid of tenderness.

Drew's eyes flew open. His kiss was electric, sending conflicting impulses from her skin to her brain. Panic raced up her spine and she pressed her hands firmly against his soft suede coat.

At the urgent pressure of her hands, Rolf drew his lips from hers. Yet at the last instant, he tugged at her lower lip softly, teasing it with his teeth. The move was so slight and quick it went unseen by those observing. But to Drew it was like a slap across the face and just as hurtful. She knew it was his way of showing her that he cared nothing at all for her feelings... or for the vows they had just exchanged.

She stepped back unsteadily, throwing him a pointed look that he returned with a wide grin. Before she could move away, she felt his arm slide to her waist as he played the part of ardent groom while congratulations were exchanged.

"My goodness," came Margaret Peabody's high-pitched voice, "that wind picked up awfully suddenly...and look at that snow come down now! And right on top of all the snow last night, too."

Drew turned toward the window. True enough. What had been a gently fluttering snowfall earlier that morning was now working itself into another real storm.

Drew viewed the weather's reaction to their wedding as an ominous sign, and while the Peabodys gathered at the window, she looked up into Rolf's roguish face and whispered harshly, "Get your hands off me!"

She jerked out of his grasp.

"I've done what I said I would. Now let me go."

A solid knock at the door caused her to jump, and brought the remainder of the party to a tense alertness.

"Remember," Rolf whispered a warning as he motioned the Peabodys toward the door, "if we are found out, there will be serious retaliations affecting us all."

The pastor and his family exchanged nervous glances.

"Don't panic, Reverend." He softened his words. "I promise you that if we keep our heads and hold our tongues, all will go well." Almost as an afterthought, he added, "You have done us both a great service." He smiled down at Drew and squeezed her waist lovingly.

The pastor nodded in sober understanding as Rolf released his wife and admitted the guard.

Drew was amazed to see how Rolf's expression could effortlessly run the gamut from enamored bridegroom to this ruthless, grim commander that stood before them now. His voice had taken on a gruff snarl as he dismissed the Peabody family to the custody of the burly guard.

An odd smirk on the bulbous-nosed soldier's face as his eyes passed over Drew made her stiffen. She felt a crawling unease, confused at his strange behavior.

When the door closed behind them, Drew jumped again at the unexpected sound of the phone ringing at her side.

Rolf moved to the low table by the door and answered it. After a few crisp sentences, he replaced the receiver in its cradle and turned back to face Drew, his brows knit.

"This morning, I issued orders to have your plane ready for takeoff by noon." He nodded toward the phone. "I have just received word that new, heavy snowstorms and high winds will make air travel impossible for the present."

Drew's dark-lashed eyes grew wide. "What? You mean we won't be able to leave now? What about tonight?"

Rolf shook his head slowly from side to side and ran long slender fingers through his thick hair.

"It appears that it will be several days, perhaps a week."

"A week!" Drew's words were a fearful squeak. "Then...you will send me back to the compound, won't you?"

Rolf's brows arched in surprise. "You? I can't chance it."

Drew took an involuntary step backward. "But—but I can't stay here. How would you explain my continued absence? Certainly not *questioning*!"

His face hardened and his voice was gruff. "I don't need to explain anything. Those whom I command here know only what I want them to know." He reached toward her and slid his hand up her arm. "In this case, they have been told that you are a very accommodating American woman, willing to give me your...charms... for a better standard of living, during your confinement.''

Drew stumbled away from his touch, putting a palm to her mouth to stifle a gasp as his meaning became clear.

He moved with her, taking hold of her shoulders, his grasp confining, yet gentle, as he continued, ''That is the impression I will continue to promote until I get you on that plane out of East Germany.''

Stunned by his revelation, Drew cried, ''You told them that I—that I prostituted myself!'' She tugged at his grip on her, wanting to get away. ''You told them that about me?''

Jerking free, she turned from him, irritably pulling a hand through her hair. ''That's just fine! Wonderful! The whole installation thinks I'm a tramp...and I'm sure they've passed that bit of propaganda along to the rest of the passengers.''

Her face burned. ''No wonder I felt like 'Today's Special' at some cheap diner when your guard looked me over just now!''

''Don't let imagined slights make you lose sight of what is important.'' Rolf's voice was deceptively quiet.

As he spoke, Drew could hear him approach her from behind. The pressure of his hands on her arms demanded that she turn back to face him. She was shocked by his face, now as glacial as the wind howling outside. His dark brown eyes held an almost insulting lack of concern for her feelings.

''You don't think that I would allow you out of my sight now, do you?'' His lashes were drawn down, narrowing his eyes; his face was hard and stony. ''I don't give a damn what anyone here thinks. My only concern from this point forward is that you are my passport out of here.''

He released her and crossed to the low table before

the couch, pointing to the sheet of paper lying face down on its surface. "Until you and this marriage certificate are out of the East, you will be in my custody— and only mine—whatever pretense I must manufacture to keep us together. Is that understood!"

It was in no way a question.

"But this wasn't part of the bargain! I can't stay here, alone with you for a whole week!" she stammered.

"Don't be a fool!" he declared bluntly. "This is the safest place for you to be. . .under the circumstances."

Drew shot back, near hysterical laughter escaping her lips, "Safe! I'd feel safer spending a week in a pit of snakes than here with—"

"Your husband?" he finished. Somehow, when he said it, the word took on a sensual connotation. "Is that what you fear? That I will insist upon my marital rights?"

The words were carefully articulated, their importance accented by the raking scrutiny of his eyes.

Drew's stomach constricted violently at his unexpected suggestion.

"That," she flared, "was definitely not part of the bargain!"

She whirled away toward the heavily frosted window. "You, Dr. Erhardt, are a predator of the worst sort. . . . A user, like all men."

She took a few brisk steps to increase the distance between them. "And since you brought it up, yes. I've no doubt that you'd take full advantage of any situation that came your way!"

Her tirade was halted abruptly by her own cry of alarm as she felt her balance being wrenched away. With some surprise, Drew realized that she wasn't falling. Just the opposite was true. Rolf had swept her up into his arms.

"What—what are you doing? Let go of me!" she cried breathlessly, kicking wildly and flailing her fists at his chest.

Rolf appeared not to be affected in the slightest as he strode with determination from the den and down the hall. His face was devoid of mercy and his eyes held a rich and unyielding cunning.

"You do not doubt that I would take advantage of you?" He kicked wide the door to his bedroom. "I am of the opinion—*Frau* Erhardt—that we should put your declaration to a test."

The sounding of the door crashing into the wall made Drew jump violently. Her eyes grew wide as she saw the rumpled bed she had vacated earlier. Turning her hot face to his purposeful one, she moaned, "You said you wouldn't. . . ."

He did not slow his stride as he crossed to the bed and dropped Drew on it.

She began to scramble up but found his large hands pressing her shoulders down as he lowered his face to hers, his lips finding her own with a bold lustiness.

His kiss was a heady mixture of subtlety and strength, more overpowering than the most zealous attempts Drew had endured at the hands of her first husband. Even in her fright, it affected her in a way that she had not expected.

Her body was tensed and ready for a fight, yet while his wedding kiss had been a shock to her senses, this pagan use of her lips stunned her into a momentary paralysis.

Her hands, fingers spread, were poised, unmoving on his chest. The warm invitation of his mouth sapped the strength of her will as her skin became charged with his touch.

With a tremendous effort, she turned her face away from his, but he anticipated it and moved with her, his lips masterful, his tongue probing, enticing.

One warm hand began to trace light strokes along her shoulder, making their playful presence felt beneath the cashmere film of her sweater as it moved silkily down her arm. His thumb grazed the womanly curve of her breast causing Drew to shudder involuntarily at the impact of his touch.

"No!" she whispered as his lips lifted from hers to follow their tormenting path along her fine-boned jaw and rest softly on her wildly pulsing throat. His tongue sent feathery spasms through her body as he teased the sensitive flesh.

A ragged breath escaped her lips. "Please..." she whimpered as her body, recovering from the initial shock of his kiss, began to receive warning signals, once again, from her brain. Fearful of her unfathomable reaction to his kiss, she pushed vigorously against him. But his strength was too much and she couldn't free herself from his encompassing frame.

Twisting sidewise she moaned, "All men are the same.... You get what you want, no matter who you hurt. *You liar!*" Tears welled up in her eyes and slid unimpeded across her cheek. "I should have known I couldn't trust you!"

Her last words were a hopeless sob as she gave one final, desperate shove at his chest.

Suddenly his masculine warmth was gone. She opened her eyes, puzzled to see him towering above her, jaw working angrily beneath flashing, narrowed eyes. "You are right in part, Drew. I *am* using you." He lifted his angular chin, but kept his eyes riveted on her face. "But only to gain my freedom. As I said before, I will not force myself on you." His lips opened in a smile, but it contained no kindness. It was a hard, forbidding smile, like that of a snarling wolf. "For a woman who has shared a man's bed, you have much to learn about making love."

"Love!" she choked, coming up on an elbow. "You call what you just did 'making love'?"

His crisp laugh was filled with malice. "Hardly. An invitation, perhaps. And one that I will not burden you with again." His carnivorous smile moved up to smolder within his eyes. "Women are not so difficult to have that I will waste my time with a whimpering wife—no matter that the carnal use of your body is now my husbandly right.''

His pointed remark brought her up to her knees, and she glared into his dark golden eyes, retorting angrily, ''Touch me and I'll tear up the marriage document. I'd rather be a political prisoner than your sexual target!''

His smiled changed almost imperceptibly, now holding a trace of genuine amusement. ''Ah, good. I see that I haven't broken your fighting spirit. I would hate to leave thinking I had cowed you into sniveling submission.''

''Leave?'' Drew's expression changed from anger to an odd panic. ''Where are you going?''

He shrugged easily. ''To assume my regular duties. At this point, I can't afford to arouse suspicions.''

He turned toward the door throwing back over his shoulder, ''I'll be gone for several hours. Have a meal ready when I get back.''

''I won't cook for you!'' she shouted angrily. But her only answer was the opening and closing of the cabin's front door.

He was gone.

Drew jumped to her feet and padded after him. Reaching the door, she rubbed at the condensate that frosted the inside of its small window just in time to see him disappear into the trees on the other side of the road. He now wore the heavy, hooded parka that had been hanging on a hook by the door.

The jeep was parked where it had been since their arrival the evening before. Drew puzzled over this, concluding that the installation must be well camouflaged...perhaps not far away, across the undulating curtain of blowing snow beyond the wall of rime-coated pines.

She bit her lip and stepped away from the door. The low howling of the wind seemed to echo her own desolation as her feet guided her listlessly into the den.

She became aware of the dull beginnings of a headache and placed her palms to her temples to ease the pain.

Sitting down heavily on the couch, her eyes dropped to the white sheet of paper lying on the table. Disinterestedly, she fingered it, flipping it over. It was all very official and legal, this marriage certificate.

For one rebellious instant, Drew wanted to rip it to shreds, severing any ties she had with Rolf Erhardt. But reason returned and she remembered that the freedom of sixty-eight people rested on the safety of that piece of paper.

Her hand began to tremble, and the document fluttered from her fingers.

Drew put her hands to fiery cheeks, allowing a shuddering sob to escape her throat. "A week..."

She slumped back into the soft cushions of the sofa and stared, unseeing, into the magenta-tipped flames of a dying fire.

Chapter Four

Drew huddled on the couch before a carefully nurtured fire, having now used all the logs Rolf had brought inside for that purpose. She felt very cold, even in her cashmere slacks and sweater, and she pulled the comforter close about her shivering frame.

The door clicked open, its loudness magnified in Drew's ears by the silent hours she had spent alone in Rolf's house. She stiffened and turned toward the door to see him enter and toss his snow-flecked parka on the hook near the door.

Fearfully, she judged his mood, noting the set, angular lines of his rugged profile and she gulped nervously, her head pounding furiously behind her eyes.

As he turned toward her and strolled into the den, she turned away, catching her breath, waiting....

"Did you get something to eat?" The question was not harsh, not even curt. He just sounded tired, weary.

She looked back up at him. "No...no, I'm not hungry."

His brows knit in a puzzled frown as he cocked his head, "No?" Lifting broad shoulders he went on, matter-of-factly, "Well, I am. Come, we can make something together."

Drew looked away from his face. She didn't speak.

"Drew?" he questioned. "It is so late, dinner will be faster if we both—" She sneezed violently, unable to hold it back any longer.

A frown deepened on his brow. "What is this?" He moved around the couch and placed his hand on her forehead. It felt cool to Drew.

Embarrassed, she tried to move away from his touch.

"I—please, Doctor. . .go and fix yourself something. I'll be all right."

"Don't be silly." He held her face firmly between both hands. "You're ill."

Drew couldn't answer. It was too obvious a thing to argue. She was ill. And most disconcerting was the fact that they both knew why. It was because of her foolish dash in the snow last night.

She ran the back of her hand across dry lips before another sneeze shook her shoulders, and then another as she put an odd, squared piece of cloth to her nose, blowing.

Rolf removed his cool hands from her head and bent to her side, lifting another square of fabric, frayed at the edges, from a large stack. "What is this?"

Drew winced inwardly. What would he think of her when she told him that she'd torn up one of his bed sheets in a moment of unreasonable irritation?

She recalled going through his dresser when she had first started sniffling and locating his handkerchiefs lying next to a color photograph of an attractive, smiling blond woman with the name "Monika" swirled in flowing, feathery script across the lower right-hand corner.

Oddly piqued by the lovely woman's photograph nestled intimately among his things, Drew had left his handkerchiefs undisturbed and chosen instead to tear up one of his defenseless sheets.

Now, though, she was ashamed and surprised by her unreasonable action, feeling like she'd once again reverted to childishness, for Dr. Erhardt's love life was certainly his own business!

She cleared her throat. He was standing silently, waiting for an explanation.

"I—I needed handkerchiefs. I know I've ruined a perfectly good sheet." Her words were muffled as she looked up at him from behind the piece of cloth and lied, "But, I couldn't find any of yours. . . ."

His smile was amused and tolerant, both of which

Drew knew she didn't deserve. He was shaking his head, chuckling. "Very resourceful."

She interjected quickly, in guilt, "Of course, Doctor, I intend to pay..."

With a slightly irritated wave of his hand, he halted her words, changing the subject. "About dinner..."

She looked away. "I—I'll just stay here. I don't want..." She coughed.

Shrugging, he said, "We'll discuss that later." He moved to flip off the lamp near the couch. "You get some rest. I'll call you when it's ready."

The room was now bathed in the muted colors of glowing embers. Drew didn't feel like following him out to reiterate her insistence that she wouldn't eat. She didn't even feel like sitting up. Sinking into the softness of the couch, she pulled the comforter about her and drifted off to sleep.

WHAT is that? Her eyes came open. The room was still dark, but something in that darkness smelled awfully good. She inhaled deeply. Even through the stuffiness in her nose, she could detect the highly seasoned aroma of something delicious.

Her stomach issued an insistent growl that she find the aroma's origin. Pulling herself up and dragging the beige comforter with her, Drew padded down the hall to its far end and entered a large square kitchen.

She blinked at the brightness of the room and stepped just inside the door looking absently around the orderly kitchen. The cabinets were all natural pine, stained a medium brown. The roof was vaulted, a heavy beam running across the center. From it, over the stove, hung a long iron bar with four hooks protruding from the lower end. Several well-used iron pots and pans dangled from them by their handles. The stove was of a German make, gas burners on the top, with a windowless door below. The white refrigerator was the most unusual appliance, for it was only counter-top high. This was,

Drew knew, because Germans shopped for fresh meat and vegetables nearly every day, requiring less storage space. All in all it was very unlike her modern, convenience-oriented kitchen in Los Alamos, New Mexico.

Rolf stood with his back to her before the stove stirring something in an iron pot. He had changed from his suede coat and gray slacks and now he sported a black and brown plaid flannel shirt, the sleeves rolled up his muscular arms midway to the elbow. And once again he wore tight-fitting faded jeans and brown work boots.

An odd feeling of normality invaded Drew's consciousness as she watched Rolf, tall and quiet before the stove. It almost seemed like home.

Home! The very idea was ridiculous. It was no home! More correctly, it was a prison. Drew shook off the foolish notion.

She tried to stifle a sneeze, but was unsuccessful.

Rolf turned at the small sound. "You're up."

Drew took a few steps forward. "What are you cooking? It smells..." She had almost said "good" when she stopped herself, refusing to compliment her captor. "...different."

"Sit down." He gestured with a long wooden spoon toward a round table near the door. "It's ready."

She lowered herself wearily into the nearest of four chairs that surrounded the pine table as he continued, "It's *Kohlsuppe*—cabbage soup with smoked sausage."

Drew wrinkled her nose, puzzled. "I thought cabbage was supposed to smell bad."

Rolf turned back to the stove, a smile playing at one corner of his expressive mouth. "I assure you, the taste will not disappoint you either."

She moved her elbows to the table, cupping her chin in her hands. The kitchen was warm and she allowed the comforter to fall from her shoulders. "You assured me once that I'd be out of here an hour after our wedding, too!" With his lack of response, she pressed on. "So, you see, Doctor, the value of your assurances is questionable.'' She blew into the crumpled cloth in her hand.

Unperturbed Rolf moved to a cabinet and opened it, removing two brown pottery plates and bowls. He didn't turn to Drew as he spoke. ''Your fellow passengers''—he began to fill the bowls with the steamy soup—''have been moved to more suitable quarters since their stay has been extended.''

He placed a full bowl on a plate and crossed with it to Drew. Brown eyes caught gray. ''The Peabodys are bearing up quite well.'' His words were matter-of-fact.

Sitting back, Drew folded her arms in her lap as he placed the bowl on the umber linen mat before her. A depressing weight had been lowered to her already pounding head. ''Then we *really* will be here for days. . . even a week?''

''At least a week, Drew.''

He turned away from her, walking back to the stove to retrieve his own bowl. Drew lowered her eyes, catching sight of Rolf's long sinewy legs moving across the floor with fluidity and ease. He seemed totally unconcerned about their living situation, one that was completely unacceptable to Drew.

She straightened in her chair. ''If the Peabodys are all right in the quarters, then why wouldn't I be?'' A sneeze burst from her lips before she could go on. ''How. . . how can you trust them out of your sight and not me?''

He turned, the guttural cadence of his accent more pronounced as he explained calmly, ''The Peabodys will not talk. They have each other to think of.'' A heavy brow arched in mocking challenge. ''You, on the other hand, have already proven your lack of ability to keep a secret. Remember, I found out who you are.''

Drew opened her mouth to protest but was cut off as he continued. ''Beyond that, Drew, you are in no condition to leave.'' His look was unreadable. ''I can give you *much* more individual attention here than you would get in the quarters.''

Drew sputtered, "That's exactly my point, Doctor. I don't want your *individual* attention!"

Rolf returned with his bowl and sat down at her left, eyeing her narrowly. "Stop talking nonsense and eat."

Drew blinked at the sudden sternness in his tone; new anger blossomed at his unyielding attitude. "I told you I didn't want anything!"

His lips twisted into a sarcastic smile. "Yes, you do." His tone had lost its harsh edge.

"Oh? And to what miracle do you owe this new-found clairvoyance, Doctor?"

Right on cue, her stomach growled angrily and she shot an embarrassed glance toward Rolf. He appeared not to have heard. Thick lashes obscured his eyes as he lifted his spoon to his lips. Drew looked down at her bowl. The soup's aroma wafted up into her nostrils, clearing her head with its spicy fragrance. Her mouth watered. He was right, of course. She was terribly hungry. She realized it wouldn't do her any good to abuse her health because of her pride. Taking up the spoon and skimming the surface, she tasted the soup. It was good...very good, just what she needed, hearty and filling.

They'd been sitting, eating in silence for several minutes when Rolf's deep voice startled her. "Would you like more?"

"No...no more." She kept her eyes averted.

He stood, taking his bowl. "You're welcome. It was no bother at all."

Drew bit her lip at his gibe. It was not like her to be ungrateful. But somehow, she couldn't bring herself to make friends with this man. And she had every reason not to, she reminded herself...after what he'd done—threatening to put her in a Communist prison, blackmailing her into marriage to gain his freedom, and now, keeping her locked up as his personal prisoner, of letting everyone think she was a—a—!

She sneezed loudly and the quiet that followed bore

heavily down on her. She decided to thrust a gibe of her own. "I'm surprised that a man in your position is forced to do all his own cooking." She lifted challenging gray eyes to his as he resumed his seat at her side.

Looking over at her passively, he spoke, "I don't do it all. Sometimes I am invited out. And occasionally, I invite someone over who cooks a meal for both of us."

"Like Monika?" The question came out without Drew's permission.

Rolf lifted a brow in surprise, but recovered himself. "Like Monika." He nodded. A slight smile passed fleetingly across his lips.

Drew compressed her mouth into a tight line, angry with herself. She was caught in her lie. He knew she had found his handkerchiefs...and Monika's photograph...and worst of all, why she had torn up his sheet!

"Monika is a good...cook, I suppose?" Drew didn't know why she'd brought this up.

"Among other things." Laughter sparkled in his eyes, making Drew grit her teeth.

Anger flared within her and she was at a loss to understand why Rolf's complimentary reference to this unknown woman irritated her so. She countered, "Yes? Well, if Monika is so *indispensable,* I'd be happy to tear up that marriage certificate and you can send me to the passengers' quarters.... We could just forget this whole thing, you know!"

He rubbed his napkin over his lips, remarking, "Haven't you done enough tearing up for one day?"

Was he hiding a smile? Drew winced, her self-respect dropping to zero.

Clearing his throat with some difficulty, he continued, "I admit, Drew, that Monika is quite a woman... in many ways." He replaced the napkin. "However, she is not an American citizen. Right now, that is all that counts with me."

Drew shot to her feet. She'd lost face with his discovery of her lie, and she was on the defensive. "You talk about Monika as though she were a thing!" The sudden move made her dizzy and she grabbed for the table.

Rolf stood quickly to steady her. "Sit down, Drew, you're not well."

She raged on, ignoring his concern, mortified that he seemed to be taking the whole situation so lightly. "And...I...I'm nothing to you either—just a ticket out!" She shook her head numbly. "Is that what women are to men—things to be *owned,* to be *used*?"

She looked up into his serious face, there were two of him—no, four. "Men! You take so much and give so little in return!" she cried weakly, running a shaky hand across a sweat-beaded forehead.

"Drew..." his hands were on her arms.

"Leave me alone!" She pushed past him into the hall dragging the comforter along behind her. In her weakened state, she had to steady herself along the wall as she returned to the den. Once there, she dropped tiredly onto the couch and lay for some minutes, wrapped cocoonlike in the down-filled quilt, listening to the clank of dishes being cleared away.

After a time, the kitchen noises ceased, and she could hear the sound of Rolf's booted footsteps as he entered the den.

She tensed, not knowing what mood to expect. His tall frame came into her view when he passed the couch and walked directly to the hearth. Placing one hand on the mantel, he appeared to be looking down into the glowing embers. Drew was startled to notice a slight droop in his wide shoulders as he released a long, slow breath. He seemed tired, or was it more? Was he, perhaps, as disturbed by this delay in the Lufthansa's departure as she?

Drew mentally shook it off looking away from his broad back. No. Why should he be worried...he had his story all worked out. It was just her imagination.

Her sneeze invaded the quiet. Drew looked back up at Rolf as he turned toward her. He was now in the process of removing his shirt. "I thought you were in bed."

He tossed the flannel garment across the back of the easy chair on his left. "I—I am." Drew pulled the comforter protectively up to her chin.

His face was serious. "You're ill. You'd rest better in the bed."

Drew stiffened. "I'm not sleeping in your room again!" She set her jaw stubbornly.

"I had not realized that my room was so offensive to you." His voice was heavy with exasperation.

Drew shot back, "It's not the *room* that's offensive! It's just that I refuse to go in that bedroom where *you* can just saunter in and out any time to change clothes. . . or whatever. There's no privacy."

Rolf's expression showed puzzled surprise. He lowered himself to sit on the edge of the table, leaning forward, his elbows resting on his knees. "I wonder if you realize that what you just said makes no sense at all." The remark held a trace of humor. "At least you have a door to close there."

Drew chewed on her lower lip. He was right. It hadn't come out exactly the way she'd meant it. . . . Maybe her fever had fried her brains and millions of cerebral cells were shriveling up, forever useless.

She rubbed a hand across her dry lips. "You know what I meant. This is your house. . . . It really doesn't matter where I sleep. . . . I can't be assured of privacy anywhere in it. So, I'm staying here."

Drew wasn't going to say it, but she also knew that since the couch was narrow, there was less danger of waking to find the tall German lying next to her than there was if she took the large bed!

Rolf lifted his bronze shoulders in a resigned gesture. The movement in the low glow from the hearth accented the ripple of muscles along his arms and shoulders. "That is your final decision?"

Drew nodded. "It is!"

"All right, then." He stood and unbuckled his belt, sliding it swiftly out of his belt loops and tossing it on the chair.

Drew's eyes grew round. "What are you doing?" she gasped.

"Undressing." His face was passive.

"Here?" she squeaked.

"Oh, yes, here and now."

Drew pushed herself up, her palms behind her on the couch, "Oh, no you're not. Go to your own room to do that!"

His lips opened into a wicked grin. "I gave the bedroom to you. The couch is mine."

He slipped the waistband button through its hole as he continued, "I admit with you joining me here, it will be a little crowded . . . but I can manage if you can."

The zipper opening raked loudly across Drew's consciousness as he prepared to remove his jeans. He was actually going to take off his pants before her very eyes!

"I—*no*—you can't—" she stammered weakly, flailing her feet to untangle herself from the folds of the comforter. At last free, she shot up from the couch and without a backward glance dashed for the comparative safety of Rolf's room, an added heat rushing to her already flushed face.

At the bedroom door, she was chagrined to hear, above the pounding of her own heart in her ears, Rolf's hearty laughter. Grinding her teeth angrily, she pushed through the door into the dark bedroom, slamming it irritably at her back. She hated him for his unfailing ability to make her retreat in humiliation and embarrassment.

SOMETHING woke Drew. Was it a door closing, or merely the spattering of snow against the window? She turned quickly toward the entrance half-expecting to see Rolf standing there. He wasn't.

But her eyes widened as she caught sight of something else, something new to the room. "My suitcase!" she breathed, unable to believe her eyes.

She'd almost resigned herself to not having a change of clothes—or even seeing her suitcase again—and her pride wouldn't allow her to ask Rolf for anything, not after that first night when he begrudgingly loaned her a towel. But her suitcase was actually here! She slipped her legs from between the sheets and padded to it.

Laying it on its side, she opened it carefully, pulling out a floor-length royal-blue velour robe and matching scuffs. She tied the soft, warm fabric about her chilled nakedness with the long sash.

A bath and a change of clothes—these were the first things on her agenda. It would be good to feel really clean again...and, too, a hot steamy room would be just the thing to help clear her stuffy head.

She quickly removed the things how would need from her suitcase and opened the door. "Rolf?"

She tiptoed into the den. He was not there—maybe the kitchen....

No. She looked at her watch, puzzled by his absence. *Eleven-thirty!*

Goodness! She hadn't realized she'd slept so late. Of course, by now, Rolf would have gone to work. *Good,* she thought resolutely. *At least, now I'll have plenty of time to myself to bathe and change.*

She sniffed as she headed back into the hall toward the bathroom. It was a small, utilitarian room. The tub was white porcelain, deeper than American tubs. As well as a faucet, there was a flexible metal tube with a shower head so that a person could shower while sitting, or it could be hand-held for a regular standing shower.

Drew switched on the water to adjust the temperature. Her head felt like a bowling ball, thick and heavy. She peered curiously into the medicine cabinet over the sink. There she found a razor, toothpaste and brush, a new bar of soap, and a bottle. Drew absently lifted the

bottle and unscrewed the lid. Sniffing deeply, she realized that it must be cologne, for the fragrance was a
pleasant combination of pine and earthy spices. Suddenly she had an uncomfortable feeling that this was
probably a gift...from Monika. Recapping it quickly,
she put it back.

That was everything there was. No aspirin, no nasal
spray...not even Band-Aids! Was Rolf Erhardt
human? Didn't he even suffer normal human failings?
Was he never sick? She closed the cabinet dejectedly.

Taking a few bobby pins from her pocket, Drew
pinned her chestnut hair up on the crown of her head. A
few errant wisps defied capture and framed her face in
impish disarray.

The water was churning near the tub's rim now. Drew
slipped out of her robe and scuffs and climbed tentatively into the slightly overwarm water.

Soon she became used to its warmth, and sighing,
leaned her head back against the pale-green tiled wall,
closing her eyes.

She breathed deeply of the steam-laden air. It helped.
She felt like staying here all day. And maybe she would,
she mused. There was certainly nothing better to do in
this—this jail.

The caressing water and the total quiet were hypnotic,
and Drew found herself nodding off to sleep. *What difference does it make?* she thought, groggily. *At least in
here I can breathe! And besides, Rolf won't be back for
hours...lovely, quiet, restful hours.*

Drew smiled to herself, her breathing less labored. At
least, at this moment, she was glad to be in Rolf's home
instead of some crowded barracks where there would be
minimal comforts. She yawned. And probably no bath-
tub at all.

"So, here you are."

Drew's head jerked up. She was confused and disori-
ented. Where was she? Tepid water sloshing over her
cooled skin reminded her that she was still in the tub.

But that couldn't be, because Rolf's voice was so near.

Rolf? Her eyes flew to the door, as she blinked to focus her sleep-blurred vision. He was there, standing just inside the door, which now stood slightly ajar.

"What—?" she gasped, belatedly covering herself. "What are you doing in here?" It was an apprehensive whisper.

He closed the door, his lips slowly twisting upward. "I thought, perhaps, now that you have your things, you decided to try to escape from me." His voice was low.

"Escape?" Drew's rosy skin deepened in color with her embarrassment. "Where would I go?" Her eyes grew wide with misgiving as a shiver danced along her spine.

His lazy look moved slowly from her flushed face to the soft curve of her breasts, exposed above the sudsy water. What was his intent? Because of the bargain, Drew had put aside her fear that he would physically molest her... but now? What did she actually know about this man? Did he too enjoy mastering women by physical force—like Jim? Her heart pounded painfully against her ribs. He could very easily rape her here, and there would be no one to lift a finger to aid her! A man in Rolf Erhardt's position made his own rules where women were concerned. Her own captivity was proof enough of *that* fact!

Her words were hushed and hesitant. "Please, Doctor, I beg you..."

He interrupted her anxious plea, hooking a thumb easily in his jeans pocket. "Are you feeling better today?"

Drew was taken aback by his casual manner. He could have been discussing the weather at a cocktail party instead of standing forbiddingly over her while she sat naked and trembling in a tub of cooling water.

She became desperate, crying, "Doctor, if you are not totally without scruples, you will leave!"

He lifted a dark brow and rubbed a lean knuckle across his square jaw. "Sometimes scruples can be in conflict with a man's best interests, Drew." He took a step forward. "With stakes this high, I cannot afford to have them."

Her eyes dilated in fear, darkening their color. "What are you going to do?" She sank deeper into the water until it licked her chin.

"Protect my interests, *Kindchen*. You're shivering." He picked up her robe. "Now, get out of that tub and back into bed."

He stood there, holding the robe like a coat, fully expecting her to obey him. She didn't move. Their eyes locked for a long moment before Rolf took action. It was quick, making Drew jump, fearful of a blow. But rather than striking out at her as she'd feared, Rolf had pulled the drain plug by its chain and the water slowly began to recede.

"You might as well get out now, Drew. But if you insist on staying, I will wait. I am a patient man." The dark eyes watching her held a dangerous glint.

She sat, feeling the water slip below her crossed arms and down along her stomach. Very little was still hidden from Rolf's all-consuming view.

She pulled her lips into a tight little frown of dismay, feeling helpless, yet her stubbornness refused to allow her to give in to his demands. "Must you shame me this way, Doctor? Does it give you a sense of power?"

"My name is *Rolf*." He sounded slightly hoarse, as though his throat was suddenly dry. Those four words, spoken with just a tinge of difficulty, sent a primitive shiver of alarm up her spine. She looked up into his eyes and gulped at the hungry new light that flickered within the brown depths, and she bit her lip.

If there was one thing she *did* know about men, it was that look. She didn't have much time. Moving quickly, she straightened and pulled the robe about her shoulders, slipping her arms into the sleeves.

Turning to face him as she tied the sash, she sputtered, "Well, *Doctor,* are you satisfied?"

"Not quite." His voice was now cold, and the light had gone out of his eyes. He scooped up the slippers and handed them to her, "I want you back in that bed."

"Oh?" She lifted her chin bravely. "And just why do you spend practically *all* of your time coaxing me into that overworked bed?"

A twitch began in his jaw and his words were measured in his attempt to keep his temper. "Drew, if you could see yourself now, you'd realize that my motives are anything but suspect. Your nose is red, your eyes, puffy..."

Drew had heard enough. Without another word she stepped swiftly over the side of the tub, brushing past him into the hall, making the bedroom door before Rolf caught up with her. He grasped her arm, spinning her around to face him. All tolerance was gone from his face.

"Here, take this." He shoved a small bottle into her hand. "I don't have time to stand here and trade barbs with you. Now get back into that bed. There is a lot at stake, and you need your health."

His eyes glittered with angry sparks as he moved his hands to her arms. "Drew, do you have any *real* idea of what you and I are involved in here?" His face was close now. "One slip—by either of us—and any hope you had for returning to a normal life is over!"

Drew stiffened at the ominous warning. "Yes, Doctor," she hissed between clenched teeth. "I'm well aware of the danger...but only to me!" She pushed against his chest, more than vaguely aware of the sheer force of his towering presence.

She wanted to get away, her heart was pounding deafeningly in her ears, and she could barely hear her own words. She raised her voice. "But I can't see any problem for *you.* You're covering your tracks pretty well, I'd say." Eyeing him evenly she lifted her face to his, jutting a persistent chin. "Remember? I'm supposed to be your *whore....*"

The word was stifled abruptly as Rolf's kiss seared across her parted lips. He moved his hands to her back, crushing her to him, molding her velour-clad curves to the granite hardness of his chest.

Drew strained away from his bruising mouth, but he would not release her lips from their captivity. Then the angry harshness seemed to melt away, replaced by a pliant, gentle eagerness as his lips separated slightly, allowing his tongue to begin its leisurely stroking of the ultra-sensitive skin of her mouth.

Drew's defenses weakened and began a slow retreat from his sensual assault on her lips.

A guttural half-moan, half-sigh escaped her throat as she felt his large hands begin to move along her back. One traveled up to stroke softly below the damp wisps of hair at the nape of her neck. The other moved down to her waist, then lower over the soft velvety curve of her hip.

Drew knew this was wrong...or it should have been wrong. But it didn't seem that way. She slid her arms up his chest and slowly encircled his neck with her hands, opening her lips to freely admit his masterful tongue.

As he pulled her close, Drew became aware of the rich, masculine scent of him, the mingling of clean, scrubbed skin and his own highly individual scent. There was no trace of the pine cologne she had found earlier, and for some wild illogical reason, that made her happy.

Her legs suddenly began to tremble and breathing became difficult. Time slowed, and Drew felt as though she were suspended in space, floating softly within Rolf's embrace.

His kiss was torrid, igniting an unexpected yearning within her. And without hesitation, she molded herself to his lean, powerful masculinity.

Why did her body feel so alive within this man's...

this stranger's arms, when with her husband she had always been hesitant of intimacy? Yet now there was a complete lack of any desire to hold herself back.

She lifted one searching hand to his curly nape, running her fingers through the thick softness of his hair. Drawing her lips from his, she moved her face to his cheek, pressing answering kisses along the hollow there, to his ear. And surprised at her own unshackled passions, she nipped softly at the inviting lobe.

A throaty laugh escaped her lips, a delighted, happy giggle of abandon. She knew a buoyant freedom and was oddly thrilled to feel his heightened desire as she actively pursued their sweet intimacy, reveling in her own womanly power over this intoxicating man.

Rolf's lips were feather soft at her throat. "The lady is amused?" His voice was deep, lazy, laced slightly with a questioning tone.

Drew moved to face him, smiling, eyes the rich, shimmering color of sterling. "Only with myself..." She felt a scarlet blush rush up her cheeks. "I—I'm sorry... I seem to have lost myself.... You have a strange effect on me." She paused, breathless, almost fearful...waiting. But for what? What did she expect him to say? What did she *want* him to say?

Thick lashes framed honest brown eyes that smoldered with undisguised desire as he placed a finger beneath her chin. "Do not be sorry, little one.... Your pleasure is my pleasure...a gift you gave to me." His smile was warm, tender as he spoke. "Do not take it back with an apology."

He moved his hand to finger the gold chain about her neck. "And lost?" He hooked two fingers under the chain. "No, Drew." Kissing the tip of her upturned nose, he whispered, "Never lost..."

His hand slid slowly down her throat and over the curve of her breast, exposed by the loosened robe. Her skin tingled in the wake of his touch as he trailed his warm fingers along, until his hand came to rest softly in the deep valley between her breasts where the infinity charm nestled. He caressed it as he spoke. "I am not sorry now that I did not have a ring to give you...." His eyes moved leisurely to her face.

Drew's blush heightened at the raw longing she could see in his eyes, but she was strangely unafraid of him. "It wasn't necessary to give me anything.... I'd understand if you took it back."

His lips softly grazed her forehead, his breath warm and sultry. "I don't want it back, Drew. It is yours."

His even breathing increased its tempo in time with her own quickening pulse as he continued, "Once you and the others are gone, I will have the pleasant memory of its new home to warm my thoughts on frigid winter nights."

He moved his hand to her chin, tilting her flushed face back up to his, his voice a husky whisper. "I may live to regret that you are not the tramp I made you out to be."

Tramp! That one ugly word brought everything back into sharp focus...exactly why she was here, why she'd been placed in this danger...all because of Rolf Erhardt's desire to defect to the United States.

And now she was actually in his arms, listening eagerly to his soft words and succumbing to the fiery message in his kiss.

She stiffened and tried to pull away. "Let me go!" she breathed, her voice breaking with the effort required to steel her body against the onslaught of his seductive powers.

His warm lips were moving down along her jaw to the hollow of her throat. "You don't really want that." His voice had thickened with need.

Something in her believed what he said. She didn't want him to let her go! Fearful now even of herself, she mentally stiffened her will against him. *You're a stupid, naive fool, Drew. Don't you see how he's worked this thing so very very cleverly to get you to this? First he*

*took you off your guard with his seeming indifference,
saying he only cared about your citizenship. Then he
topped it all off by telling you you're too unattractive to
bother with... then—bam! He's whispering in your ear
that he wishes you were a tramp. He wants everything—
your citizenship and your body! And God forgive you—
you almost gave in to him, you almost allowed your
emotions to be swept away by this—this scoundrel!*

Near panic with the awful realization of his scheming
duplicity, Drew flailed out wildly, hitting his cheek with
the forgotten bottle. "I said let go of me!" It was a
miserable wail.

He pulled away, startled at the unexpected blow to his
face.

Taking advantage of his surprise, Drew spun around
and darted through the bedroom door, closing it solidly
between them.

"Drew!" His voice was uncannily close to the snarl of
a wounded animal. "What the hell—?"

"Get out of here and leave me alone!" she sobbed into
the back of her trembling hand as she leaned against the
door. "I can't stand the sight of you." Her voice broke.
"Don't you ever try to put your"—a slam of the cabin's
front door cut through her verbal attack—"hands on me
again...." It came out in a long, desolate sob.

Her hand shook badly as she wiped at the steady
stream of tears that rolled down her heated cheeks.
With a frown, Drew realized that she still clutched the
small glass bottle, the weapon she'd just slammed into
Rolf's face.

Squinting, she tried to clear her vision. The label was
small and blurry before her, but the content description
was easy enough to read... even in German.

It was aspirin.

Chapter Five

Drew tossed restlessly in the bed and peered at the luminous dial of her watch. 2:00 A.M. Rolf was still gone. It seemed that he was always gone now...since that ugly scene four days ago when she'd marked him with the bottle of aspirin.

Turning to her stomach, she pushed her pillow away and lay with her head on the back of her hands, eyes wide, recalling Rolf's face the first evening after their fight. She had been sitting in the den when he returned. Flinching even now at the memory of his face, Drew recalled the vivid image of the large, swollen bruise that blossomed along the ridge of his cheekbone, ending near his eye. She had been horrified to realize that she could have done such a hurtful thing to anyone and had automatically risen to her feet, miserable with guilt.

"I...I..." She bit her lip and moved hesitantly toward him, lifting her hand toward his face. For an instant she thought she saw him wince as her fingers gingerly grazed his injured cheek.

"Oh, God, Doctor..." she gasped, turning her shimmering eyes to his, dark and brooding. "I...I am so sorry.... I didn't realize what I was doing..."

She finished weakly, in an anguished whisper, her tear-filled eyes searching his features for some softening, some forgiveness.

She recalled how he had just stood there, unmoving, watching her for a long moment as his shadowed eyes held her like a bird caught in a hunter's snare, leaving her unable to speak, or even turn away from the pull of his stare.

Then he had quietly nodded. His words low and without malice, broke the spell as his fingers gently encircled her wrist, pulling her hand away from his face.

"And I, too, am sorry, Drew...for many things." His eyes moved away from her to roam aimlessly about the room. But his hand continued to possess hers as he spoke. "I now see that my involving you in this plan was foolhardy at the least, and perhaps even criminal at its worst. You had every right for your anger."

His eyes, seeming almost tormented, returned to her face. "Yet you must believe that I did not anticipate the circumstances that required your continued stay here. I would not have endangered you had I known...."

Drew lowered her eyes, not knowing how to react to his unexpected confession. She couldn't answer, her throat was swollen with a sudden, overpowering compassion for this eminent man.

His voice was quiet and controlled as he continued, "But the deed is done, and we are caught in it. Even so...I feel that I can rectify matters somewhat, by relieving you of my further unwanted presence."

Drew's head snapped back up to his serious face. "What do you mean?" The question was an anxious whisper.

Was he now sending her back to the passengers' quarters? Her heart fluttered wildly—was it anticipation or dread? She could not fathom her own confused reaction.

She put her question to words. "Are you sending me back?"

He shook his head slowly. "No."

Releasing her, he continued, "I will go. I have a cot in the laboratory and enough work to fully occupy my time...."

Drew's limbs grew weak, and she could do no more than lower her body to the nearby couch, listening in silence as he said, "I will of course come back from time to time, to keep up the pretense that we are lovers...."

He did not look at her now, but moved silently about the room, gathering up papers.

"But, Doctor, please—this isn't necessary. I don't want to put you out of your own house!" She was amazed that she was pleading with the man to stay, the man that she had so recently injured and told she hated the sight of. But he didn't seem to hear her at all.

At the door, he had turned back. "Rest." A weary smile played across his lips. "I will be back for a while this evening to see to your needs."

Before Drew could speak again, he was gone.

And he had been true to his word. For the past four days she had been left almost totally alone. She sighed, running a hand through her hair, recalling how he had come home in the evenings for a short period to shave, change clothes, and sort through papers. Then with a few polite words, he would leave.

Drew turned in the bed, an arm draped over her tightly closed eyes. She shivered involuntarily as she thought of Rolf's cool, withdrawn attitude, and for some reason, it saddened her.

Though the continual rest had all but cured her, she had been invariably miserable and alone, or miserable and politely ignored. For when she wasn't alone, she felt almost invisible as Rolf moved quietly about his business, saying little. Oh, he had been kind, and solicitous of her health, almost as though she were a small child or a visiting maiden aunt—either of which was a depressing substitute for being recognized as a desirable woman. That, somehow, bothered her more than she had realized it possibly could.

Looking at her watch again, she sighed, long and low. He would be with Monika now. There was no doubt in Drew's mind about that. Where else would he be at two fifteen in the morning? He had married Drew to gain his freedom, but he was in Monika's bed, Monika's arms.

She gritted her teeth, feeling suddenly bitter, angry. A man like Rolf Erhardt used women like most people used towels. He put his hands on one and she ended up in a crumpled heap on the floor!

Drew felt the treacherous trickle of a wet tear slide across her cheek and flicked it away, angry at herself for dwelling on the arrogant Doctor's amorous escapades. What did his indifference matter to her? At least he was leaving her alone!

Her mind thundered with that understatement and she abruptly sat up. It was useless to try to sleep. She flipped the covers back, deciding to go and heat some milk. Maybe—

Suddenly the door to her room burst open and the overhead light was flicked on. Rolf's tall frame filled the door, his rugged, bruised features intent. "Get up." He strode across the room to the bed and bent to reach underneath it, sliding out a brown leather suitcase.

Drew sat stunned, rubbing her eyes against the brightness of the light. "What—what is it?"

He pulled open the case and walked to his dresser. "The West German and United States governments are applying strong pressure to the East to get the Lufthansa passengers released. They don't like the Communists' continued story of unfavorable flying conditions." He pulled a stack of shirts from a drawer and returned with them to his suitcase. "They think it's a stall."

Drew's eyes grew wide. She hadn't realized this would become a high-level battle between governments.

"Where are we going?" she asked with nervous anticipation.

"A train is being prepared at Eisleben to remove all of you to East Berlin where you will be released into the West.

"We'll go there by car, the rest of the passengers are being loaded on a bus right now." He moved back to his bureau. "Snow plows are clearing the route."

"Are. . . you going to Eisleben to see us off?" Drew asked in a whisper.

He stopped, his arms loaded. "I'm going to Berlin."

"No!" she breathed fearfully.

His brow lifted and his dark features were set as he turned his face toward hers. "I told you that I would not let you out of my sight until you were safely out of the East. I meant it."

Drew's mouth dropped open. "But won't they think that it's odd—you going along?"

He frowned. "I often go to East Berlin on business." His jaw worked angrily as he stared at the girl poised in his bed. A scalding gaze raked her before he spoke again, his voice harsh and thick, "Put on some clothes!"

Drew looked down at herself, for the first time since his abrupt entry. She realized that she was woefully under-dressed. The low-cut nightgown with a bodice of transparent lace clung artfully to her full breasts. And the peach-colored silky gown, slit up one side, lay invitingly open to his blistering stare.

She quickly flipped the sheer fabric over her exposed hip and jumped out of the bed. Scurrying to her suitcase to get a less revealing change of clothes, Drew removed herself, in a blush of embarrassment, to the privacy of the bath.

After a few moments, she had changed into an off-white silk blouse, military in detail with roll up sleeves and matching front-pleated wool gabardine trousers. Slipping her wool-stockinged feet into bone ankle boots, she hurried back to the bedroom.

Just fastening his case as she entered, Rolf turned toward her. "Here." He extended a folded sheet of paper.

"This is the marriage document. Make a slit in your coat lining and slip it inside." The words were a crisp order, devoid of emotion.

As Drew took the paper from his hand, her fingers grazed his, causing an unexpected voltaic surge to careen through her body. Surprised by the impact of their small contact, Drew lifted light-gray eyes to his, dark and unreadable. For the briefest instant, she thought she saw a shadow of regret, even pain, pass across his face. But too quickly, it was gone—if it ever had really been there at all—for he had dropped his hand and turned away.

"Hurry, Drew." His urgent tone made her jump. She noticed her white lamb jacket draped across the freshly made bed and rushed to it, taking up the fur piece with trembling fingers. Working with a small pair of fingernail scissors from her suitcase, she slit open a two-inch space at the base of her hood, slid the folded marriage license protectively between several layers of wool fiberfill and painstakingly restitched it.

"There," she breathed, smoothing the lining.

Rolf closed the distance between them and looked critically down at the coat. His nod was curt, "Good." Picking up the bags, he headed for the door. "Come on. We'd better get started."

Once on the plowed road, Drew bolstered her courage to ask, "If there's been such an outcry about all this, then won't the passengers' identities be in the papers?"

Rolf kept his eyes on the road. "I assume so." Turning slightly toward her he went on, "Mrs. James Pollard will no doubt be an instant celebrity when released." He didn't smile.

"But. . . isn't there the danger of the press releasing my relationship to Dad? That would be news, wouldn't it—American scientist's daughter held by Soviets."

Rolf's face closed in a deep frown. "It hasn't happened so far, Drew, or you would have been arrested." He pumped the brakes on an icy incline before continuing, "Let us just assume that your American intelligence department is not made up of fools. As long as they feel the Communists don't know who you are, they are not likely to let it slip."

Drew sat in silence, allowing this thought to ease her qualms a bit. Nearly an hour later, Drew broke the tedious quiet again. "How much farther?"

"Not far. We passed the ten-kilometer marker some time back."

The terrain had become increasingly hilly and the road began to curve, hairpinlike through a virgin wood. Rolf's face was a study in concentration as he maneuvered the jeep over the ice-glazed road. And Drew, agitated by the precarious route, sat in nervous silence.

Rounding a treacherous bend, Drew's eyes grew wide with horror and a scream was torn from her throat as she grabbed at Rolf's arm. "Watch out!"

Before them in the wavering headlights stood a motionless shadow, its thick coat almost silver in the reflected light. An animal, close to six feet in length, gaunt and long-legged, turned its wide head toward them, eyes glowing iridescent.

Rolf's quick reflexes had already maneuvered to miss the awesome creature. But Drew's excited pull on his arm overcompensated, and they skidded sideways toward the statuelike beast.

Drew realized her mistake too late, and cringed, covering her eyes to the imminent impact. The car, now hopelessly out of control, speeding sideways like a gigantic bullet, could not be stopped on the slippery road, though Rolf used all of his expertise to slow and turn the vehicle.

Suddenly, a spark of self-preservation flickered to life in the wild eyes and it sprang out of the jeep's path and loped into the safety of the dense pines. Instead of colliding with the huge creature, the jeep slid quietly off of the road's solid surface into a snow-filled ditch, lifting the passenger's side off the ground and throwing Drew onto Rolf's lap.

A moment passed when Drew was sure she was dead, as a total unearthly silence blanketed them. Then she became aware of Rolf's voice, deceptively gentle. "Are you all right?"

She lifted her head, surprised that his face was so close to her own, and that she lay in his arms like a baby...or a lover. "I—I think so. Yes." Her voice was shaky.

"You don't deserve to be, you know. That was a stupid thing to do."

Shocked by his coldness, she turned her eyes up to his, her lips trembling. "I—I just didn't want you to hit that animal."

"I wasn't going to."

Drew looked away. "Can we get out?"

Rolf scanned the windshield. They were tipped over at such an angle that snow rose up over part of the front window, as though they'd been dipped on their side into a vat of icing. "Yes, we can get out." He paused. "But the jeep can't."

Drew's eyes grew. "You mean we have to walk?"

She could feel his shrug. "Or sit here and miss the train."

"The *train*!" Drew gasped. In the face of their present calamity, she'd forgotten. She moaned, "They'll go without me!"

Rolf put his hands about her waist and gave her a little shove upward toward the passenger door. "I doubt that, but sitting here wailing about it isn't going to get us there."

Drew moved quickly now and took hold of the latch. She pushed, but the door stuck. She couldn't budge it. "I—I can't get it open!"

He slowly untangled himself from behind the wheel and crawled up beside her, pressing her into the seat back. They were chest to chest as he examined the door handle, his weight pressing down on her as he worked.

Drew was grateful for the thickness of his parka and her jacket between them. But the nearness of this man still sent her pulse to racing as she felt the raw power of his muscles pushing against the jammed steel of the door.

"Drew, you'll have to turn the handle for me while I work with the door."

She did as instructed, reaching up to turn the handle. But, in order to do it, she was forced to encircle his neck, almost in an embrace. He did not look down at her as he said, "When I say *now*, let go. I'll be pushing outward, and I don't want your weight pulling against me."

Drew nodded numbly.

Rolf looked down. "Did you hear me, Drew?" Their eyes met. He hadn't seen her nod.

His lips were only inches above hers, and without reason Drew had the most overwhelming urge to lift her face to his, to merge her lips with his, slightly parted and sensuous above her.

"Drew?" She slid her view from his lips to his dark eyes. There was a question in them. "Did you hear me?" His voice had thickened slightly.

"I—I, yes." It was a stammer. "I heard you...."

His face seemed to move closer as he spoke, in a whisper, "And do you understand me?"

"I..." What was he saying? Her chest tightened and moisture beaded her forehead. His lips were moving... he was speaking with his mouth...yet he was also speaking with his eyes, and the message in them was much clearer, much more eloquent. They were saying, "Kiss me, Drew. Put your lips to mine. I promise you it will be good. Let yourself go and kiss me."

She wet her lips in anticipation, her breath came in short, dizzying pants. When his mouth was softly grazing hers, Drew noticed his lips, turned slightly upward at the corners.

Something tipped the delicate balance in her mind. He was smiling. He knew exactly what he was doing. He was manipulating her into the gaping maw where, with one false step she would lose herself to him and become just another link in a long unbroken chain of Rolf Erhardt's conquests.

"No!" she breathed, pulling away. "No!"

He drew back slightly, his expression guileless, questioning. "You don't understand?" He began again, his voice businesslike and instructive, his eyes distant. "It is really quite simple. Just let go of the knob when I say *now*."

Drew stared up at him in disbelief. He was speaking as if nothing had happened between them, as though it had all been her own overactive imagination! It hadn't been! It couldn't have!

She said through clenched teeth, "Yes, Doctor, I believe I understand. Now will you just get it finished?"

With a humorless half-smile he turned back to his work. Drew was acutely conscious of the sound of his breathing, and his soft breath feathering her hair. Her heart pounded maddeningly against her rib cage with the long, lean touch of his body against hers, his closeness remarkably disquieting. She didn't like the effect his nearness had on her senses. She didn't like it one bit!

She cried out in frustrated exasperation, "What's taking you so long?"

"Now!" he shouted in answer, and Drew released her hold on the latch as the jeep door swung up and out, freeing them.

Rolf quickly climbed out, leaning back inside for her. "Give me your hands."

Drew obliged, and he pulled her bodily from the overturned car.

"What about our bags?" Drew gestured toward the back seat.

"If there's time, someone will come back for them. If not, we do without."

Drew opened her mouth to protest, but he took her arm, silencing her with his words. "Look, I'll probably end up having to carry you. So I'm not about to concern myself with suitcases!"

Drew's spine stiffened with indignation. "Don't count on it, Doctor. I can take care of myself!"

His sidelong look was narrow. "You think so?"

Her eyes moved involuntarily, almost guiltily, to the ugly mark she had made on his face, starkly visible in the reflected moonlight.

The corners of Rolf's mouth lifted cynically as he ran tentative fingers across the tender discolored cheek. "I find no pleasure in subduing a frightened kitten just because she bares her claws, Drew." He spoke evenly. "That door you put between us had no lock. If I had wanted to, I would have had you then and there."

There was no harshness in his voice. But the words, spoken with a calm conviction sent a quiver of fear up her spine. She swallowed hard as his grip tightened on her arm. "We'd better get started."

At that moment, a baleful howl tore through the virgin quiet of the wood. Drew jumped, stifling a cry with the back of her hand. Nerves wound tight to the point of fraying, she whirled in panic to the protection of Rolf's arms.

Sliding her hands about his neck she asked in a fearful squeak, "What was that?"

Rolf lowered thick lashes over velvet-brown eyes in a frown of surprise. He spoke near her ear, "That was the wolf whose life you so spectacularly saved a few moments ago." His hands rested lightly on her waist as he went on, "Let's hope he was returning to his den from a filling meal."

Drew bit her lip, her eyes competing in size with the round, full moon above their heads. "It was a wolf? I didn't realize . . ."

He nodded. "I know."

"Do—do you think it might . . . attack us?" She clung ferociously to his wide shoulders, her face buried in the softness of his parka.

His shrug was noncommittal. But his arms were not as they tightened about her, pulling her into the lean hardness of his body. "I thought you were the girl who could take care of herself."

"I—I can." Her breathing was suddenly erratic. "I was just startled, that's all." She moved in his arms, pulling her hands from his neck, embarrassed by her fright-induced weakness. She blurted defensively, oddly breathless, "Don't jump to any incorrect conclusions about this, Doctor. It was an instinctive reaction. I would have jumped into anyone's arms just then!"

He gently released her. "Ah, Drew, such flattery will turn my head." There was a tinge of laughter in his deep voice as he took her arm to begin their long, cold walk.

Because they had wasted precious time, the pace Rolf set was rapid and single-minded. Drew's leather-soled boots were more hindrance than help and after sliding and stumbling for over a kilometer, her feet seemed like clumsy blocks of ice.

Since the accident had been her fault, Drew was surprised and thankful that Rolf chose to walk in silence rather than berate her for her rashness. She wondered why.

Looking up at his rough-hewn profile, she asked, "Doctor?"

He slid his eyes to her, raising a questioning brow.

She cleared her throat and said, somewhat out of breath with the effort of walking in the frigid night, "I'm sorry...about the car..."

He didn't exactly smile. But there was a change in his face, a pleasant change.

Lifting his shoulders, he commented without rancor, "It was an accident."

Drew grimaced, not satisfied, her guilt making her go on, "I know...but you were right. It was foolish of me to grab your arm."

His well-formed lips parted in a friendly smile. "I won't argue that."

She frowned. "Aren't you angry? I mean, Jim would have been—" She bit her lip at the unpleasant memory of her first husband's terrible temper.

The mention of the other man's name brought Rolf to an abrupt halt, forcing Drew to slide to face him. His features had darkened into a deep scowl. "This Jim." Brown eyes were not careless in their perusal of her face as he continued, "Has it ever occurred to you that he might *not* be the best model for you to judge all men by?''

Drew opened her lips to reply, but nothing seemed appropriate. She shrugged, lowering her eyes in thought as Rolf once again set a breathtaking pace.

Some fifteen minutes later, he spoke again. ''I see the lights of Eisleben.''

''Thanks Heavens!'' Drew breathed, bone-tired.

Rolf turned to her as they trudged toward the outskirts of the town, his face serious. ''I know I haven't made this easy for you.'' He slowed his pace to a more comfortable stride. ''Would you like me to carry you the rest of the way?''

Stubborn pride fired Drew's flagging strength. ''I've come this far on my own power, I can make it all the way!''

He nodded, his eyes narrowing reflectively. ''I never doubted that, Drew, or you would not be here with me now.''

His words pierced her cold numbed brain. Was that a compliment? Perhaps a glimmer of respect for her as a person? She stole a look at his face but had no time to reflect further, for suddenly rounding a corner, the train loomed before them.

In the muted light of the moon, it looked like a gigantic sleeping python, long, black and sleek. All windows were dark and lifeless because, as Rolf explained, blackout curtains had been installed to keep curious eyes from peering in along the route.

Nearing the lighted platform, they were halted by an armed soldier in gray. Rolf spoke in curt German and the guard quickly passed them through. He had taken on the role of the grim-faced, powerful Dr. Rolf Erhardt she had first met, once again resuming the intimidating aura of command that sent East German soldiers scurrying to do his bidding.

''What did you tell him?'' Drew asked in a breathless whisper as they mounted the steps to their assigned car.

"The truth." He steadied her on the icy steps with a hand at her back. "That we slid off the road."

At the car's entrance, she turned to face him. Since he had not stepped up with her, they were literally face to face. "What"—she blinked, catching her breath at their sudden closeness—"what will they do?"

A wayward smile slashed his lips. "Do? Well, now that I am here, they will prepare to get us under way."

"What about the bags?" she gasped worriedly.

"They will try to get them before we leave. But I can't make any promises." Gentle hands at her waist turned her around. "This is not a good place to talk, love."

Stiffening at his use of an endearment, she stepped briskly away from him. But she immediately stopped short, surprised to see, not rows of seats, but a narrow hallway, flanked on either side by four numbered doors. With an exasperated breath, Rolf took her hand, pulling her down the hall to the last door on the left. Opening it, he gestured for her to precede him.

She hesitated. "What is this?"

"Our compartment. I usually stay in the command car when I travel by train. But this time I decided it would be best—"

She stammered, interrupting, "Our—*our* compartment!" Her eyes were fixed on the bunked cots inside the barren, narrow room.

He placed his hand at her back and pushed her into the room, closing the door.

Drew turned and flared resentfully, "Must you *shove* me?"

"Drew"—something glittered in his eyes, something vague and frightening—"a man's harlot does not stand in the hall in shocked indignation over the prospect of sharing a room with him. Remember, you are playing a part now. Play it well."

"But I'm not staying in this—this overgrown closet with you!" She threw her arms wide. "Why there isn't even a chair, just those''—she dropped a reluctant nod toward the cots—''narrow beds!''

''Keep your voice down.'' He moved toward the lower bunk and, tossing his parka to the upper, sat down near its foot.

''Join me. I won't bite you.'' He gestured broadly making it appear that there was an abundance of unmolested space.

Suddenly Drew was very nervous at being thrust into such close quarters with Rolf. Staying in his house was one thing, but this tiny room was another matter entirely! She let out a long sigh. Dead on her feet—her frozen feet—all she wanted in life was to curl up in a ball beneath that green wool blanket and sleep...preferably for days and days. But she decided, chewing her cheek, sitting next to Rolf on the narrow cot would have to do, as a distant second...though being this close to him on a bed would be far from *restful*!

She laid her coat near Rolf's on the top bunk and sat down beside the pillow of the lower, putting as much distance between them as possible.

A movement caught her eye and she shot a sidelong glance toward her husband. He had leaned back against the wall, folding his arms across his broad chest. ''Tired?''

Drew shrugged. ''I suppose...a little.'' Tugging off her boots, she tucked her feet up under her.

''I have to be gone for a while.'' He paused. ''Why not try to get some rest?''

She turned toward him, barely able to make out his face in the darkness.

''When do you think you'll be coming back?'' Why did she ask *that* question? Surely that was what she wanted—for him to go.

''Late.'' He unfolded his tall frame from the bed and moved to face her. ''Or should I say early?''

Tucking a finger beneath her chin, he went on, ''I'll check on the bags. Now promise me you will try to sleep." His voice was low and disconcertingly intimate in the darkness.

Nodding, she whispered, "I'll try."

"Good." Sounding satisfied, he removed his warm finger from her chin, turned quietly, and left the cubicle.

Drew stared blankly after him, her thoughts in turmoil. Why did he have the uncanny ability to always put her emotionally off balance?

Just when she thought she had him pegged, he changed. The arrogant, untouchable commander became the seductive male animal, bent on having his way with her; then, too, he could be this image of a concerned big brother, solicitous of her health. Drew shook her head numbly. Where in all these dissimilar characters was the real Doctor Rolf Erhardt?

She wasn't sure if she could trust herself to sleep, knowing he would be coming back any time. And who would he be then? She didn't like the idea of being defenseless, asleep before that changeable man. But, surely he wouldn't force her against her will in this thin-walled compartment. He had said himself they must play-act the part of lovers.... *Lovers!*

A chill rushed through her at the thought of Rolf lounging naked beside her in the narrow cot, his eyes soft with desire, expert hands exploring the secrets of her body. His well-formed lips, sensuous and tender one moment, hard and demanding the next, leaving their smoldering trail along the rise of her breast....

An odd warmth replaced the chill, spreading rapidly through her body bringing her back to reality as an embarrassed heat flushed her cheeks. What had prompted that contemplation?

She brushed irritably at a strand of hair, pushing it behind her ear. She wouldn't allow herself to be dominated by Rolf Erhardt either physically or mentally. She needed rest and wanted to sleep... so she would!

Looking down at her clothes, Drew grimaced at the idea of sleeping in what could be her only remaining change of clothes. She made her decision, unbuttoning the soft beige shirt front. Rolf wouldn't dare accost her when the chance of discovery was so great, for he must know her struggles would definitely bring out the curious. Besides, there were two beds. Rolf would probably take the upper anyway; after all, his attitude toward her lately had been more like a brother than. . . a mate. . . .

Nodding her head with finality, her mouth set in a determined line, she finished undressing. Moments later, slacks and blouse neatly folded at the foot of the bed, Drew was curled between clean, muslin sheets and a faded wool blanket, sound asleep.

The train was moving. Through the fog of sleep, Drew could feel a slight rocking motion as the wheels moved over uneven track. She drowsily lifted heavy lids. It was pitch black. She decided the train must have just pulled out, awakening her. Did it really matter? Yawning, she pulled the sheet closer about her and drifted back into a fatigue-drugged sleep.

SOMETHING soft caressed her cheek and her eyes fluttered slowly open. What had seemed like moments must have been hours, for on the wall was a narrow shaft of rosy light. It was dawn.

"Good morning, love." Rolf's voice was soft and very near. Drew started and tried to raise up on an elbow, but was thwarted in her effort as long lean fingers firmly pressed her shoulder down, turning her on her back.

"Did you sleep well?" He smiled easily down at her as he lounged on his side.

Drew gasped, eyes wide. "What are you doing. . . .?" It was a terrified whisper. "You can't sleep here!"

He raised a well-shaped brow. "Sleep? I wasn't planning on sleep, *Kindchen*."

Her mouth gaped with realization. "You. . . you can't mean. . ." Panic sent a raging blush to her cheeks.

"You have no right!" She edged toward the confining wall. "Get out or I'll call for help!"

"And if you do, questions will be asked. I would hate to be forced to reveal your true identity."

"You couldn't!" She grasped the sheet up about her chin, trying to remain logical. "You're in this as deep as I am!"

His smile was knowing. "Drew, my work is important to the East. Granted, they would watch me more closely if they knew of my desire to defect, but my life would change little. On the other hand, yours would be altered drastically."

She chewed hard on her lower lip, deciding to try another tack. "I'm getting up!"

Rolf increased the pressure on her shoulder. "No, little one." Slipping a finger beneath the strap of her bra, he went on, "Neither of us is leaving this bed...not yet."

His face was serious now, and his eyes, dark and fertile held hers in their hypnotic grasp. "The time has come for us, Drew." Her eyes widened at his pause. "I am going to make love to you."

She swallowed. "No..." It was soundless in the sudden dryness of her throat.

Brown eyes flickered with a new heat as a hand slid to her back. One jarring instant later, the undergarment went slack.

"Do you know how lovely you are?" His voice had deepened with the smoldering color of his eyes.

She couldn't move. Her eyes, huge and glowing, read the truth of his intent in every line of his handsome face. She cast her glance away where it fell over wide bronze shoulders and slid on down to the dark mat of hair that covered his chest, narrowing over a flat belly....

She caught her breath at the awesome, naked splendor of the man beside her.

He slipped the straps of her bra and removed it quickly as he said, "You are a beautiful woman." Her eyes

flew back up to his face. "And you are my wife...."
His tone held a finality that shook her to the core.

"But this wasn't part of the bargain." An ache in her
throat made it a harsh whisper as the rational part of her
mind rebelled at what was happening. But her body,
with maddening disobedience, hesitated to act as his
hand slid silkily up, cupping a round breast.

Drew inhaled sharply at the warmth of his bold
touch.

"Don't speak to me of bargains!" He lowered his
face to her invitingly parted lips in a long, leisurely
feast.

His mouth, soft, sure, held the richness of morning
coffee, the revitalizing taste of a new, fresh day...a
birthing.

The contours of his lips, the perfect teeth, masterful
tongue, all made his kiss as individual as any finger-
print. It was his and his alone to give.... Not Jim's kiss,
demanding, selfish, or the tentative kisses of other men
of her acquaintance—or even the rash, lustful kind of
kiss she had sometimes endured at the hands of less than
gentlemanly suitors....

No, Rolf Erhardt's kiss was the scorching signature
of a man born to passion, a man who knew well the
ways of women and how best to please. His lips, wide
and bold, moved lingeringly, possessing by soft seduc-
tion. He inspired warm response, induced heightened
returns, aroused and thrilled.... And, to say the least,
Drew was not unmoved.

With deliberate languor, Rolf implanted his searing
brand along her cheek, and then up, softly kissing one
tentatively closed lid and then the other.

"Our bargain"—his whispered baritone was rich with
emotion—"did not take into account the desirable
woman you proved to be."

A gentle hand, moving softly over the taut crest of her
breast sent a delicious quiver through her as her lips
throbbed with the memory of his touch. Flaming bright-

ly in her mind was her earlier vision of Rolf's long, lean nakedness next to her in this bed. And now he was really here, his virile masculinity weaving its sensuous spell about her like the tantalizing warmth of a raging fire drawing the foolish moth, once singed, heedless of her own impending destruction, back into the flames.

She could feel the doom of surrender settle about her as the wanting within her body rose to fever pitch. He was a devastating adversary, one she could not win against. He had trapped her within a marriage assuring his freedom, and she had no card to play against him. And now he was equally as devastating in his sexual power over her. She did not have the strength of will to defend herself against his passionate mastery of her body. She was falling, losing everything. . . .

And yet in the face of this mortal disaster, her womanly spirit soared wildly overhead, uncaring, thrilling to his burning touch.

Thrilling, too, in the glorious splendor that brought men and women together in this most primitive of acts. . . the same act that had, in Drew's past, been distressful. Yet now within Rolf's arms, all was right. She felt surrounded by an aura of something mystical, spiritual, almost divine. . . the essence of being man and woman.

His lips were moving down now, nipping at the soft flesh of her throat. And his hands were caressing, sure in their mission as the last barrier of clothing was swiftly disposed of. They were flesh to flesh as Rolf slid to blanket her with his body.

Their eyes met. His were strangely glazed, soft and vulnerable, and his face had lost some of its angular sharpness in the muted light of morning.

She could feel the sledgehammer pounding of his heart, increasing in tempo against the hummingbird flutter of her own. His soft breath on her cheek was reminiscent of the first warmth of a spring breeze, bringing life to the dormant land after a long, barren winter.

Something pagan and uncivilized, at cross-purposes with her whole life plan, tore madly through her every fiber. Her body glowed with it.

She wanted him! More than life, more than freedom...she wanted him to make love to her. With a low moan, Drew encircled his broad back with her arms, reveling in the raw strength in the play of his taut muscles. "Rolf..." The word was a desperate sigh.

A tender smile parted his lips at the sound of his name, his eyes glowed with an erotic promise....

Their joining was like the first taste of rain after an earth-parching drought. It began slowly, with the leisurely taste of renewal, then built from that to a wild, unrestrained storm, filled at its peak with the thunder and lightning of fulfillment as Drew, her fingers digging into Rolf's all-embracing shoulders, cried out in her ecstasy, arching up...up to complete the merging, the melting until for the raging eternity of an instant they were one.

In the stillness that followed, Rolf lowered his lips once again to hers, kissing her gently. "I could not let you leave...without this." He smoothed a damp strand of hair from her face and kissed the flushed cheek where it had been. "This was our destiny, *mein stürmisches Fräulein.*" The provocative statement made her shiver as her numbed mind stumbled back into a semblance of control.

What had he said? He couldn't let her leave without...this? *Leave!* A knife-sharp pain shot through her breast with the truth of it. Rolf Erhardt couldn't let her go without taking his pleasure with her.... He couldn't let any woman get out of his grasp without... She closed her eyes to the hurt of reality.

That is all it was to him, an opportunity too good to pass up! And she had actually wanted him. Her arms slid listlessly from about his broad back.

How could she have allowed him to so easily take her by the hand and lead her away from her own convictions not to become involved? Now she was what she had most feared—a trophy for his wall, a game, easily won, important only as a tantalizing bit of locker-room trivia to be chuckled about. . . and then forgotten.

Desperately ashamed of her weakness, she choked out bitterly, "You. . . won, Doctor. I hope it makes you happy."

She turned her face away, unable to do more, for he still lay on top of her.

"Please. . ." Her voice cracked with emotion. "Please. . . just go. . ." It trailed off in a hopeless whisper.

She did not open her eyes, so she could not guess his expression. Was he smiling, triumphant in his victory? Perhaps, already bored with her, he was planning his next conquest. . . in Berlin!

A tear slid across her burning face. Of one thing, Drew was sure. Rolf would not be feeling remorse or guilt about her tattered emotions. He would probably be thinking only one thing: that the defenses of Drew McKenna Pollard Erhardt, his hostage bride, had been successfully and expertly destroyed. He was no doubt, quite proud. . . .

Now Drew knew the real Rolf Erhardt, the ruthless commander. A man that got everything he wanted. Oh, he played other parts well, when it suited his cause. But they were not to be confused with the true man—heartless, cruel and cunning.

She became vaguely aware that Rolf had left the bed and was dressing. After a moment, the door of their compartment opened and closed, and she could hear his footsteps echo dully along the hall as he walked away.

Chapter Six

The train had been stopped for some time. Drew pulled the heavy blackout curtain aside again, trying to determine why. Surely this mountainous area could not be their destination.

Her suitcase had arrived mysteriously during the night... probably at the same time Rolf had returned to their compartment. An involuntary heat rushed up her face at the memory of awakening within his possessive and all-encompassing warmth.

She pondered her sudden decision to wear all white; the hand-knit sweater vest and cardigan she had chosen were wool, knitted in a distinctive popcorn and cable design, paired with suited flannel trousers and spool-heeled pumps. Wondering if her choice was a Freudian desire to erase the reality of this morning's surrender to Rolf's passionate lovemaking, she drew a shaky breath.

Of course, this morning had not been her first time with a man. After all, she had been married before. But she had never—Drew bit her lip—never reacted quite so... Recalling her wild abandon, her blush increased to furious proportions.

Trying to push thoughts of Rolf from her mind, she forced herself to concentrate on the scene before her. A soft flutter of snow drifted down as far as the eye could see, across forest and field to the snow-capped peaks beyond the valley.

Off in the distance, in the direction from which they had come, Drew could see a village, patches of red-tiled roof showing through the snow. Smoke curled lazily from the brick chimneys giving the little East German town a charming postcard look of placidness.

A shouted order from a soldier leading a Doberman pinscher on a length of chain almost directly below Drew's window startled her. She stepped abruptly back and dropped the curtain. Turning away, she leaned listlessly against the smooth paneled wall.

"Did you eat?" A masculine voice split the silence.

Her eyes shot up in surprise. Rolf was just inside their compartment door. He stood, legs astride, looking down at her, his face stern.

She found her voice. "Some time ago. A soldier brought coffee and rolls."

Lifting her chin in an attempt to seem calm, she turned back to the window. Her fingers trembled as they curled around the curtain and she leaned heavily against the sill for support, the bones in her legs suddenly liquid.

"The town is Aschersleben," he offered. "We're still in the Harz Mountains."

Drew did not turn, but heard him move to the cot and remove his parka.

"Why have we stopped?" Her voice was carefully controlled. She had decided to treat Rolf with the same attitude of indifference that he obviously harbored for her. She would act as though his lovemaking that morning had meant no more to her than it had to him! She could be as callous and unfeeling about this breach of the bargain as he seemingly was.

What had happened between them had happened, and she had let it, but now it was over. Tears and recriminations would do no good. Besides, Drew had never been the kind of woman to resort to such tactics. As a mature adult, she would not allow herself to act like a wronged schoolgirl.

Clearing her swollen throat, she repeated, "Why have we stopped?" It didn't come out quite so well this time.

The creak of the metal springs on the cot told her that Rolf had seated himself. "Snowslide ahead. I've just returned from there.'' She turned to face him as he continued, ''It shouldn't be much longer.''

''And the soldiers and dogs? What are they doing?''

Rolf leaned back against the wall, hooking one booted foot, still glistening with melting snow, on the metal edge of the cot.

One corner of his mouth lifted. ''I see you made the bed.''

Drew stiffened and turned abruptly back to the window.

Rolf's low voice broke the mounting silence. ''The soldiers and dogs are checking the train for possible stowaways. They will be checking at every stop.''

''Stowaways?'' Drew was puzzled.

''East Germans trying to get to Berlin.''

Drew watched as the soldier and his dog disappeared around the bend. ''Why—why would they want to go there?''

''To attempt to escape.'' He let the statement lie.

Drew turned back toward the bold man on the bed. ''Are there so many? Escape attempts, I mean.''

''Yes, Drew, there are.''

Rolf laced long fingers across his raised knee. As he made the slow move, Drew was struck once again by his dark good looks. His deep brown curls and eyes blended successfully with the bulky black turtleneck sweater that accented the lean suppleness of his shoulders and arms and showed to good advantage his narrow waist. Slim-cut black trousers and well-polished ebony boots did nothing to mask the raw strength of his long legs.

Drew felt a blush rush up her neck as she recalled him stretched out like a primeval beast next to her on the bed.

As her cheeks flushed scarlet, a puzzled expression passed across Rolf's eyes. ''What are you thinking about?''

She pulled her lips together in a tight line, piqued at herself for the unruly turn of her thoughts. ''Nothing!'' She lowered her eyes.

He shrugged it off. "To pass the time, I'll tell you about a few of the successful escape attempts, if you'd like."

His voice was quiet as he gestured toward the cot. "Join me."

She eyed him narrowly for a moment before he spoke again. "You can't remain standing all the way to Berlin." A slight twitch in his jaw set off a warning bell in Drew's head. He was barely controlling his temper. He was angry with her. *Angry with her!*

Of all the— What possible reason could he have for being angry? He'd gotten what he'd come for! It was she who had a right to be angry. She was the one who had been used, lied to and seduced!

"I'll manage, thank you." It was a short, definite reply.

The rage in Rolf sparked to life in his eyes as he pulled himself abruptly up causing Drew to take a defensive step backward.

"All right! The evil defiler of semi-innocents is off the bed." He stood; one arm was draped across the upper bunk as he gestured broadly toward the bunk with the other. "It is *all* yours. Though for the life of me I was sure that you enjoyed the sharing of it earlier!" His eyes shot challenging sparks.

She felt that insidious weakness invade her legs again and decided to voluntarily sit down before she fell. Outwardly ignoring his blatant reference, Drew spoke evenly, "I thought you were going to tell me about some successful escapes." She pushed off her white pumps and crossed her legs Indian style on the cot. "I could do with a good story about *escape* right now!"

Her inflection was not lost on Rolf and his eyes narrowed, thick lashes masking angry fire.

"Very well." A humorless smile twisted his lips as he lowered himself to sit beside her.

Surprised by his unexpected return to the bunk, she

tried to rise. But her yogalike position slowed her just long enough.

His fingers curled around her wrist. "Stay here, Drew."

She tried to jerk away, but he tightened his grip. "There's no reason we can't both be comfortable. I won't attack you."

Drew met his eyes. They were dark, brooding, and his face was serious. He was telling the truth. She could read it in every line of his strong face.

Too, she had already vowed to herself that she would pretend an aloof indifference to him. And so far this wasn't turning out to be a very convincing indifference.

She looked away. "I'll sit. . . if you talk."

He released her, his softly accented voice was instructive as he began: "The subject is escapes. . . ." He paused in thought placing his hands behind his head as he lounged back. "There was one man—a circus performer—who, with the help of a relative on the west side of the Wall, merely strung a tightrope and walked over it." He chuckled softly, shaking his head incredulously at the vision it conjured.

"It sounds pretty easy to escape to me." Drew mused aloud.

Rolf lifted a questioning brow. "Would you prefer to know of the many who have died in their escape attempts?"

She shot a sidelong glance toward his solemn face as he went on, "In West Berlin did you not see the floral wreaths set up along the wall?"

Drew gulped, turning her face to his. "Yes," she breathed. "And those were—?"

"Failures," Rolf finished for her.

"Please," Drew winced. "Surely there were other successes?"

"Well"—Rolf rubbed his chin with fisted knuckles—"there was another man who had a friend in West Berlin who operated an earth-moving shovel.'' He paused, tapping a finger on the bridge of his nose. ''On the appointed day, this friend drove his machine up to the Wall and dropped its large bucket over to the East side. The refugee jumped in, the shovel was clamped shut and he was swung to the safety of the West as a hail of bullets ricocheted off the steel sides.''

Drew's mouth dropped open at the vivid picture of the man's daring. She shook her head and lowered her eyes to her hands, saddened at the reality of the Wall. ''The desire for freedom can breed unbelievably irrational acts, can't it?''

His voice came softly. ''Yes, Drew, it can.''

She lifted her face to his. There was something odd, almost sad in his eyes.

Her chest constricted and she found it hard to catch her breath while his brooding eyes held hers in their spell. Was he trying to make her understand why he had done what he had done? The blackmail and forced marriage, the threats of exposing her identity, were these all the rash acts of a man wanting desperately to gain his freedom? And was she to excuse everything because she could now understand something of a man's basic need to be free?

Drew bit her lip and pulled her eyes from his. No matter what his reasons for their bargain, no matter how fierce his desire for freedom...none of it excused his actions of that morning. *That* was not something to be explained away on the grounds of a desperate desire for liberty. No, *that* was nothing other than his own selfish, animal lust. And she could not forgive him that. She steeled herself, drawing a deep breath, ''You know, Doctor, it is interesting to compare the two stories you just related to me with your own case...I mean, both those men also required help from someone on the outside.'' She straightened, staring ahead, ''However they were friends, not victims! I wonder if you can recognize the difference?''

A knock sounded at the door making Drew jump in surprise.

"*Herein!*" Rolf's curt reply held a bitter edge that she had not noticed before.

The door opened slowly as he strode across the room to meet it. A smallish, hawk-nosed soldier spoke quietly to his superior. Rolf nodded briskly. "*Gut, danke schön.*"

The door closed solidly after the departing soldier before Rolf spoke again.

"The track is cleared. I will need to be gone for some time now." He moved to retrieve his parka. Though he had spoken to her, he had not looked in her direction.

"Where are you going?" Drew couldn't restrain the question.

He slid into the jacket. "The command car."

Turning to the door, he paused, not looking back. "We should be in Berlin in two or three hours. I am sure you will be relieved to know *your* captivity is near an end." The words were shot like bullets from a silencer.

He walked out, leaving Drew to stare at the blank door panels long after the dark image had faded.

THE train was chugging along the outskirts of Berlin when Drew could finally see it: the border Wall, a ten-foot high, flesh-cutting, steel-mesh fence.

It was an ugly scar across a field, disappearing into the nearby forest. The closely spaced concrete posts held antipersonnel mines set to explode at a touch.

Drew's eyes filled with tears at the awesome monument of man's inhumanity to man as she scanned the shadow of the antivehicular ditch, designed to prevent motorized vehicles from reaching and breaking through. And now, looking ironically toylike in the distance, a tall watchtower dominated, an unnatural, dark protrusion from the pristine snow, the snow that knew no geographical boundaries, but fluttered down equally beautifully on the faces of both East and West.

Drew remembered her West Berlin friend, Megan, reminding her that the purpose of the Wall was to keep people of the East *in*. The death fields of land mines were strung all along the inside of the 800-mile Wall, a powerful, mutilating deterrent. She wiped away at a tear that slid down her cheek as the door clicked open at her back.

Rolf's voice was low. "We are entering East Berlin."

She straightened, turning. He filled the door, tall and solemn.

"I know.... I saw a sign."

He nodded. *"Berlin, Hauptstadt der DDR."*

"Yes, I guess. What does it mean?"

"Berlin, Capital of the German Democratic Republic." His conversation was polite; yet his brown eyes held a wilderness that Drew did not want to explore.

She decided it would be best to keep talking. "And all the red banners I've seen, what do they say?"

"Sowjetisch, DDR, Freundschaft." He smiled wryly. "Soviet GDR Friendship. You'll see that often." He closed the door quietly.

Drew pursed her lips in thought, turning back to the window. "Don't they protest a bit much?"

"A bit." He closed the space between them, turning her to face him. "Drew"—his features were taut—"there is not much time now. Once we arrive at the station you all will be taken by bus to Soviet Security Headquarters for out-processing." He paused. "My authority ends here. I can go no further."

Drew could see a rigid tightening of the muscles of his body. "You have made your feelings about me quite clear. So I musk ask"—he sounded doubtful—"are you going to turn the marriage document over to the American authorities?"

Drew was taken aback by the question. It had never occurred to her not to. Dr. Erhardt's defection to the United States was too important to ignore, or hamper, no matter what her personal feelings were. It was vastly more important to get this man to the United States than to allow his authoritarian tactics to color her judgment. For with him working alongside her father on the problems of fusion reactors, the eventual practical application of this energy source could be moved forward by a number of years. And in a world close to war over the need for energy, a new, safe source was desperately being sought.

No, it was unthinkable, even in the face of everything he had done to her, to spitefully reject him in his bid for freedom.

"Drew?" It was an urgent whisper.

She found herself staring into his eyes against her will as his hands tightened on her arms.

"I made a promise to you, Doctor. I will not break *my* word." The train began to slow in contrast to the sudden quickening of her pulse as she felt the warm maleness radiate from this man, her husband-captor who would so soon be gone.

"How—" She gulped to ease the sudden ache in her throat. "How dangerous is this...really...for you?" Some small corner of her brain required an answer.

His dark eyes slowly took on a golden light, and white even teeth gleamed from behind a reckless grin. "Do I dare hope the lady cares?" It was a light, buoyant question.

Drew became defensive. With that unplanned question, she'd handed him potent ammunition for his inflated ego, and he was firing it back at her now—teasing, taunting, insinuating that she was not as immune to his advances as she pretended.

Pushing a strand of russet hair behind an ear, she averted her eyes, surprised and angry with herself, and completely baffled by the feeling of impending loss that had come over her upon entering Berlin.

Why? It couldn't be because she was leaving Rolf! *No!* She pushed that insane thought from her mind, gritting her teeth. The man meant absolutely nothing to her.... *Nothing!*

And, besides, now that he had American citizenship, his release would probably be no more difficult than crossing a street. It was absurd for her to be concerned for this provokingly self-assured man's safety!

She pulled abruptly away from him, determined to prove his assumption wrong.

She spat, "Care!" Stormy gray eyes flew to meet his like lightning striking ground. "Yes...yes, I guess you could say I care! But not for you! I care about the importance of my father's work...and how your knowledge could benefit that work!"

Through gritted teeth she hissed, "Personally, I can only hope that I never have the misfortune to lay eyes on your egotistical face again!" Drew foolishly ignored the warning muscle tautly kicking in his jaw as she raged on, "You are conniving and unfeeling, and I will make every effort to forget this whole, ugly episode!"

With the swiftness of a lightning bolt, she found herself crushed into his steel-bound embrace. His lips imprisoned hers, bruising, angry, devoid of mercy or tenderness. It was a plundering debauchery, an uncaring ravishment of her mouth.

Drew pushed wildly at his chest as tears of pain and confusion squeezed from beneath tightly closed lids. His kiss was filled with a passionate hatred, and that knowledge tore through Drew's soul like a rapier. He didn't require words to insult her; his contempt seared through her body with the torched fire of his touch.

Her tormented mind became aware of his hand beneath her sweater, slipping the hooks of her bra. Her eyes flew open and she groaned against his lips.

Suddenly his kiss was less harsh, more giving. He moved his lips across hers, nipping softly. Then as his hand slid forward to cup a breast, his lips moved down to her jaw, his tongue slid teasingly to her throat.

The protests that had clamored behind her lips died a shuddering death, and her eyes fluttered closed.

He moved lower. His warm hand on her breast was

replaced by soft moist lips, tasting, sampling its taut tip. A warmth overflowed from the depths of her body and moved like molten lava through her veins. Drew slid her hands over his shoulders and down his back, lowering her face to the clean softness of his dark hair. She pulled him close and sighed with the delightful sensations that his kisses were sending through her. She pressed her mouth to his curly head and let a throaty moan escape her lips. Her legs trembled in their weakness and she longed to be lifted to paradise within the circle of Rolf's arms, longed for the complete fulfillment that she knew he had the power to give.

He lifted his face to hers, the hard angular planes were softer, the deep brown of his eyes shining with want. Their lips came together in unbridled passion as he straightened, taking her in his lusty embrace.

Both of his hands were beneath her sweater at her back, leaving their warm imprint against her tingling skin. She clung to his broad frame, pulling herself up to mold to his long lean masculinity. Lifting his lips from hers, he gently kissed the tip of her upturned nose. Drew was surprised to feel him slip her bra back together and raised her eyes to his to see them sparking with amber fire, a knowing smile curving his finely sculptured lips. "I think, *Liebchen*, you will find me harder to forget than you realize."

Rolf's shrewd appraisal, spoken in a husky whisper, was like an icy shower, sobering and painful. Drew's heart stopped, dead, at the same instant as the train ceased its motion. She had been fighting hard to keep the unwanted truth of his statement from surfacing, but now it hit her between the eyes. She knew, no matter how she tried, she would not be able to erase this vigorous man from her memory.

Rolf stepped away from her. The place they had shared grew noticeably colder and Drew shuddered involuntarily as he moved to the bunk and removed her lamb jacket.

As he placed the coat across her stiffened shoulders, she choked, "How could you play with my feelings that way?"

He shrugged easily. "As is the way with scientists"—he spoke low, near her ear—"I was conducting a small experiment." The easy baritone was soft as he continued, "Would you care to know the results?"

Drew stared straight ahead. "You're a cad!"

She felt him drape his arm about her shoulders as he steered her toward the door. His parting words were gentle. "That is not a well-kept secret, my love."

DREW stared unseeing out of the bus window. The Peabodys had anxiously searched her out, and now the reverend sat beside her, patting her hand and talking softly, reassuringly. But Drew's mind wandered away, back to her last vision of Rolf, standing silently on the snow-swept ground beside the bus.

In the last instant, as the bus had pulled away, Drew thought she could detect a slight nod of his head. What had he meant? Her brows knit in confusion. Could he have been wishing her well?

Otherwise, he had been the image of the unperturbed commander as he looked up at her, his lids lowered slumberously over dark eyes, his face a mask, showing no emotion.

Regarding him from the window, Drew had been acutely aware of the singular magnificence of the man as he stood there, tall and cool, legs braced wide, and an errant curl brushing his forehead. She had watched his unmoving figure recede until the bus, rounding a corner, obscured her captor-husband from view. . . perhaps forever.

Now the large bus crawled along a nearly deserted, icy street toward some unknown destination. Their conveyance was being escorted by two dark green Volga police cars, one preceding it, and one following. Within minutes, they were passed through a high gate into what they heard whispered among several of the English-speaking Germans as the police headquarters and offices of the *Staatssicherheitsdienst* —the State Security Service. Drew and the Peabodys learned, too, that this grim, fortresslike building once housed Hitler's SS operations.

Armed, green-uniformed *Vopo, Volkspolizei*, lined the way as the passengers disembarked and were led up a wide, creaking staircase to the third-floor offices of the *SSD*. The hallways were eerily lit by yellow and green fluorescent tubes, giving everyone a sickly pallor, only serving to accentuate the stark and fearful expressions on the already harassed captive faces.

They were stopped to wait in a long hall. Names were called, and as the captives stood restlessly, a few at a time were admitted into an office. The door was unlocked and relocked after each new group entered. But, as a source of added worry, no one ever exited.

The four Americans were called together. Drew and the Peabodys entered a small, sparsely furnished room where a bushy-haired man with his shirt sleeves rolled up above his elbows sat at a wooden desk. He looked up as they entered and pushed a pair of glasses up to his wide forehead, sitting back. His homely face was carved into a permanent scowl.

Propping his elbows on the table and placing his fingertips together, he spoke; the deeply accented voice rumbled like distant thunder. "You are the Americans of the Lufthansa." He surveyed the quiet group slowly before moving a hand to a stack of passports. Lifting one he continued, "Reverend Peabody?" His small eyes met the pastor's. "Were you treated well during this unfortunate delay?"

His scowl deepened. He was obviously expecting a positive answer.

Norman Peabody spoke quietly, "Why, yes." He cleared his throat. "We were given adequate housing and food."

The bushy-headed German nodded, replacing the passport and retrieving another. "And you, *Frau* Pollard?" He looked up. "You appear fit. Do you concur with the reverend?"

Drew gulped, shifting her weight nervously. What was the purpose of this type of questioning? Did they know of her living arrangements with Rolf? Did they possibly suspect the marriage—or the escape plot? She must keep calm, she ordered herself. She could not allow the raggedness of her emotional state to cause her to slip, endangering the Peabodys or herself or—she realized in some awe—Rolf Erhardt. "I—I have no complaints." She managed in a voice that sounded more secure than it had a right to.

The German scooped the passports into his hammy fist and pushed himself up. "You understand, of course, that this delay was not the desire of the German Democratic Republic." He circled the desk, crinkling his face into a devastatingly poor attempt at a friendly smile. "We regret that the weather was so inclement. And we hope that you understand." Leaning back against the desk, he continued, "Even your own government would have diverted such an unidentified aircraft as the Lufthansa. This I am sure you realize."

Drew doubted that, considering the obvious lack of Air Tunnels over the United States, but she kept her silence along with the Peabodys, as the man moved forward and handed them their precious passports.

"Now"—he paused, walking toward a side door and turning the knob—"two members of our people's police are waiting to take you to the American Checkpoint Charlie. Your bags are in the car." He stepped back and opened the door. "Good day to you."

Relief rushed over Drew as they were escorted from the building by the two uniformed *Vopo*. They were actually on their way to the American sector of Berlin— and freedom!

Once in the assigned Volga police car, the driver

turned toward his passengers, and offered in the now familiar guttural cadence of English spoken by a German, "I will give you an explanation of our wonderful East Berlin."

More propaganda, Drew sighed to herself as the car was pulled slowly out onto the snow-cleared road. An icy mist had begun to trickle down, and the police officer flicked on the wipers. "We will be passing through *Alexanderplatz.* It is the forty-block center of East Berlin. You can see the clock tower which is our city hall."

Drew absently looked out of the foggy window in the direction he gestured, not really interested in the scene before her. Instead, her mind's eye centered on a dark, brooding face with brown, gold-flecked eyes, eyes that could reach deep within her and pull her out of herself beyond her will into his own. Her heart increased its tempo, and an odd lump formed in her throat as she thought of the man, Rolf Erhardt, and wondered for the first time what dangers he really might encounter in his bid for liberty. She was jarringly brought back to reality by the pain in her lower lip, realizing that she had bitten down hard on it, drawing blood.

"And you will notice the needle-shaped tower, the *Fernsehturm.* That ball, near the top, houses our television broadcast studio and a restaurant." There was obvious pride in the policeman's voice as he continued, "It is three hundred and sixty-five meters tall, and the view is spectacular."

Drew licked at her lip as she peered skyward into the freezing mist. A dim outline of the tower disappeared into the low clouds, with the ball barely visible near its top. An awkward silence had fallen over the occupants of the car, broken finally when Reverend Peabody commented, "Most impressive. Your city is most impressive."

Both policemen straightened noticeably, and Drew had to smile at the minister's gesture of friendship.

"As we pass across the *Unter Des Linden,* you will look to your right to see the *Brandenburger Tor,* Berlin's triumphal eighteenth-century entryway." The silent policeman on the driver's right cleared the window of frost, and they all squinted into the distance along the wide principal avenue of the prewar capital.

The Brandenburg Gate was an impressive structure, its six Doric columns forming part of the stone arch walls supporting an antique-style coping. The driver explained that the gate, inspired by the Propylaea of the Parthenon, was surmounted by a reconstruction of the Victory Quadriga, a victory chariot drawn by four prancing horses.

Drew was saddened by the fact that now the gate, though historically inspiring, was a symbol of the divided Germany, a stark reminder of the tragedy of an imprisoned people. For it was permanently blocked off to all traffic by the Wall, which ran only a few yards beyond it, enclosing it on the extreme edge of Communist East Berlin.

"Checkpoint Charlie is just ahead." The talkative policeman was now more businesslike, dropping the casual tour-guide facade. "We will depart the car and walk across."

The police car was pulled to a halt and both *Vopo* stepped out, pulling the bags from the trunk and placing themselves on either side of the four charges. "Your bags will be checked and forwarded to the checkpoint by guards in a few moments."

As they walked the fifty yards, Drew noticed three brick barriers across the road which required auto traffic to weave slowly and carefully between them, preventing a vehicular dash for freedom.

A tall fence separated the road they walked from the actual "death strip" along the East side of the Wall. To reach the safety of the West, a refugee would have to run a gauntlet of tank traps, which looked like giant jacks from a child's game, strung end to end; but the sinister weapons would never have been mistaken for an innocent toy. Next there were mine trip-wires, police dogs, and guarded watchtowers with orders to shoot to kill.

As they silently walked, Mrs. Peabody nudged Drew and whispered, "Look at that!"

A small Volvo leaving the East was being checked out by armed border guards in their traditional jack-booted uniforms. One guard was rolling a wheeled mirror under the car while the other was checking under the hood.

The two occupants were standing outside as a uniformed woman checked their papers.

Drew knew, as she turned away from the scene, that this vivid picture of the East German side of Checkpoint Charlie was forever branded in her mind, a symbol of the almost unbelievable reality of totalitarian control of life behind the Iron Curtain; a life, not really your own, but the property of an unfeeling state.

She chewed the inside of her cheek, realizing for the first time that if Rolf had not been at her interrogation to handle her slip of the tongue, the military would have checked the name "McKenna," and discovered her identity. Her fate would have been much worse than this.

No matter what Rolf's reasons had been for keeping her secret, he had kept his word, and she was now being freed. A choke blocked her throat, and she coughed, masking the desolate sound as she thought of her husband. Feeling a sudden, overwhelming surge of gratitude to him, Drew wished for just one more moment alone with him...to tell him...to thank him for her freedom. For, once almost lost, it had become very precious to her, and Rolf Erhardt had helped her regain it.

She sighed heavily. Looking back over the past week, Drew realized that the price he had asked had not been extreme.

Drew's thoughts were interrupted when suddenly two border guards appeared from behind the final brick blockade in the street, confronting them. "We have to check your passports."

The two East German policeman halted. "And we must leave you now." Their expressions were official as they saluted the guards and turned in unison, beginning their walk back.

"You will turn over your passports." One gravel-voiced guard put out his gloved hand. Reverend Peabody complied, laying his passport in the taller man's hand.

After opening it, scanning its contents, and looking from the picture to the minister's face, the guard handed it back. The identical procedure was followed with Mrs. Peabody and Sarah. Then, it was Drew's turn. She handed over her passport. "You will remove your hood!"

Remove the hood? Panic restricted Drew's chest. "What?" It was a weak question.

"You must remove your hood, *Fräulein.*" He paused to look down at the passport. "*Frau* Pollard. It obstructs your face."

Drew's lips opened in a soundless "oh" as she lowered her hood to her shoulders.

The guard scanned her picture, nodding. "Good, you may pass." He gestured toward the remaining fifteen yards to the American entrance.

Ahead of them stood the complete opposite of what they had just passed through. There was a small, windowed booth housing one American soldier.

Across the Checkpoint entrance was a lowered barrier, if you could call it a barrier at all. For it was no more than a single wooden plank, painted with alternating black and white stripes. The soldier lifted the small barrier and stepped out, extending a welcoming hand.

"Well, well," he beamed, his face young, friendly...and refreshingly American. "Welcome, folks. Let me shake your hands. We've been waitin' for you!" He cocked his head toward a long black limousine with small American flags flapping from the front bumpers.

Standing in restless groups around the car were a number of people, some with cameras, some with tape recorders.

The soldier spoke again: "You've been anxiously expected for nearly a week now. Hope you're up to the press." His smile broadened. "You folks may not know it, but you're pretty famous now!"

Drew's thoughts tumbled back to Rolf's words: "Mrs. James Pollard will, no doubt, be an instant celebrity when released."

She mused sadly, that the really important story could not be told.

Chapter Seven

Drew sat alone in the quaint Oberammergau *weinstube* toying absently with a delicate goblet. Her father had been called away to greet the Canadian delegation that had just arrived for the fusion conference.

She nibbled on a pretzel, not tasting it, as her mind traveled back a month, to the day she and the Peabodys had been released into West Berlin from Checkpoint Charlie.

The furor had been unbelievable—a whirlwind of photographers and interviews, their faces splashed across front pages of newspapers around the free world.

Fortunately, the story of Drew's seeming indiscretion in living with Rolf never came out. She was not sure if it was because the others aboard the plane did not want to distract attention from their own stories or if the United States government had kept it quiet. But whatever the reason, she was grateful.

The story of the marriage hadn't been told publicly, for any leak about that might have jeopardized Rolf's escape attempt. However after presenting the marriage document to the American authorities in West Berlin, Drew and the Peabodys were flown to Washington, where they testified before a closed, top-level security committee.

Drew remembered her conversation with Security Secretary John Standish after the committee had heard the evidence. He was most solicitous and as reassuring as a governmental agency representative could afford to be. But no promises had been made.

She took a sip of her wine and she relived his remarks. . . .

"My dear Mrs. Erhardt"—he paused, picking up a gold pen and weaving it between his fingers—"your testimony, along with the marriage certificate, has given our government all the ammunition we require to make Dr. Erhardt eligible for our most diligent efforts to remove him from the Communist East."

Drew sat back, relaxing a bit as he went on, "Now that he is a citizen of the United States by marriage, we can claim him as such." He cleared his throat, his jowly features clouding. "However, I'm afraid in this case, gaining your husband's release will be much more dangerous than if he were an ordinary citizen."

She sat back up, erect, expectant, breathing the question, "What do you mean, more dangerous?"

Dropping the pen to the top of the expansive rosewood desk, he leaned back and moved his hands to the arms of his chair, grasping the pliant black leather.

"Your husband, Mrs. Erhardt, is a very valuable man. . . to both sides. The truth is, the Communists will not voluntarily allow him to leave. Therefore when the escape attempt is made, they will react with the same brutal methods they use to block any escapes to the West."

She interrupted, shaking her head, confused, "I—I don't understand. Before I left he told me they would not hurt him, even if they discovered his desire to escape. He admitted only that he would be *watched* more closely!" She lifted bright, cold eyes to his face. "Surely, Mr. Secretary, you exaggerate the danger!"

The ruddy-faced man lifted a halting hand; his smile was sad. "Mrs. Erhardt, your husband is a gallant man, not wanting to worry you. I, however, can't afford to be so charitable with your feelings."

Drew's heart began to hammer painfully against her ribs as she remembered the floral wreaths that she had seen along the Berlin Wall—the escape attempt failures!

Failures! The blood froze in her veins.

Vividly looming into her mind's eyes came the vision

of armed watchtowers, the mined death-strips, vicious guard dogs...and Rolf, meeting these deadly obstacles.

She inhaled sharply, unable to speak. Somehow the danger of his position had not really penetrated until this moment, and she was truly afraid for him.

Her face must have spoken volumes, for Secretary Standish hurried on, a worried frown deepening on his forehead, "Please, Mrs. Erhardt, don't jump to desperate conclusions." He stood up from behind the barrier of his desk and moved around it to face her directly. "I can't of course go into security details with you. But I will say that we have *very* talented operatives in the East. And since Dr. Erhardt is a well-trusted man, we may be able to utilize that trust to gain his eventual release."

Before he went on, he reached out and patted her shoulder tentatively. "I promise you, we will be very, very cautious in our efforts."

Drew realized that she had been holding her breath, and she exhaled heavily. "I—I should have realized—should have seen! But I was too concerned with my own problems...." She shook her head in dismay, unable to finish.

He moved both hands to her shoulders. "Mrs. Erhardt—Drew—I'm afraid, like a doctor, I feel that you must know the worst that *could* happen." His face brightened slightly in his effort to cheer her. "When in reality the chances are—are good that we will be successful in getting your husband out unharmed."

She nodded dumbly, not knowing if he was being truthful, or just kind. "Thank you." She stood. "You will let me know...as soon as...anything happens?" There was little hope in her voice.

"Of course." He pursed his lips. "But don't expect news very soon."

Releasing her shoulders he sat back, leaning against his solid desk. "These things take time to prepare.

Meanwhile, you understand, your marriage must remain a State Department secret.''

Drew nodded in understanding.

A belated thought struck him and he lifted a finger of reminder. ''Though I'm sure you told your father. That would be the obvious exception.'' His expression was sympathetic.

''No-no.'' She averted her gaze, staring blankly out of the large arched window of his office. Her vision had turned inward, a dark, brooding face filling her brain. ''I decided not to say anything to anyone until... Rolf...is safe.''

That had been the first—the only—time she'd used his given name since the morning on the train when he'd made love to her, and she felt her face grow warm with the haunting memory of his touch.

''Well, naturally that is your decision.'' He took her arm, leading her toward the door as he continued, ''Now try not to worry too much. We will treat this situation with the utmost care.''

She repeated her thanks and smiled tiredly, leaving his office with some difficulty, for their conversation had made her limbs as weak as her hope of ever seeing Rolf Erhardt again....

LOOKING back now she felt a stab of guilt for never relating the truth of the ''bargain'' to the security committee, and allowing everyone to go on believing that she and Rolf had married for love. But she knew it would have benefited no one to reveal the truth. After all, the United States government cared only about the *fact* of the marriage, not the circumstances of it.

As to telling her father! She certainly *never* planned to let him know anything about her intimate relationship with Rolf! No. Drew had made the decision before she even turned over the marriage certificate, that once she was informed of his safe release, she would initiate proceedings for an uncontested divorce through State

Department channels, ending the brief marriage quickly and quietly.

That had been then, a month—an age—ago. But what of now? Today was April 17th and the Oberammergau Fusion Conference would officially begin at the formal dinner that evening. She recalled that Rolf had told her that, had he been able to leave the East on his own, he would have defected at this conference. *This conference!* Allowing her mind to wander, she couldn't help but wonder what might have happened if they had met here—under totally different circumstances. She sighed heavily, saddened by her helplessness. She had no way of knowing if Rolf were alive or dead. Up to this point, she had heard nothing from the State Department about him.

A prickly sensation between her shoulder blades made her reach up to rub the back of her neck. She grimaced at the odd, tense feeling of expectancy that had come over her. And a peculiar racing of her heart was accompanied suddenly by a queer dryness in her throat. She gulped. Why it was almost as though—

"Good afternoon, *Frau* Erhardt." The voice, deep and slightly accented, was spoken barely above a whisper, but the feather-soft words boomed through her brain like a clap of thunder over a parched desert. Her gaze shot upward to see her husband, his gold-flecked eyes, serious, questioning, as he moved to face her.

"Rolf!" His name slipped from the depths of her throat in an awed murmur of disbelief. He was here! After all the doubt, all the secrecy and worry. He was free, and he was here. He looked remarkably handsome, even more so than she remembered, though there was a slight gauntness in his angular features, and a tinge of shadow staining the skin below his deepset eyes.

He was an incredible sight standing there looking down at her. His dark-brown leather flight jacket, and muted gold crew-neck sweater fit snugly across generous shoulders, and the soft brown whipcord slacks hugged his muscular hips, accenting the strength and suppleness of his long legs.

Seating himself, he asked rhetorically, "May I join you?"

Her heart skipped a beat with his nearness. During the past month, that week in East Germany, her marriage, and Rolf's powerful lovemaking had become unreal, dreamlike in her mind. Yet seeing this magnetic man again, hearing the so familiar accent of his baritone voice, brought it all back to her in a rush of luxurious sensations.

She found her shaky voice. "Y-yes, of course, Rolf." His features softened into a smile at the mention of his name. Clearing her throat nervously, she hurried on, "I wasn't told you were out."

His deep umber eyes settled on her wide gray ones. "I know. I asked John not to tell you."

Her brows knit in confusion. "Why?"

Lacing long fingers together under his chin, he answered, "Because I knew you would be here, and I wanted to tell you myself."

She felt an embarrassed warmth flush her cheeks and her lips worked silently for a moment before she admitted, "I'm glad you're safe. I—I was very worried."

"Were you, *Kindchen*?" He paused, waiting, his eyes softly inquiring.

Inhaling slowly, Drew lifted her chin, unsure of how to continue. When she did speak again, it was not an answer, but a sidestepping question. "How...long have you been...free?"

He lifted broad shoulders and let them drop tiredly. "Nearly twenty-four hours."

She scanned the rugged lines of his face, wanting to touch them, smooth them, and somehow comfort him. But she knew she had no right. "Was the escape difficult?"

Rolf's face darkened into a craggy frown and he shook his tousled head slowly, his eyes never leaving hers. "Don't ask me that, Drew." Running a hand through his hair, he concluded, "I'm free, and it's over. That is all that matters."

His words held a tone of finality and she knew he would never talk about what he had gone through to gain his freedom. Whether his reasons were personal, or for the sake of security, she did not know, but she realized that it would do no good to press him further on the subject.

She looked down at her hands, flattened atop the table so that their trembling would not betray her nervousness.

He was first to break the silence. It was an unhurried question. "Drew?" Their eyes met. "You are still Mrs. Erhardt?"

She tensed even more, her heart fluttering in an haphazard rhythm. Very uneasy now, she moved her eyes from his, taking a tremulous sip of her white wine to ease her throat before answering, "I—I couldn't get a divorce until I knew you were safe."

His nod was thoughtful. "I see." There was a pause. "I want to thank you for what you did for me."

She was surprised by the intensity of his voice and moved her gaze back to his face. Some private emotion glistened in his eyes, one that she couldn't quite define, and her throat closed with an overwhelming tenderness for this man, her husband.

She couldn't utter the words that crowded her brain...not here, not in public. Though she knew she must tell him what she felt. But it was so important, so very important to find the right time, the right place to reveal to him that *she didn't want to divorce him*. Rather, if he would have her, she was willing to remain Mrs. Rolf Erhardt for the rest of her days. For like a blinding flash of lightning coming after the crack of thunder—reversed, out of sync with the natural order of things—she suddenly knew that she was helplessly, hopelessly in love with the man she had married, not so long ago, under extreme protest!

Yes, seeing him like of this, being with him again—Drew had to admit it to herself: She was in love with Rolf Erhardt! She should have seen it coming, should have known before it hit her between the eyes. But, she had misread her feelings, believing that they were merely concern for the safety of another human being. But, no. Being with him now was more than just relief in the knowledge that he was safe. It was an overwhelming sensation of returning home after a long absence, a comfortable, joyous return to cherished ties—and the ties were real, strong now, bound tightly through the month-long separation when her mind had drifted back to memories of their time together, of his gentle concern for her when they were alone. Even his lovemaking had been as much her own desire as his. She had lost every shred of bitterness and mistrust long ago for the blackmail marriage. Rolf was her husband, the man she loved, and that fact was all that was important now. No matter how it began, she did not want to see it end.

She ached to tell him all this, to thank him for the awakening he had inspired, a dawning within herself to understand and value her own femininity. But how could she find the courage to tell him of her love, and thank him for teaching her the joy of being a complete woman?

The warm strength of his hand settled over hers as he quietly spoke, breaking into her thoughts, ''Now that our bargain is met, perhaps we can begin again.''

Drew's heart stopped in anticipation. Was it possible that he, too, loved her? And was he about to tell her so?

She became almost giddy with girlish excitement. Of course he loved her too—he had to! That must be why he had come here himself—to tell her!

His face was unreadable as he began, ''Now that I have no further hold on you, and there is no more need for us to be married...I hope that you can forget the unpleasant things that happened between us in the East, and that we can go on now as friends.''

Her breath caught sharply in her throat and something akin to pain filled her breast.

Unpleasant things!

His face blurred and she pulled her shining eyes away, staring instead at the well-manicured fingers that held her hand.

He was speaking. "As you know, I hope to work with your father. And since we will probably be working closely with each other, I think that that would be best."

The warmth of his hand mutated from a secure haven for her smaller one, to a fiery, imprisoning kiln, and her breathing was suddenly labored. He was telling her the way it was with him, what he felt...and what he felt was definitely not love! Closing her eyes, she pulled her hand from his.

Friend! The ordinary word seemed so sterile, so wrong when it was used to connect her with Rolf Erhardt. He wanted her to be his friend, in a platonic, chaste, day-to-day working relationship. She couldn't bear the thought, knowing that other women would take her place in his arms while she was expected to be nothing more than a cheerful co-worker! He would be so near, and yet, so very far away.

Steeling herself, she looked up into his solemn face, her voice barely audible, "Friends, Doctor?"

A puzzled frown creased his brow. "Have I said something wrong? Perhaps I used the word incorrectly."

She shook her head, lowering sooty lashes over tear-filled eyes. "No." A hard, heavy knot had formed in her stomach. "Your English is impeccable. I am sure you meant exactly what you said."

Gathering all of her self-determination, and clearing the tightness from her throat, she spoke, her words sounding surprisingly calm. "If you work with my father I will do my best to be...an effective co-worker."

She moved her eyes, lackluster and leaden, reluctantly back to his face. Her mind cried in anguish at what was happening. She was telling her love good-bye, and it was what *he* wanted.

Pride would never allow her to let him know how this hurt, how she didn't want to say good-bye, how this was killing her soul. Though she had once thought their forced marriage was unthinkable, this separation, this rending between them was far and away the more terrible. For now she knew the *man*. And since their marriage, he had catapulted her into a wonderful new awareness, where once, just once in her life, she had been his woman, his lover, and had known the tempestuous erotic storm of his passions. *That* she could never forget, didn't want to forget.

Her husky whisper quivered with emotion, "No, Doctor, do not ask me to be your friend." The statement lay there flat and dead between them.

A shadow enveloped Rolf's eyes as a light was extinguished somewhere in their depths, and Drew could detect no emotion in that vast darkness.

After a moment of tense silence, Rolf slowly pushed himself up from the small table, his voice taking on a crisp edge. "That is it, then." His fingers curled around the edge of the chair back at his side, the knuckles whitening as he continued, "As I promised in the beginning, I will leave the divorcement to you."

Drew gulped convulsively, her gaze fastened on the crushing anger in his fingers. He had obviously not expected her to reject his proposal of friendship.... But why anger? Was it pride? Had she pricked his male ego? She was amazed to discover that she had the ability to affect him, to hurt him...even in so small a way as this. But it gave her no satisfaction. Quickly she moved her eyes to his face as he continued, "I am staying at the chalet at *Dorfstrasse* 48." His lips twisted in a sardonic smile. "I was going to ask you to come by for a... friendly...drink before the dinner tonight."

She flinched at the coolness that now marked his manner as he spoke, "But I believe I know what your answer would be. So I will not burden you with the necessity to decline."

He looked down at her, his stance aloof yet noble as he pulled several deutsche marks from a leather-lined pocket and placed them on the table, "Instead, allow me to get your wine."

Drew started to protest, but halted, realizing he was gone. Two broad strides had taken him through the door and out of hearing.

She heaved a long, ragged sigh. The picturesque little *weinstube* had become drab and lifeless, and Drew felt drained, completely empty.

"That is it, then... I will leave the divorcement to you."

Recalling his words, she stared vacantly at her nearly empty wineglass, feeling numb. "That is it, then." She breathed to herself, closing her eyes and feeling very foolish.

What had she expected from him? Flowery speeches of undying love? Hysterical laughter welled up inside her. But all that survived to reach the surface was a slight, melancholy upturning of the corners of her mouth.

No, not love... never love! Rolf Erhardt had made his wishes perfectly clear. Now that he was free, he wanted no more from her than he had wanted from any of his past conquests! She ran a hand through her chestnut hair, slipping a long silky strand behind one ear, very much wanting to bury her face in her hands and cry. But she couldn't give in to her feeling of loss. She wouldn't add to her humiliation by being reduced to tears in a public place by an arrogant, willful man!

She exhaled heavily. Why, oh, why did Rolf Erhardt have to be so typically male? Would she never realize that they were *all*—every last one of them—self-centered opportunists! Clutching the delicate goblet in trembling fingers, she lifted it to her lips to finish her wine and go, to get away to be alone with her shattered hopes. As she swallowed the last, somehow bitter dregs of her wine her eyes grew wide over the glass's rim, and she froze. There before her was a face she had not expected to see—or wanted to see—ever again!

Approaching coolly, tall, blond and cocky as ever, a wide grin splitting his good-looking face, strolled her ex-husband, Jim Pollard! He was a bit shorter and stockier than Rolf, and very much lighter in complexion with the type of skin that pinkened and burned in the sun. He sported a green plaid sports coat and green slacks, the off-white dress shirt lay open at his wide neck. He wore his most charming smile, deeply dimpled, a feature, Drew remembered, that had always pleased him.

"Hi, sugar!" The offhand intimacy of the tone was gratingly familiar.

She lowered her empty glass to the table as he took a seat in the same chair that Rolf had recently vacated.

"Drinking alone?" He cocked his white-blond head. "Thought you always told me that was a bad sign."

She balled her hands in her lap and looked up into his green eyes, ignoring his remark. "I didn't know you were going to be here, Jim." Her voice was quietly controlled.

Lifting a sandy brow, he quipped, "Right, and you also didn't remember I work for *Science and Engineering Magazine,* and that we *met* four years ago when I was covering that fusion conference in Chicago. Besides"—his eyes narrowed as he peered closely at her—"I've found that letting you know I'm coming doesn't insure a warm welcome."

She could feel her nails cutting into her palms with his sarcastic reminder that he knew she had run to Berlin to avoid his last announced visit. Counting slowly to ten, a difficult control-gathering exercise considering her present mental state, she managed to remain civil. "Actually, Jim, I just didn't think. I've had my mind on other things." She let it drop. She wasn't required to explain her actions to Jim, and she just didn't feel up to an argument.

He put an elbow on the table and toyed with one of the *marks* Rolf had left. "No doubt. An international celebrity like you has probably got fan mail to answer, speaking engagements. Hell, sugar, you've really come up in the world since we split!"

Drew fought a crazy urge to smile at the irony of his remark. She wanted to say that she had nowhere to go *but* up after leaving him, but she restrained herself. "That's all pretty much died down now." Shifting uneasily, she mused that soon the news of Rolf's defection must come out, and if a connection were made between them, it all might be stirred up again. She added, "Besides, it's all over and best forgotten." Her thoughts took her a step further. *Like our marriage!*

"If that's the way you feel," he winked, "but if it were me, I'd milk it for all it's worth!"

Drew let out a slow breath rather than answer. Jim hadn't changed at all—he was thirty, still going on thirteen.

"Well, I hate to leave so soon, sweets, but I've got to go. Covering a swank cocktail party this afternoon." He paused and looked pointedly at her. "Will you be there?"

He meant, of course, the welcoming party for the delegates at the Hotel Alois Lang, which had been booked entirely by the convention to handle their conference activities. Drew's mind raced toward an escape. She had planned to be at the party, but now with both Jim and Rolf in Oberammergau, and most likely in attendance there, she cringed at the thought of going.

"No. No, Jim. I don't believe so."

He shook his blond head and made a clucking sound with his tongue. "Too bad. Well, no problem. We've got plenty of time to get together during the next couple of weeks.'' He tossed the last over his shoulder as he left, ''I'll catch ya later...when we can have more privacy.''

Drew bit her lip. She had no intention of ''getting together'' with Jim Pollard ever again, in public or private! She hated the thought of spending two weeks at the conference avoiding him. And then there was Rolf; he could very easily decide to remain at the conference for the entire time. After all, as one of the world's leading authorities on fusion reactors, he would be a sought-after celebrity.

She ran a hand across her forehead, pressing her lips tightly together, the only visible sign of her inner turmoil. Within just a few moments, she had been presented not only with an all-too-friendly ex-husband who seemed perfectly contented with the idea of getting back into a husbandly role, but also a real husband, however temporary, who seemed more than willing to be nothing more than a casual acquaintance!

After some moments, her emotions still in a disheveled heap, she stood up from the table feeling numb and walked on leaden feet out of the small *weinstube*.

She wandered aimlessly along the narrow lanes of the picturesque village for several hours. To others, Drew appeared merely to be window-shopping, yet inwardly she was anything but placid as her mind conjured up scowling visions of Rolf that changed, melted into Jim's lighter, leering image...and back again to Rolf. Though in different ways, thoughts of both men were equally disquieting in their effect on her. More than anything she wanted to catch the first flight back to the States. But she discarded that thought immediately. Obviously, running away was not the answer. Jim still refused to believe that it was over between them. Besides, she was here at the conference, not only as her father's assistant, keeping report paraphernalia organized for him, but also to cover the conference for the *Scientific Monthly*. She looked down at her watch—

nearly six o'clock—time to get ready for the opening dinner. She must attend. It would not do to behave like a frightened little girl, always running away from her problems. She had to face things as they were, the reality of Rolf's rejection as well as Jim's unwelcome interest. And she had to handle things as an adult—talk it out with Jim, and then go on with her life as best she could. And her life at this moment required her to be at the fusion conference's opening dinner.

Sighing, she entered the quaint *Gasthaus* where she and her father had acquired rooms, and trudged tiredly up the central staircase shrugging off her down-filled bubble jacket. Rummaging in her bag for her room key, she walked to her door. Unlocking it, she entered, stopping short. She was not alone.

"Jim!" It was a surprised gasp. "How did you get in here?" Her jacket slipped unnoticed from her fingers to fall to the polished pine floor.

As he slid off the bed, carefully balancing a full highball glass in one hand, Drew leaned back against the door, unconsciously wanting to put distance between them.

"Hi, sugar." His smile was confident. "Said I'd see you later." He raised his glass in a salute. "Let me fix my pretty lady a drink." Gesturing toward the half-empty bottle of rye on the dresser he went on, "You're behind."

Drew's chest rose and fell in her agitation. Ignoring his drink-lightened banter she retorted resentfully, "Jim!" Her voice rose with the angry color in her cheeks. "I asked you how you got into my room?"

He gave her a smirking look. "It's not hard for 'Mr. James Pollard' to get a key to 'Mrs. James Pollard's' room, sweets. Just told 'em I'd arrived on a later plane 'cause of business delays." Nodding sagely, he went on, "Seeing that you'd registered as my *wife* was the best news I've had in a coon's age!"

His features creased into deep dimples as he walked

toward her, taking a swallow of his drink. "Tells me a lot about how you feel."

Not wanting to be trapped against the door, Drew moved away, circling into the room's center, near the foot of the bed.

"Don't be absurd, Jim!" It was a rasped, irritated whisper.

He cocked his head. "What's absurd? You've had a year to get that passport changed. You may *say* we're through"—his wink was as wicked as his leer—"but your actions, or lack of them, speak pretty loudly too, and they say you want me back."

She closed her eyes in exasperation, irked by his unbounded conceit. Before her fateful trip to Berlin, she'd never given her passport a second thought, and was forced to travel under her married name, having had no time to get it changed. But as it happened, the name "Pollard" had proven to be a blessing of sorts, disguising her relationship to Dr. Drew McKenna. . .to all but one.

Since her return, she had purposely hesitated having her passport changed. Certainly not for Jim's reason! She knew that the last person on earth she wanted a relationship with was her ex-husband! But since becoming Mrs. Rolf Erhardt, she had hesitated officially becoming Drew McKenna again. At the time she had refused to analyze this lack of logic, but now she knew why. She had wanted to be able to change her passport to read "Mrs. Rolf Erhardt." She had wanted their marriage to be real, lasting. . .but after her encounter with Rolf in the *weinstube,* she had been forced to see that that hope had been a flight of fantasy all her own, a completely one-sided desire. Dejectedly, she realized that she would never be Mrs. Rolf Erhardt, not in any real sense of the title—not a woman *loved* enough by a man to give her his name forever.

Her mind caught on the fact that Jim was still talking, his words now slightly louder as he rambled on. "The way I figure it, sweets, we could use these two weeks to get reacquainted, sorta' like a second honeymoon.'' He emphasized the last word and reached out, touching Drew's cheek with the knuckles of his hand, fisted about his glass.

He was very drunk, she could tell, remembering all too well how he was when he'd been drinking, a little too loud, and a *lot* too confident! To anyone who didn't know him well, he appeared to be completely sober, a man who could hold his liquor. But Drew knew better. She knew when he drank, his temper became thin-walled, and expanded like a balloon, easily pricked by opposition, exploding into violence.

She stiffened, backing away from his unwanted touch. "Jim," she started nervously, "please understand. There's just no *us* anymore—and there never will be again. It's over. We're not married." She gulped as the last slid out quietly, her heart hammering heavily as his face darkened in an ominous frown.

"There's where you're wrong, sweets." Cold dread stabbed through her midsection at his icy tone as he slowly ground out his words. "I figure I've been pretty patient, letting you run home to Papa and pout." He took a step forward, swallowing heavily on his drink. "And letting you file for that damn divorce!" He growled the words, gesturing broadly, sloshing rye on the colorful braided rug that brightened and warmed the rustic room. "Then you ran like a scared rabbit when I came to get you." Green eyes narrowed between sandy-brown lashes, "But hell, Drew! I figured by now you'd know that no stupid piece of paper can take you away from me!"

Taking a final swallow, he slammed his glass heavily down on the nearby dressing table, the ice landing and settling with a loud clatter, like an earthquake's aftershock, startling Drew jarringly in the room's foreboding quiet.

"You're mine, Drew"—it was an ugly snarl—"and you're gonna stay mine."

He grasped her arms with fists of cold granite, the one that had held the glass burning icily against her skin.

"No!" she cried, as raw terror slithered up her spine.

The balloon had burst. There was no reasoning with him now. It would do no good to bring up old wounds. All the other women he had flaunted in her face, nurturing his macho ego, while at the same time, in unreasoning jealousy, he had condemned every innocent encounter she had with men—and then the final straw, when he knocked her to the floor in a drunken, possessive rage!

"No!" she repeated in a flat, fearful breath. Her only thought now was to escape, to get away.

Placing her hands, fingers spread against his barrel chest, she pleaded, "Jim, let me go! This is no good!"

His lips peeled away from his teeth in a sneer. "The hell it isn't." He snorted, "I'm gonna prove to you once and for all that you *belong* to me. You're mine...and I'm not about to let you forget it!"

"Jim—I—I...don't," she gasped in a pain-filled whimper, as his hands bit mercilessly into her arms. "I don't belong to you. You're not thinking clearly."

She suddenly staggered back as Jim's hand struck her savagely across the mouth.

"Shut up, you damn tease!" he hissed, his eyes strange, wild. "I'm thinking clearer than I have in a long time!"

She stumbled back, the force of the staggering blow spinning her away from him. Stunned, unable to speak, she ran an unsteady hand across her throbbing lip. It felt damp, sticky. She licked it as her vision cleared, and then scanned the room in panic, locking her eyes on the door—and her only route to freedom! She knew that Jim was bent on hurting her now, and her sense of self-preservation told her that she must get away, and quickly.

An uncomfortable unease prickled her flesh as she realized how silent the room was. She gulped, not knowing what Jim was planning. Her throat was dry with apprehension, and what was worse, her legs wouldn't move, wouldn't respond to her mental command to *run*! She suddenly understood the reality and total helplessness of being paralyzed with fear.

Before she could make her traumatized body respond to her shock-dulled mind, she felt a sharp jerk on her hair, pulling her head painfully back, and forcing her to stare up into Jim's sneering face.

He spat out, "Listen to me, Drew, and listen good." His liquor-coated breath turned her stomach. "I do own you! You became my property when you promised to honor and obey me." His features were twisted into a vicious mask, an evil caricature of a man. Yet, it was the identical expression she remembered from the night she had run away from him, numbed, bruised, and fearing for her life.

Once again she was in his power. And once again he was capable of harming her to get his way, and her blood ran cold with terror.

He raged on angrily, "What the hell do I care about some slip of paper saying you divorced me? That was your idea, not mine . . . and as far as I'm concerned, it doesn't exist!"

He grasped her arm with his free hand and jerked her to face him as he pulled his face into a taunting smile. "Don't be such a cold fish, baby." His lids lowered as his hungry gaze dropped to pass slowly across her heaving breasts, partly exposed at her open shirt-neck as he held her in the twisted position. "Guess ol' Jimmy'll have to warm you up."

She was revolted to be held so closely in his rough grasp. Her neck ached sharply from being pulled so far back. "Jim . . ." It was a faint squeak, and she closed her eyes to block out his crazed face. "You—you need professional help. This—this isn't right, it's not normal."

Her desperate attempt to talk rationally to him was

stifled as he lowered his broad lips to hers, muttering, "Shut up!" He devoured her mouth with moist zeal. It was a sour, offensive kiss, making Drew's stomach churn in disgust. She hammered her fists against his chest and tried to turn her face away. But he tightened the hurtful grip on her hair as his groping mouth held hers in agonizing imprisonment. To Drew, his unwanted embrace was like being wrapped tightly in a hot, damp blanket on a muggy day, stifling and afflictive. In desperation, she raised a hand to his face and slapped him hard.

Abruptly pulling his lips from hers, his eyes sparking angrily, he hissed, "So you want it rough!" His mouth twisted into a misshapen smile as he dragged her toward the bed, his hand still clutching the mass of tawny hair at her crown.

She was flung roughly on the brightly colored quilt spread. An instant later, Jim's bulk landed heavily on top of her, knocking the breath achingly from her lungs.

"N-no—Jim...you...can't...." she choked out with tremendous effort.

"The hell I can't! I've waited a long time for this!"

He fumbled with the top button of her blouse with one hand, while the other searched intimately beneath her pleated skirt and up the inside of her thigh.

Shuddering with revulsion, she tossed her head convulsively, catching her lips between her teeth. Her mind was on fire, terrified by the realization that Jim would resort to criminal rape to have his way with her!

At that instant, her eyes fell on a heavy crystal **ashtray** on the bedside table. Without hesitation, she flung her hand out, grasping at it in reckless abandon. Jim had opened the front of her blouse and moved his clammy hand inside to cup a breast, his breathing now heavy with desire. As he lowered his lips to the soft rise of flesh, the moan that escaped his throat began as lustful anticipation, but ended in surprised disbelief as Drew hit him sharply on the forehead with the heavy piece of leaded crystal.

He went limp over her, and Drew gasped, horrified, and lay in shocked stillness beneath him a moment before she was startled into action as the ashtray dropped from her fingers and landed with a loud thud on the floor beside the bed.

Pushing frantically at his prostrate form, she squirmed free of his cloying, sweaty warmth and rose weakly to stand at the edge of the bed. Tentatively, she lifted his wrist, feeling his pulse. It was strong; he was just stunned.

He groaned. Wild alarm stampeded through every fiber of Drew's body and she dropped his hand as though it had been red hot. She had no intention of being there when he regained consciousness!

Pulling her blouse together with trembling fingers, she dashed from the small room, running full-tilt down the curved staircase to the rustic lobby and through the nearly empty *Wohnzimmer*—a sitting room—where a cozy fire blazed in a smoky, ancient stone hearth.

The small scholarly group of guests sitting in casual camaraderie around the fire, started at her rash intrusion, and stared curiously after her as she fled the warmth of the old-fashioned *Gasthaus* and ran instead out into the growing chill of an early spring evening... without even a coat.

Chapter Eight

Dorfstrasse 48.

Drew hugged herself, rubbing icy hands along her bare arms, suddenly aware of the encompassing chill... and of where she was!

In a daze of panic she had run from Jim's punishing advances, away from him, the room, and the *Gasthaus*. At the time, she had let her tormented body move her onward, getting her instinctively away from the immediate danger. But now her rational mind had taken control, and she was appalled to realize where she had run: *Dorfstrasse* 48. Rolf's address.

What irony that her mind, hearing the number only once, would cling to the memory of it like an emotional lifeline, and then, unconsciously, even in these strange surroundings, take her directly there!

She was standing, shivering from the rapidly dropping temperature on the low curb fronting the charming, Bavarian country house. In the growing dusk she scanned its outline. The low-pitched roof was decorated with a little belfry, and at regular intervals along the wooden-shingled roof were blocks of stone.

A long balcony ran the length of the upper story, with two multipaned doors leading out onto it. There were six small windows on each story fronting the house. Their colorful shutters were flung wide revealing the lower floor lit from within with a flickering glow. And three of the windows above were flushed with a brighter, steadier light. Rolf was, no doubt, at home.

She gritted her teeth, angry with herself. This was insane! He had made it clear that he wanted nothing more to do with her... except in the most godforsaken, barren way. Why couldn't she accept that and stay away from him? She shook her head, sighing heavily. Lowering her eyes from the closed, blank door, she turned away.

Who then could she turn to for help? Why hadn't she simply run up the *Gasthaus* stairs to her father's room instead of making this paradoxical rush to a man who could not care less about becoming further involved in her personal life?

Her bottom lip trembled slightly as she recalled why she did not automatically go to her father with this. Though she loved him dearly, and he, she knew, loved her, he was not an adequate confidant. Of that she had become painfully aware all too often after her mother's death.

As a scientist, Dr. McKenna could not be surpassed in the logical, intelligent way he attacked and surmounted a problem, but in everyday, person-to-person relationships, he was admittedly at a loss.

When Drew had come home after leaving Jim and needed desperately to talk it out with her father, he had cut her off, stammering out self-consciously that the break-up was her affair, her decision. If the marriage was over, he would accept it without question. Then he had excused himself, mumbling that he was needed in the laboratory. Drew let a sad smile alter her lips. She could not fault her father, he was what he was, and she understood and accepted him, valuing his many accomplishments. For anything he might lack as a parent, he more than made up for as a pioneering physicist. And she was proud of his achievements.

No. She could not burden her dad with this, it would serve no constructive purpose. But, still, she *needed* someone... someone who could understand her fear of Jim's sick possessiveness, and help her—even protect her, if need be.

The local authorities were out of the question because the notoriety any complaint would cause would leave a terrible blot on the conference, and an ugly embarrassment for her father and the American delegation. It would leave a pall on the proceedings which would overshadow the importance of the paper her father had worked on for so long in preparation for this presentation. She imagined the newspaper headline: "Attempted Molestation of Ex-Wife, Ex-Hostage, Alleged at Fusion Conference." Squeezing her eyes closed, she shuddered at the thought.

Though she had every right to notify Jim's employers of his attack, she didn't want to revenge herself by permanently harming his career. After all, in two weeks the conference would be over. She would return to Los Alamos, New Mexico and Jim would go back to San Francisco. And, he was not really a dangerous man—not to anyone but her.

But how then could she protect herself from him in the meantime? She stood, hesitant, unwilling to return to her hotel room where Jim might still be angrily waiting for her. But where could she go? Completely at a loss, knowing only that she couldn't just stand there forever, she sighed deeply and took a slow, retreating step away from Rolf's home.

"Drew?" The deep voice called questioningly from some distance away.

Stiffening, she stumbled to a halt, her heart catching in her throat.

Turning tardily, feeling almost as though she were in a dream, she blinked her gaze back up toward the shadowy house. The door had been flung wide, and almost filling its rosy opening stood Rolf, a deep frown creasing his craggy features. He stood very erect and still, one hand resting on the door's brass knob while the other curled around the door jamb. His legs were braced wide, as though it were necessary as a balance for the aristocratic breadth of his shoulders. Handsomely cut dark tuxedo trousers fit to perfection over his flat belly and down along the curve of his well-developed hips and thighs. The white shirt he wore sported tiny knife pleats along its front and was opened half way down to his narrow waist, revealing the wiry dark mat of hair that, from this distance, sharply deepened the color of his muscular chest.

"Drew?"

Repeating her name, he moved quickly across the wooden porch and with long-legged strides closed the distance between them and lightly touched her shoulder. "Do I flatter myself to think you changed your mind about that drink?"

Momentarily confused, she shook her head. "Drink? I—I—no. I came here for another reason. But I—it was a mistake." Lowering her gray eyes from his dark, searching ones, she continued, "I'll just go."

He didn't release her arm. "You're cold. Where is your coat?"

She couldn't think of an appropriate, believable answer without telling him the truth. Keeping her face averted, she moved her shoulders helplessly.

"Come inside." It was not a suggestion, and Drew found herself being pulled along in his fast-paced wake.

She did not want this and tried to pull away. "No, please, Rolf. It would be better if I—I just leave."

Once inside the semi-dark, rustic living room, he led her to a dark-brown, deeply grained leather couch that faced a newly lit, crackling fire.

Completely ignoring her protests he commanded quietly, "Sit down."

Openmouthed, she lowered herself to the rich leather cushion as he picked up his dinner jacket from the back of the couch and draped it across her slender shoulders before moving to a tall liquor cabinet that stood beside the hearth. It was open. A brass bucket filled with shimmering cubes of ice sat next to a variety of bottles.

"I was just about to fix myself a drink." He lifted ice tongs and turned back over his shoulder to speak. "You look as though you could use one, too."

Not really wanting anything, she turned her eyes to the blazing fire. Her mind tumbling critically in her anxiety over Jim's attack, she did not even have the mental capacity to make a decision one way or the other about something so unimportant as a drink. Nodding weakly, she whispered, "Thank you. Whatever you're having will be fine."

He chuckled, drawing her curious stare. Startlingly white teeth were revealed in an outright humorous grin. "I doubt that, I'm having tomato juice. You look like you could use something more substantial than that."

Her lips parted in a surprised, "Oh," but she recovered herself quickly. Being around Jim for so long, she had just naturally assumed... "Tomato juice would be fine, really."

Turning back, he confirmed easily, "Whatever the lady wants."

After a moment, he returned to the couch with two tall tumblers of juice, each wrapped in a small white napkin. Drew was surprised to see that a sprig of celery sprouted from each glass, a colorful, unexpected addition.

She took it gratefully, her spirits somewhat lightened by Rolf's amicable reception. "Thanks."

Lowering his long-legged form to the cushion next to her, he leaned back, making himself comfortable and draping a relaxed arm behind her, warming her with a heat quite different from the fire's.

He looked at her quietly for a moment before asking, "Am I right in assuming you were leaving when I came to the door?"

She nodded, nervously putting the glass to her lips to avoid speaking, then winced, the salty juice smarting as it invaded the cut along her lower lip. Hoping he had not noticed the reaction to her injury, she glanced quickly up at him. His eyes were on her hands. Good! He had not noticed. In some surprise, Drew realized that she was ashamed—ashamed for Rolf to know that

Jim had struck her and treated her so cruelly. And that fact made her feel even more positive that she had been wrong in coming here.

Her fingers began to tremble under his inspection of them, and she had the wild feeling that in his quiet concentration he was listening to her thoughts!

That fear was calmed, however, when he asked gently, "What has happened since I saw you this afternoon?"

She looked down at her shaking hands curled about the frosty glass, sighing, "Rolf, if you'd just let me leave, we could forget this whole thing."

In a surprise move, he lifted the tumbler from her fingers, and reached across her to place it, as well as his own, on a marble-topped end-table. As he leaned past her, Drew became awkwardly conscious of his heady scent and had to fight the urge to lift her arms to his neck and draw his face to hers, begging him to help her. No—to love her and keep her forever as his wife!

He sat back, putting space between them, and leaving her with a feeling of immeasurable loss.

"Now, let's start again." His tone was purposefully stern. He wanted answers, and his patience was wearing thin. "Why did you come here tonight?"

She knew he was determined to get an acceptable explanation, and would not let her leave without giving him one. Staring unseeing into the flames dancing in the hearth, she hoped that her expression didn't mirror her turmoil. How much would she have to reveal to satisfy him? Would he make her tell him the whole humiliating story? Not if she could help it! She began, vaguely, unsteadily, "I—I came here because I wanted"—she cleared her raspy throat—"I wanted to ask a favor." Without looking up to read his reaction, she hurried on, "And I was leaving because I—" She almost said, "came to my senses." But to save face she finished, "I changed my mind. The less involvement I have with you the better." The sentence died in a whisper.

A long drawn-out silence followed in which Drew could hear nothing but her own racing heart hammering in her ears, and the occasional protesting crackle of the fire.

Finally, Rolf asked, a fine edge tingeing the question, "And just what was this favor?"

"Nothing," she tried. "I—I can take care of it."

"Drew." His voice was now merely questioning, and he sounded a bit tired. "Something upset you enough to make you come to me in the dark, without a coat, on foot. If it was important enough for all of that, surely you can tell me what it was."

With the softening of his manner, she became aware that he had moved closer, the hard strength in the muscles of his thigh now pressed against her hip. With his unexpected nearness, her breathing became uncontrollably erratic, and she couldn't think clearly. Abruptly, she stood up, putting a cooling distance between them.

Shrugging off the coat, she lay it in the seat she had vacated. Exhaling dejectedly she spoke, a little more sharply than she had intended. "All right!" Unable to hold it in any longer, she blurted, "Jim is here."

He inclined his head to look up at her, his face losing expression. "Jim?"

A sharp pang stabbed at her insides and her mind reeled. *He doesn't even remember who Jim is!* Had she been of so little importance to him that his recollection of the fact of her former husband was totally nil?

The horrible thought struck her that if she told her story to Rolf, he might agree that she did indeed have a problem, but he could very easily suggest she seek out the authorities, leaving her no better off than she was now! Swallowing hard, she wished she had kept her wits about her and never come!

Turning away to face the bar, she explained without emphasis, without hope, "Jim Pollard is my ex-husband."

There was a pause. "He is a physicist?"

She shook her head. "A reporter for a scientific magazine. I—I didn't realize he'd be covering this conference... but he is."

Her eyes moved aimlessly over the ornately carved bar, from the bottles and ice bucket to the several glasses arranged near the ice. Suddenly it occurred to her that Rolf was expecting company. Could it be that after their meeting in the *weinstube* this afternoon, he had decided to invite another woman to his home for that drink?

Her insides churned with that possibility. Of course! Why not? There was no moral obligation in the vows they had exchanged. She cringed inwardly, knowing now just what an unwanted intrusion her appearance must have been!

"Oh, God!" she groaned, running a hand through her hair, mumbling in a pitiful squeak, "Forget it. I shouldn't have come!"

Pivoting on her heel, she headed single-mindedly toward the door, her pride shoving her toward the nearest exit. She couldn't beg this man to protect her from Jim, no matter how fearful she was of his raging temper. She'd just have to think of another way out of this mess. Involving Rolf when he didn't care to be involved would be just too humiliating!

Her hand closed over the door knob. It clicked open loudly with a light turn, giving her easy access to the dark street.

Rolf had said nothing, done nothing and she heard no sound from him now. He was letting her go without protest. She had been right, he was in a hurry to have her out of his way. But when she left, where would she go? Something deep inside her arrested that first step as her pride struggled against her need. Her common sense warred angrily with her desires, pulling her mentally to and fro. She must go! She must stay!

She did not leave. The battle ended without a winner,

without rejoicing, when the door clicked again as it closed. Drew's shoulders slumped forward as she pressed her forehead to the smooth panels of the door. "I don't want to ask this of you," she moaned in abject misery, "but I really need your help."

"What kind of help?" The question was spoken softly, yet so near her ear she started, astonished at the soundlessness of his approach.

She took a deep, shaky breath. "Jim. He wants me back."

Rolf's touch was gentle as he fingered a smooth curl of hair at her shoulder. She felt him lift it, and as he did she could hear him inhale deeply of the light floral perfume that wafted from it.

Caressing the silky lock between his fingers, he murmured, "I believe I understand." Why did he suddenly sound so somber? "You don't want him to find out about what happened between us in the East." He sighed heavily. "Do you really think I am a man of so little integrity that I would tell anyone about that?"

She was surprised by his assumption that she had come here to extract a promise of silence from him—a promise she would never in her wildest dreams have thought necessary.

Turning abruptly to face him she exclaimed wide-eyed, "No!" Instantly regretting her move, she retreated defensively from his dusky face, only inches above hers, flattening herself against the door before she continued in a self-conscious breath, "It's not *that*—just the opposite!"

He straightened, a flicker of surprise danced across his dark face and a crooked smile twitched at the corners of his mouth. "I'm afraid you'll have to explain that, *Kindchen.*"

She swallowed, concentrating her gaze on his cleft chin, for his eyes were too hypnotic to stare into, and his lips overly inviting. . .and the broad, bare chest open to her view beneath the wide vee of his shirt was excessively sexual for her peace of mind. So she concentrated all of her attention on the clean-shaven chin, stammering, "Well—you see, Jim won't believe—it's—our marriage, that is, is over." She shifted her weight, but not her eyes. "He wants me back, and he won't take no for an answer. His...insistence frightens me."

Rolf moved his hand to cup her chin, lifting it as he scrutinized her face closely for the first time. She watched as his jaw tightened, and a muscle began an erratic twitching in the hollow of his cheek.

Moving his thumb to tentatively trace along the slightly puffy lower lip, he questioned in a low growl, "Did he do this?"

Lifting sparkling eyes to his, her throat closed with mortification. She could not answer.

His dark eyes, now brittle and cold slid from her eyes back down to the vulnerable curve of her mouth and the bruised wound *"Verflucht!"* The curse was expelled in a snarl. "The bastard!"

Drew's eyes grew round with surprise and her cheeks burned fiery within the cool, firm grip of his fingers. She was embarrassed, dumbfounded at the vehemence of his reaction.

"And your father? What does he say of this?"

"I—I didn't tell him. I can't." She barely whispered the words under his glowering look.

"Yes," he nodded. "I can understand that. Were I your father I would kill *der Teufel*!...the devil.... And the *Polizei*, you did not choose to involve them." It was not a question.

"No. I—I don't want him arrested. I just want him to leave me alone." At last, with the truth out, she could not keep her battered emotions in check a moment longer. A tear slid down her cheek, and she inwardly damned her show of weakness.

His features softened noticeably with her distress. "What do you want me to do?"

She breathed a long apprehensive breath. "I

thought—hoped—you—you'd pretend to be..." she stopped, unable to bring herself to say "in love with me." Trying again, she altered her words. "If we could continue this farce of a marriage," she amended, "just for the conference. I'm sure if Jim thought I were married, he would realize it is all over between us, really over. And he'd leave me alone."

She pressed her lips together, enduring the relatively unimportant physical pain in her lip without notice. The emotional pain of his looming rejection of her proposal bore through her wrenchingly, and she tried to steel herself for his negative reply.

"Farce?" His voice was questioning. "Drew, our marriage is not a farce. It is real, at least for now. You told me that yourself this afternoon."

She squared her shoulders bravely. "You know what I mean. If Jim believes we're married—"

"But we are," he interrupted calmly.

She blustered, hating him for forcing her to be blunt. "Oh, please, Rolf, don't play with me! You know what I mean!" Anger came tremulously to her rescue. "For two weeks you—we would have to pretend to be happy... happily married! That's it! That's the favor I came here to ask. If you would pretend that we're happily married for two weeks! Could you do that... for me?"

Something changed in his eyes as he stepped back, lifting a heavy brow. "So, suddenly our positions are reversed." He paused for one heart-stopping moment before going on, "Now it is *you* who needs this marriage to gain your own freedom, of sorts, from an over-possessive, brutalizing ex-husband."

She stared blankly up at him, shocked at their unexpected role reversal, struck for the first time by the irony of it.

Pulling herself together with effort, she countered, "Er...yes, I suppose so...." Her reply grew taut as she went on, "But I am only asking for your help. I would never demand anything of you!"

His lips parted in a crooked smile. "Nor could you, *Kindchen.*"

She sucked in a sharp breath, her hopes crashing to her feet. "So, you are refusing to help me?"

Slowly he moved his curly head from side to side. "No." His look was intent, earnest. "I merely meant I do not require demands to help you. I am willing to publicly acknowledge our marriage if you think it will help rid you of your Jim Pollard." His eyes narrowed in a sardonic half-smile. "You could say I owe you this much for what you did for me. . .on the train."

Drew gasped, throwing him a grim look. "That doesn't enter into this at all!"

He shrugged, looking into her angry eyes calmly. "It does to me. And because it does, you needed only ask."

Suddenly, Drew felt very weak, not having fully understood just how desperately she had wanted this until now. No matter the reason he gave for helping her, he was still willing to help. That was all-important. She must have grown very pale, for Rolf immediately moved forward, the sharp planes of his face once more molded into a deep frown as he slid a supportive arm about her waist.

"Damn! Is the memory so painful that you prefer unconsciousness to remembering?"

Guiding her to the couch he spoke, his voice taking on a decidedly serrated tone, "I'll send for your things."

She pulled weakly back, protesting with a start, "Now?"

Momentarily ignoring her outcry, he seated her on the cool leather and moved to the nearby phone. Lifting the squat, gray receiver, he paused and looked narrowly down at her. "Drew, it is now or never. Either we announce to the world that we are married tonight, or we keep it a secret until it is no longer fact. The conference officially begins this evening, at which time I will acknowledge my defection." He continued, his voice stern, instructive, "Tonight my life will become an open book for the press. You can't suddenly appear on the horizon as my wife tomorrow, or next week.''

He held the receiver poised over its cradle as if he would hang it up with one word from her. ''Now, make up your mind. Do you want my help or not?''

With her hesitant, but positive response, Rolf took quick charge, first calling the *Gasthaus* for her things and then coaxing her up the stairs, insisting that she soak in a hot tub until her luggage arrived.

That had been an hour ago, and now, she sat before the dressing table of the small, well-ordered guest bedroom. Her mind drifted back to what Rolf had said as they reached her bedroom door.

''Don't worry, *Kindchen*. You have not run from the snapping fox into the jaws of the hungry lion. Even though we are man and wife, I'll not take from you what you do not care to give.'' He pursed his lips and lifted his shoulders almost wearily, handing her the room key before he went on, ''But, then, I don't believe I ever did.''

He turned quickly, and exited down the stairs, leaving Drew to herself. Now, she absently scanned her solemn reflection in the mirror. Unusually pale, her gray eyes seemed extraordinarily large within the ebony frame of lashes. Her hair, flowing softly to her shoulders, was a bright, coppery contrast to the milky pallor of her skin and the rich pearl-gray, cotton lace jabot blouse and long gray silk taffeta skirt.

Very tentatively she smoothed a coral lip color over her injured lip. Leaning forward, examining her glossy mouth closely, she felt a degree of relief to note that the puffiness and bruising around the cut was undetectable beneath the frosted, womanly camouflage.

With her earrings already in place, she lifted a matching strand of pearls to her throat to complete her toilette when a knock at the door startled her, causing the pearls to fall from her fingers. She was bending to retrieve them as Rolf entered.

Seeming to sense her difficulty, he moved to her side and took the pearls from her hand, and turning toward her back, he slipped them about her neck, his fingers softly grazing her throat before moving back beneath her hair. With the pearls in place, he rested his hands lightly on her shoulders, and looked down at her reflection in the mirror. "Most of my guests have arrived. Are you ready to be introduced as my wife?"

She lifted her eyes to his image, momentarily overcome by his dark, lean good looks. He now wore the black cotton velvet dinner jacket which fit snugly, yet flawlessly across his wide shoulders. The stark-white shirt was buttoned, and the black tie in place. His hard, male potency seemed to reach out and ensnare her heart, causing it to hammer unmercifully against her rib cage.

Unable to bear the pain of seeing him there like that—so perfect, wanting him beyond all else, yet knowing he cared nothing for her, she lowered her eyes, noting instead the flush of color that suddenly darkened her cheeks.

His hands, lingering softly along her shoulders burned through the light fabric, marking her skin with the treacherous memory of his touch, leaving her strangely light-headed and dizzy with the disturbing contact.

Taking a deep revitalizing breath, she found her unsteady voice. "Yes, Rolf. I'm ready."

As he took her arm, helping her to her feet, she queried, "Who am I meeting?" She wasn't sure she cared to know the answer, and his response was little help.

"I'll introduce you."

Feeling the hesitancy in her step, Rolf whispered, his voice taking on an amused note as he led her through the door toward the stairs, "Don't worry, love, in the East you played my mistress expertly."

She shot him a quick, unsure glance and caught a flash of startlingly white teeth in his grin, followed by a reassuring wink. ''I'm sure you will be a most—convincing wife.''

At the foot of the stairs, they rounded a corner to the living room. Drew stopped short, surprised to see three pairs of eyes staring in their direction in varying degrees of bewilderment.

A silver-haired man of average height, clad in formal black, stood beside a tiny, graying woman in a long tailored grown of black wool. These two, Drew surmised, were a married couple. But the other, the third person, was the one her eyes were immediately drawn to like a mouse in a room with a hungry cat. The eyes of the two came together with something akin to the clash of swords, and Drew was momentarily halted in her tracks by the sharpness of the contact.

Her blood ran cold with envy, for she recognized the signals which passed from this stranger to herself. . . the age-old instinctive reaction to a rival. Tall and strikingly attractive, this woman was obviously Rolf's intended companion for the evening.

Drew's heart sank as she stood across the room from this shimmering blond beauty, her long hair pulled back in a severe, but becoming French twist. The blue eyes were slanted slightly upward at the outer corners, and her nose was straight and well-formed. Red, full lips opened slightly as she blew out a stream of white cigarette smoke. But the lips did not smile.

Her voluptuous figure was shown to its utmost advantage as she stood before the fire almost glowing golden in the slim-cut, lamé evening pajamas.

Drew gulped at the comparison everyone must be making between them—herself, pale, even gray, like a cloudy, winter day, cold and lifeless next to this sunny, glittering vision. And she wondered what Rolf's thoughts were just then. Was he disappointed to be holding her arm instead of the other woman's—the woman he had intended to spend the evening with, perhaps even the night.

She wet her lips nervously, casting a sidelong glance up at her husband. On the surface, at least, he seemed not at all affected by the fact that both his wife and his date were standing in the same room, staring suspiciously at each other.

With the beginnings of an introduction, getting no further than, "Drew, may I present—" Rolf was interrupted by a melodic chiming of the doorbell, announcing the arrival of another guest.

He nodded to Drew excusing himself and, releasing her arm, moved to the door.

For a fluttering instant, Drew rallied in the hope that this new guest might be the late arrival of the blond woman's escort, even husband, but the man that did appear at the door was definitely not that, but a totally different and unexpected surprise.

"Father!"

Her astonished gasp grasped his attention, changing the puzzled expression on his rawboned face to a wide smile that split his long features. Altering the course of his lanky frame, he moved swiftly to his daughter's side.

"Why, Drew..." He took her cold hand in both of his. "So it was you who left me that cryptic message to come to this address." He shook his head, chuckling. "I should have known when I couldn't find you in your room. What's this all about?"

Before she could question her father about the unknown message, Rolf moved to her side and extended his hand. "Forgive me, Dr. McKenna, but I sent you that message."

The older man's reddish brows knit as he took Rolf's outstretched hand. "Oh?" he queried. "I don't believe I've had the pleasure."

"Allow me to introduce myself." His smile was warm. "I am Rolf Erhardt."

Drew could see the immediate electric flicker of excitement in her father's dark-gray eyes, and he straightened noticeably, opening his lips in an awed whisper,

"You? You're Dr. Erhardt? But...that's impossible...he's..."

Rolf shook his head. "No. Not anymore, Doctor." He lifted his eyes to include the others as he said, "Dr. McKenna, please meet my other guests." Still in a state of confused shock, Drew's father turned around to see the three others for the first time as Rolf continued, "This is Dr. Gieslbert Hartmut and his wife Kristel."

They nodded, smiling as Rolf further explained, "As you know, Dr. Hartmut is our conference chairman, and director of nuclear sciences at the University of *München.*"

"Ah, yes, Doctor. I have heard fine things about your Munich University." Dr. McKenna returned their smiles as Dr. Hartmut acknowledged the compliment.

Then all eyes moved expectantly to the other guest. Drew sucked in a nervous breath as Rolf went on to introduce the golden woman before the fire. "And this is Ilka Markus, a research assistant to Dr. Hartmut."

Drew sagged inwardly. His explanation was totally devoid of any reasonable explanation of why she might be here other than as Rolf's guest. For, as a rule, the numerous research assistants were not included in these illustrious affairs.

Barely aware of what was going on around her, Drew took little notice as her father chatted momentarily with the lovely young lady. Only when Rolf slipped an arm about her waist did her attention move away from Ilka Markus's placid face up to his.

"And now"—he paused, looking down at her, brown eyes holding gray; the quiet smile he bestowed on her could only have been described as husbandly—"may I present Drew McKenna...Erhardt, my wife."

There was a clock ticking somewhere in the silence, callously unaware of the sacredness of this moment... of the words Rolf had spoken.

No one in the room moved for what seemed to Drew like a long time. But she didn't care. She didn't care if this moment never ended. Rolf was holding her near, his eyes were warm, deep and glowing with something she couldn't quite read. Why, it almost seemed as though...

"Wife!"

Her father's exclamation brought everyone instantly to action in a buzz of congratulations. Everyone except the glittering Ilka Markus who, Drew noted, stiffened and took a deep draw on her cigarette before tossing it, in what seemed to be excessive irritation, into the flames.

Dr. McKenna grasped his daughter's shoulders, blocking her view of the other woman. "My Drew? Wife of Dr. Rolf Erhardt?"

An astonished, almost dream-come-true expression changed his features to an openness of boyish joy, shedding years from his face.

Unable to remain unaffected by her father's uncharacteristic effervescence, she smiled bashfully, confirming his wide-eyed question with a quick, but enthusiastic nod.

He took her in a light embrace. "Why, my dear. But how? When?" Releasing her, not waiting for an answer, he turned to Rolf, declaring with a puzzled shake of his head, "Dr. Erhardt, I can't express my...my feelings." Taking Rolf's hand between his, he began to pump it heartily in a substitute for vocal congratulations. Rolf smiled broadly, apparently pleased by Dr. McKenna's reaction to the news.

Yet, watching her father's animated face, it suddenly occurred to Drew that what they were doing was terribly unfair—not to have told him the truth about the marriage. She had not thought to lie about the arrangement. She had assumed that they would confide to him that their marriage was only temporary. But, then, if they did that, he would have to know everything—about Jim—and she desperately wanted to avoid telling him that! Also, what would the truth have done to her father's state of mind, just before giving an important speech—knowing that his only daughter was temporarily living with one man as protection from another? No! It definitely would be better to leave it this way. At least her father could be genuinely contented while they were at the conference.

Out of the corner of her eye, Drew could see the three German guests converging on them. The elderly man spoke first; his smile was a bit sheepish. "Well, Dr. Erhardt. I must apologize to both you and *Fräulein* Markus." He bowed slightly toward Drew. "And to you, *Frau* Erhardt. I am most embarrassed that I did not know of your marriage." He lifted his shoulders in a small shrug as he continued, explaining to Drew, "You see, as your husband's host, I took it upon myself to provide him with a companion for the evening." Clearing his throat, he cocked his silvery head toward the other woman, who stood, looking thoughtful, a few feet away.

Ilka lifted her chin and opened her lips in a stunning smile. But Drew could detect no sincerity in the icy-blue eyes as they passed disdainfully over her before moving to Dr. Hartmut.

The soft voice was a pleasantly accented purr. "Do not apologize, Gieslbert." She turned back, looking directly at Rolf. "I am gratified to be among the intimate few with advance knowledge of Rolf's defection to the West."

"Defection!" breathed Dr. McKenna. "Why, of course. I'm afraid with all this excitement about your marriage, I didn't think—"

Before he could finish, Ilka single-mindedly went on, "I would be interested to know your plans, Rolf. Perhaps you will join Dr. Hartmut in his work at the university?" Her full lips curved in a knowing smile. "I would be most pleased to work under you."

Drew balled her hands, the nails cutting into her palms at the other woman's barely disguised invitation.

Under him, indeed! She moved her eyes quickly up to Rolf's face to judge his reaction. A slow grin spread leisurely across his lips as he contemplated the lovely German woman. He, too, had received her message.

Dr. Hartmut cut in, "Ah, yes, Dr. Erhardt. It would be my fondest hope—"

Rolf's attention turned to the man speaking and he held up a halting hand, "Thank you, Doctor. Your offer is greatly appreciated. However, my field is research, not teaching—at least, for now." He moved his eyes to Drew's father before going on. "If it is permissible to Dr. McKenna, I would like to go to the United States, and perhaps find a position on his staff at Los Alamos."

Dr. McKenna inhaled sharply. "Well!" He clapped his hands together. "I had no idea, Doctor. I am honored!" He shook his head, looking incredulous. "With all that has happened to me this evening, I must say, I am a most fortunate man."

Dr. Hartmut said, "Well, of course this is understandable." He shrugged, smiling the smile of a good loser.

Ilka's smile, however, was not in the least that of a loser—more a sarcastic smirk as she nodded sagely. "Yes, I believe it is quite understandable—a marriage, a defection, and now the offer to work with the bride's famous papa in America. A most interesting coincidence." Raising a well-manicured brow toward Drew, she seemed to be saying that she was very well aware of just why Rolf was her husband, and she would not let a little thing like that stand in her way. It was a message so clear to Drew, that she wondered why no one else in the room appeared to have received it.

Dr. Hartmut took this opportunity to cough importantly into his hand and looked down at his watch. Taking the cue, Rolf offered, "Yes, we should be on our way. It was not my intention to make us fashionably late, only to allow Dr. McKenna some advance notice of his daughter's marriage."

"And I truly thank you for that, Dr. Erhardt." He squinted sideways down at Drew. "At least someone decided I had a right to know!" Drew winced slightly at his fatherly chastisement and answered him with an impish shrug as he went on, "Now, Dr. Erhardt, tell me how this all happened."

Rolf smiled at his father-in-law, placing a friendly hand on his shoulder. "All will be clear soon, I promise you, Doctor. And please call me 'Rolf.' "

"And I'm 'Madder' to my friends," Dr. McKenna offered in return.

With Rolf's quizzical turn, the doctor explained, running a hand through his shortly cropped head of gray-streaked, carrot-colored hair, "It means 'a moderate to strong red.' But I'm afraid it's getting more and more"—he paused for emphasis—"moderate as the years go by." He finished with an embarrassed chuckle that infected the whole party as wraps were gathered, and they made for the door.

In a rare bubble of enthusiasm, Dr. McKenna offered his arm to Ilka Markus as they left the country house. They set off in Dr. Hartmut's BMW for the Hotel Alois Lang in a relatively festive atmosphere; that is, all but Drew, who appeared happy enough to the others. But in reality she recalled little of the trip to the hotel, for her mind held only the memory of the meaningful smile Rolf had directed toward the golden German woman.

Chapter Nine

As would have been appropriate in any nightmare, the first person Drew saw upon entering the large, rustic dining hall was a glowering, sullen Jim Pollard, a very visible gauze patch taped on his forehead. Though he remained in the background, his eyes bore combatively through Drew during the gala dinner, leaving her with little appetite for the grandly prepared banquet.

"I think I see him," Rolf whispered as they sat, very conspicuously, Drew thought, at the head table.

She turned worried eyes to meet Rolf's clear ones. "Who do you mean?" she asked weakly, wanting to avoid the subject.

He pursed his lips, ignoring her sidestepping question. "It looks to me like *he's* the one who needs protection." The sensuous lips curved upward into a teasing smile. "Perhaps justice would be better served if I offered Mr. Pollard my services."

Her shoulders sagged and she averted her eyes. "It's not funny, Rolf."

His fingers curled beneath her chin, forcing her gaze back up to meet his. "No, *mein Kindchen,* you're right." His brown eyes were soft and lazy, and looking into their fathomless depths was a dangerous undertaking.

He spoke again, this time a small gleam flickered to life in the earthy darkness, giving his eyes a golden cast. "It is no joking matter. Yet I can't help but recall a time you left your mark on me." A low, masculine chuckle escaped his throat. "Weaker sex, indeed."

Her jaw dropped and a scarlet heat flamed her skin at his jolting reminder of the time in East Germany when she had hit him with the aspirin bottle, but before she could retort, Dr. Hartmut took the podium, calling for quiet.

A few moments of welcoming preliminaries preceded the introductions of those at the head table, other physicists like Drew's father, who would be making presentations during the coming two weeks.

And when the applause had died away after introductions of the guest dignitaries, Dr. Hartmut, with a degree of enthusiasm that had not been in his voice up to now, called the body's attention to the couple sitting at his near right.

Drew and Rolf.

Then it was happening; he was announcing to the world Rolf's defection to the West, as well as his marriage to the daughter of Madder McKenna.

With that revelation dropping like a bomb, all hell broke loose, and chaos reigned as reporters flooded forward to get the story, now turning this conference into a much more important assignment than they or the papers and magazines they represented could ever have imagined.

Questions were fired simultaneously at both Drew and Rolf: How did they meet, marry? How did he make his escape, and what were his plans for the future?

Rolf fielded most of them himself, calmly relating the facts about the Lufthansa's forced landing, meeting Drew at the interrogation, enlisting the help of the Peabodys, but there he changed the story slightly, saying that Drew volunteered to the marriage, performed secretly at his home.

Inevitably the question Drew dreaded was asked— and by none other than Jim, himself. Shouting above the din, he demanded, "Dr. Erhardt! If it is as you say—the marriage was simply a means to an end, aiding you in your escape, you will be getting a divorce. I mean"—his sharp look was aimed pointedly at Drew— "now that *Mrs.* Erhardt has served her purpose?"

An expectant hush fell over the large body, and Drew's heart pounded wildly and painfully against her ribs. Her throat, stingingly dry, closed, and she could barely get her breath. Paralyzed with foreboding, she was unable to move her gaze from Jim's self-satisfied sneer.

Rolf's intelligent eyes narrowed as he seemed to size up the man before responding. He nodded, "Yes, that was our plan."

He moved, sliding a casual arm about Drew's shoulders as he said, "Yet because she could not immediately leave, as we had at first hoped, we were forced to share rather close quarters for a time. And"—he paused, turning to look at her, a strange and tender smile curving his lips—"I grew to know her."

Returning his attention to Jim, he answered, yet didn't answer, the question with one of his own. "My friend, if you were fortunate enough to have such a lovely lady consent to be your wife, would you be so foolish as to let her slip through your fingers?"

Jim's mouth sagged at the unexpected rejoinder, and before he could recover himself, the pregnant silence was filled with the clamor of new questions, questions Drew did not hear. For her mind remained behind, echoing Rolf's soft query.

She knew her own expression could not be far different from Jim's at that moment, and she turned her face to her husband's strong profile, nonplussed by his uncanny ability to manipulate the English language to suit his purpose. He had not lied to Jim. Yet he had not given him any hope that she would ever be free for him to victimize again.

She felt herself smiling, and her breast filled to almost bursting with gratitude for his chivalrous handling of the entire interview.

Her thoughts were interrupted when Dr. Hartmut pounded the podium with a wooden gavel, trying to regain some semblance of order so that the remainder of the evening's program could continue.

Placing a slightly trembling hand on Rolf's, she whispered, "Thank you."

The planes of his face grew solemn as he dropped his gaze to her hand, resting tentatively on his, yet not half covering it. His only response was a slow nod.

Much later, with the program concluded, the gathering milled about the room in an excitement-charged atmosphere with an international flavor.

Unfortunately, it wasn't the excitement over her sudden importance at the conference that most affected Drew. More than that, it was Jim's scorching stare that followed her unfailingly about the room.

Several times, she realized he was making his way through the crush of well-wishers toward her. But Rolf, though not obviously watchful, would always guide her skillfully away, to yet another of the countless groups that insisted upon toasting the happy couple with champagne that flowed as freely and never ending as the Rhine.

Drew began to feel that she and Rolf had been congratulated and toasted by every one of the two hundred guests...and by some more than once! And she was chagrined to discover that her champagne glass had been filled and refilled countless times as the evening progressed.

And now she was less than pleased with the unbalancing effect the sparkling wine was having on her nearly empty stomach. Adding to her discomfort, Drew was distressed to note that Ilka Markus was constantly near at hand—or more correctly, near at *Rolf's* hand. And now as Kristel Hartmut attempted to converse with her in halting English, Drew had to watch as Ilka sidled silkily up to Rolf, taking his arm and murmuring something near his ear, instantly drawing his interest. He smiled, nodding, speaking in low German. His positive response moved her to laugh. It was a husky, purely feminine sound of delight.

Gritting her teeth, Drew tried desperately to keep her mind on Mrs. Hartmut's fragmented sentences, when she suddenly became aware of Ilka's presence beside them.

Looking up, she saw that Ilka was smiling, not at all pleasantly. "Drew, may I offer you my very best wishes?" She paused, dropping her eyes from Drew's face to her left hand, which held a full champagne glass. "I would love to see the ring. I know it is an American custom to wear the ring on the left hand...." The words fell away, and she moved her slanted eyes to Drew's right hand, also bare of jewelry. Meeting Drew's eyes, one of Ilka's softly sculptured brows went up in mock surprise. "What? No ring?"

Drew swallowed hard. What did she mean by this charade? What had passed between her and Rolf? Had he assured her of the truth—that the marriage was a pretense, and that her advances would be welcomed, later, in private?

Stumbling over her words, she began, "I—we—that is Rolf didn't have time to—"

Ilka interrupted, her tone vaguely hostile, "My dear girl, do not feel you need to explain to me. It is none of my concern." Shrugging prettily, and examining her perfectly manicured nails she went on, appearing quite indifferent, "Perhaps Rolf will remember that detail, soon. I wouldn't worry." Their eyes met again. Drew could see a malicious gleam in the glacial blue depths as she concluded, "He does not appear to be the sort of man to forget something important to him."

She turned her back, obvious in her attempt to exclude Drew, as she exchanged a few polite words with Mrs. Hartmut, whose confused expression revealed that she had not understood much of their English conversation. Then, in a golden fluidity that turned more than a few heads, Ilka walked away.

Drew put a hand to her throat, tugging nervously at the chain that held the token Rolf had given to her at their wedding as a substitute for a ring. She wanted to rush after Ilka and pull it from beneath her blouse to show her—to prove to her—but what?

Her anger faded in the face of her frustration. She dropped her hand listlessly to her side. What was the point? After all, Ilka was right. She knew the truth. The necklace she wore was not important to Rolf as a symbol of his love for her. To him, it was merely a symbol of their legal marriage. So why bother to argue the point with Ilka. It hurt, yes. But, then, sometimes the truth did.

Drew bit her lower lip to keep it from trembling, feeling totally deflated, and suddenly very woozy. She knew that she couldn't stand much more of this, and turned toward Rolf. He was deeply engrossed in a conversation with several Oriental men, and even in her cotton-headed state, she was amazed to realize that he was conversing with the men in their native Japanese. She stood for several moments, quietly waiting, listening to this strange tongue, in awe. Finally, one of the Japanese men acknowledged her presence with a polite bow and Rolf turned, a question knitting his brow. He took her hand, "What is it, *Kindchen?* You look tired."

"Rolf?" she whispered, her lips oddly numb. "I'm—" A tiny hiccup escaped, silencing her, and she pulled her lips together in a tight embarrassed line before continuing, "Could we sit down? I feel a little...funny."

Cocking his head to the side, he eyed her closely. "Would you like to leave?"

Inhaling slowly and feeling very light-headed, she nodded. "Yes, could we?" She squinted up at him. "I guess all this ess—essitement has made me tired."

A lazy smile softened his features. "That, too, perhaps."

She screwed up her brows in confusion at the remark and at his odd tone. He almost seemed to be fighting a battle to keep from laughing.

In a mellow fog, she realized that Rolf was making their excuses, and she was being pulled along toward the exit amid good-humored nudging and friendly, knowing glances as everyone bid the newlywed couple a hearty good-bye.

Very fuzzy now, Drew was thankful that all that was required of her was a pleasant smile and an occasional nod, and at last, they were outside and alone.

Rolf hailed a taxi. Once inside, he pulled her shivering frame close, where she stayed, enjoying his encompassing warmth.

He gave his address to the driver and turned to Drew, relaxing against her as he said, "Well, are you satisfied with the charade, so far, *Kindchen?*"

She hesitated, trying to recall some vague remark Ilka Markus had made. But it was too hazy and she couldn't concentrate on it, didn't want to. Besides, it had appeared that everyone else, including Jim, had believed them. And for that she was grateful.

Turning her face up to his, she sighed. "Yes...you were wonderful."

Lifting a brow in some surprise at the unexpected warmth of her words, he shot her a crooked half-smile. "As wonderful as the champagne?"

She giggled, not exactly sure why, and snuggled more deeply into the inviting crook of his arm. "Yes, just as wonderful...but in a...different way."

"Oh?" he queried. "How so?"

She shrugged beneath his arm. "Well..." She ran a curiously numb tongue over tingling lips, frowning with the effort of thought. Why were her reasoning processes so irritatingly slow tonight?

"Let's see.... You...Rolf Erhardt...Doctor... genius...You are a very clever man with words.... You make me feel"—she sighed, compromising her choice of words—"safe."

They passed beneath a lamp post, and Drew's eye was caught by the flash of embossing on a brass button on his overcoat, and she idly began to toy with it as she went on. "But, the champagne..." She smiled, remembering the sparkling, effervescent rich taste of it. She rarely drank and had only sipped from a glass of it at her own wedding with Jim as pictures were snapped.

But being from a practically teetotaling, scientific-minded family, she had never been inclined toward drinking it again, for Jim's habit of heavy drinking soured her on alcoholic beverages as an everyday necessity. But tonight was different, special. She concluded, "It makes me feel...happy."

They sat in silence for a moment before he murmured, "A good marriage could make you happy, too."

She thrust out her lower lip, suddenly irritated. "You should talk!" It came out in a somewhat snappish slur. "The confirmed womanizer...lech—" She fumbled, trying again, enunciating carefully: "Lec-tur-ing on love, no less!"

His muscles tensed about her, but by this time Drew didn't really care if she spoke out of turn or not. After all, he had hurt her terribly today with his proposition of detached friendship and even his offer to help her hadn't blotted out that pain.

Her champagne-charged mind shifted into high gear, and she felt herself smile, an impish, go-to-the-devil smile. She'd show him just exactly what he'd tossed aside! She was a woman, and he was, after all, only a man! It almost made her laugh out loud now to think about it. But really it was Rolf himself who had taught her just how much of a woman she could be!

Well, she'd just use a little of what she'd learned. She'd tease him just a bit on the drive home. And then, when they were inside, she'd draw coolly away, and lock herself in her room. That would serve him right!

An odd warning buzz went off somewhere in a remote, cautious corner of her brain, but she quickly smothered it. She was going to enjoy herself with a vengeance. She heard another giggle escape her throat. *And why shouldn't I!* she thought. *Why shouldn't I give Rolf Erhardt a little taste of his own love-'em-and-leave-'em medicine!*

She whispered almost soundlessly, yet in her most seductive voice, "Well...we're married." She paused, moving her lips up to brush against his ear. "Make me happy."

The hand on the brass button, warmed from contact with her skin, moved up his chest, slipping quickly beneath the heavenly softness of his cashmere overcoat. Finding the black tie, she tugged, loosening it, and bubbled over with laughter at her success.

"Drew?" His whisper was questioning.

"Shhh," she admonished thickly. "'M'busy!"

She then slipped the button beneath the tie out of its opening and slid her hand eagerly down to the second button, unfastening it, boldly pushing her hand into the curling spring of dark hair that covered his broad chest.

He inhaled sharply, shuddering with her touch...or did he? It was all rather mixed up now and she couldn't quite be sure of anything.

Frowning, she cocked her head. Had the cab come to a stop?

"We're home." It seemed like an oddly hoarse whisper.

Shaking her head dejectedly, she moaned, "Nooo...I don't want to go in...." Winding her arms about his neck in an effort not to be separated from his warmth, she blurted, "Let's just sit here for a while. It's...so... cozy...."

His voice was very, very low. She knew he must be near, but he sounded so far away. "Too cozy, *Kindchen*. We have an audience."

She screwed up her face in a confused grimace. "Hmm?" She couldn't see his features now, but she knew he was still very near. Her arms remained wrapped possessively about his neck, and his sultry breath tickled her cheek. She couldn't quite remember what he had said. But it didn't really matter.

She snuggled up against the cashmere, murmuring a contented sigh.

It was so hazy now, and dark, and in a slow realization, she became aware that her arms were empty—she was

alone! How had this happened? Flinging out a searching
hand, she felt nothing but the coolness of clean linen
sheets. She was in her bed. Though she couldn't remember getting there. Of one thing she was sure. Rolf had
gone!

A low moan escaped her throat, coming out in a whimper as she turned on her side. Gone. . . always gone!

Well, what could she expect? He was just doing her a
favor. He'd said himself that he was doing it because he
felt he owed it to her. After all, she reasoned groggily,
to put it bluntly, he'd had her once. . . and once had obviously been enough!

She moved with some effort to her stomach, fuzzily
conscious but terribly heavy-lidded. A tear dampened
the sheet at her face. She had wanted him to at least try
something. . . to be interested, so that she could put him
in his place by soundly rejecting him. But, it hadn't happened the way she'd planned. Once again, he'd rejected
her, even after she'd made such a fool of herself in the
cab! She closed her eyes. If only she could go back to
sleep. At least there would be peace in sleep. . . .

Soft fingers of fire slid along her back and down over
her hip. Stretching languidly beneath the phantom
touch, Drew sighed and moved with it, turning on her
side. The softness of the touch stayed with her and slid
up from the feminine curve of her hip, along the valley
of her waist and forward to the waiting ripeness of one
round breast, cupping it with gentle warmth.

She covered the larger hand with hers as she molded
herself to the warm, male contours at her back.

He was here. His velvety breath feathering the hair
along her temple, his lips nipping at the naked lobe of
her ear, sending chills of delight rippling along her
spine.

He was loving her again, the way she longed for, the
way she so foolishly yearned for him to, and she vowed,
this time, she would not spoil it. . . by waking up.

In the past month she had begun this same tangible

dream of Rolf returning to her bed and making intense, vigorous love to her. But she had always awakened prematurely—fearful of her unconscious wanderings—in a cold, trembling sweat, to find herself in the forbidding emptiness of her lonely bed.

And she always followed these heated dreams with hours of wakefulness, feeling desolate, frustrated and incomplete, unable to comprehend her emotions—until today when she so suddenly discovered her love for Rolf.

She had fought the dream then. But not this time! This time it was reality she would fight! Tonight she would dream this dream through to its completion. She would will herself not to awaken this whole cherished night. And just this once, she would allow herself a respite from reality, of remembering Rolf's disinterest! Yes. This night would be one of letting go to her flight of fantasy with Rolf, and she would fill the hours with her own passionate, desperate dreaming...and leave tomorrow's light for facing the truth.

Squeezing her eyes tightly shut, not daring to open them and have her phantom lover melt into vacant darkness, she lay, mesmerized by the magic of his ghostly touch, caring only for the perfection of his caresses as his body molded itself with her own, like two parts of a puzzle, long separated, finally joined to complete the desired image.

As he moved her through the ancient rhythms in love's dance, Drew floated along, enthralled, matching kiss for kiss, touch for touch as she explored the stirring hardness of his body, delighting in the supple tautness of his muscles and the completely male roughness of his strong jaw as his mouth seared along her shoulder.

He was an artist at his craft, a virtuoso, with full knowledge of the instrument she was, as he gently stroked, played her, leaving her nerves humming in a rush of melody as his hands moved along, bringing every fiber of her being alive with rich harmonious sensations.

His hands touched her everywhere at once. . .or at least, it seemed so. Yet if they did not, her skin could not bear witness, for it sizzled delightedly, making past and present contact melt together in a thunderous orchestration moving her quickly to forte, and her heart hammered out the percussion in throbbing palpitations beneath his eloquent, sensual direction.

This gentle, yet firm command he had over her body was intriguingly different from any other touch she had ever known; and it set her aflame with wanting, needing him, that mounted, at last to a crashing crescendo. Pulling him to her, she cried out fervently, "Please. . .oh, please. . .love me!"

He then guided her through a universe of unearthly emotions, and the dream became so passionate, so palpable and real within the cloudy champagne-washed darkness, thrilling her beyond reason, she found herself doubting her own sanity. And at the zenith of their joining, she cried out tearfully as her body shuddered beneath his in victorious surrender.

In the pleasurable stillness that followed, she felt at peace, aglow with love's embers as she lay entwined in the arms of her shadow love. . .miraculously content for the first time in so long. . . . She slept on, happy with the dream, for it was all that she had.

SHE stirred, snuggling in the cocoon warmth of the bed, blinking her eyes open. Bright light flooded in the glass door which opened out onto a narrow balcony, and she winced at the small pain it precipitated behind her eyes.

Turning to her back, she squinted down at her wrist. It was quite late—after 10:00 A.M. The conference breakfast meeting was long over, and she worried that her father would be wondering why she had not been in attendance.

Sitting up quickly, she swung her legs over the edge of the bed, then stopped short.

A gasp escaped her throat as she looked down at herself. She had nothing on! Confusion sent a needle of apprehension painfully through her mind as she looked slowly about the large room. The bed she perched on was long and wide within massive, beautifully carved head and footboards. Along the opposite wall sat two German closets, or *Schrankes,* large, double-doored chests used for hanging clothes. These too were richly adorned with carvings—clusters of grapes, cherubs, mountains and various other symbols that Drew did not recognize. But they were lovely.

Sitting between them stood a matching dresser, over which hung an antique beveled mirror.

She saw herself framed in the glass, wide-eyed, still as an alabaster statue and almost as pale, but for the fiery highlights of her hair, glowing a gold-red in the broad shaft of morning sunlight that fell on her there, singling her out in the lovely room like a spotlight illuminating the most important element in the opening scene of a play.

Just then, the sound of booted feet bounding up the stairs pulled Drew from her shocked paralysis. Hurriedly she pulled the sheet up before her bare breasts as the bedroom door swung wide.

A smiling Rolf entered briskly, moving toward the bed. Dumbfounded by his unannounced entry, Drew instinctively backed away, until she was halted both by the bed's sturdy headboard and by the fact that the sheet she clutched, tucked securely at the bottom of the bed would move no further.

"Good morning, wife." He stopped below the bed's footboard and hooked a thumb in his belt, then just stood, smiling for a moment as his eyes moved slowly over her. When he spoke again, his voice had taken on a husky tone. "I hated to leave you so early, but I had business in town that couldn't wait."

Drew's open mouth was prickly dry. "Leave. . . me?" It was a hushed question. She swallowed, afraid to ask any questions that might lead him to explain his remark.

Why? Never in her life had she felt so helpless. He obviously knew something that she didn't. Something, it seemed, which was very significant. How else could she explain his familiarity. . . entering her room. . . or. . . any room she was sleeping naked in as though he owned it!

Her fearful turn of mind was interrupted as he circled the end of the bed, still smiling. He sat down on the bed near her covered feet, pulling a newspaper from his hip pocket. Unfolding it, he laid it in her lap, tapping the image that faced her. It was a picture taken last night after the dinner. She saw herself smiling up at Rolf as he faced an unidentified reporter.

"You see, my love. Now the world knows our secret."

She shot her eyes back up at his face, amazed at his casual intimacy; his unconcerned use of her room and her bed. She bit her abused lip and winced.

No. This wasn't her room, she recalled again, and icy dread of the unknown moved along her spine, stiffening her back.

Unable to withstand his intent gaze, she lowered her eyes to the paper. The image before her faded as her mind took her inward, and she was suddenly very unconcerned about the fact that she was, once again, front page news. Right now, she had deeper concerns, problems. . . questions that needed answers, no matter how painful. . . questions, it appeared, that only Rolf could answer.

She let the words come, but half-heartedly and in a small, almost little girl voice. "Rolf? Did. . . did anything"—she cleared her swollen throat, and toyed nervously with the sheet she held tightly to her chest— "unusual. . . happen last night?"

He cocked his head, his broad smile diminishing slightly. "Unusual?"

She could only nod.

His brows knit, and he eyed her closely for a moment before asking, "Don't you remember?"

She tried to focus on the newspaper resting in her lap

as she whispered, "Not...not clearly." She knew she could have said *not at all* after a vague recollection of being bundled into a cab—or was that just part of her dream, too? She hesitated.

He shook his head, chuckling. "I think I am offended. But, to answer your question, no, I can't say anything unusual happened."

Hugging the sheet close about her, she relaxed slightly, expelling a long breath as she let herself slide slowly down, until her elbows, and a pillow at her back halted her. She just lay quietly for a moment, puzzled gray eyes meeting steady brown. Her mind tried to pick up loose ends, fragmented mental pictures of the night before... but all she could recall was a night of wonderful imaginings.

Regaining some of her confidence, she lifted her chin and spoke, trying for sternness, however belatedly. "Then—then you have your nerve, coming in here!" She moved her eyes about the room. "Are we still in the Alois Lang? Why didn't you take me back to the chalet?"

A slow, easy smile replaced his thoughtful look, and he surprised Drew by moving his hand to her ankle, resting it warmly on the sheet, his fingers gently massaging her leg. "This is the chalet, Drew. It's my room." He paused. "Try to remember."

With the electric contact of his hand, coupled with the soft order, her jaw dropped as overwhelming disbelief numbed her brain.

"No!" She pulled her leg away from his charged touch, jumping to her knees. "It wasn't...it couldn't have been...not *you*!"

Yanking hard on the sheet, she managed to pull it free from its confining hold and scrambling farther from him, she cried breathlessly, "It just couldn't have been you!"

An uncharacteristic flicker of surprise danced across his eyes. "No?" His smile was crooked. "Were you expecting someone else?"

In heated but graceful fluidity, Drew swept the sheet and herself off the opposite side of the bed, retorting hotly, "That remark is not worthy of an answer. Just what kind of a woman do you take me for?"

His eyes held a meaningful golden glint as he husked, "Actually, Drew"—white teeth flashed in a quick grin—"you are a most appealing kind."

She avoided his knowing eyes. "This is all a terrible mistake! I—I thought you were all a—a dream..." she let out helplessly. It sounded so ridiculous now, after the fact. For if dreams were really capable of that degree of fulfillment, man would have died out aeons ago—most probably, peacefully, in his sleep!

He stood and thoughtfully rubbed a fisted knuckle along his square jaw. "Well, I've been called many things in my time, but never a dream." He nodded his head, amusement lightening his words. "I believe I like it."

Drew sputtered at his contrary lack of repentance, "You told me you wouldn't take advantage of me!"

His look held a disturbing candor. "And I won't."

"You won't!" she fumed, her body going taut in her fury. "But—but—you did! Last night you—you knew I wasn't myself!"

His eyes seemed to brand her with his ownership as he answered, "No, *mein stürmisches Fräulein,* my stormy woman. I would say last night you were very much yourself."

She sobered instantly, eyes growing huge at his unexpectedly gentle remark. She moved her lips to retort, but no sound came. For some ridiculous reason she felt as though he had extended her a great compliment, and with it thrust right in the midst of her mental turmoil and righteous indignation, she didn't know how to react.

Suddenly he was rounding the bed, coming nearer. With his approach, uncertainty sharpened her words as she fleetingly scanned the neat room once again. "Where are my clothes? I want my clothes!"

"They are in your *Schranke.*"

"In the other room?" She was positive now of how all of this must have happened. "So, you came into my room when I was helpless and asleep, and carried me in here!" She tossed her fiery head, confident of the accuracy of her accusation. "Can't you get a woman to come to you without sneaking up on her while she lies in oblivious sleep?"

His eyes narrowed slightly, but he ignored her gibe. "I put your clothes away this morning." The remark was matter-of-fact. "You were in too much of a hurry last night to be concerned about them."

"I?" Her voice rose an octave and was slightly thready. "What is that supposed to mean?"

His eyes, far too penetrating for her peace of mind, passed over her thinly clad form as he moved to face her. "You seduced me, you know." He reached out, lazy fingers tracing along her cheek. "I will admit, I was quite surprised." His face changed as a seductive smile softened the angular planes.

Moving long fingers to her chin, he tilted her face up to his, grazing her lips with his own as he concluded, "Surprised, but very pleased."

His mouth consumed hers, his possessive lips held an urgent fiery demand that caused Drew's legs to grow weak.

A supportive hand slid to her back, pressing her to his long, hard frame. The move told her with graphic accuracy that he was a man aroused.

The scorching kiss, the ardor of his bold touch on the bare skin of her back was quickly drawing all resistance from her. In his arms, the memory of the night just past blazed to life in her mind. This man was a lusty, potent lover, inflaming her to white-hot passions instantly, like a fragile match easily struck to flame against the proper friction.

In his arms, she burned, and was consumed by him, totally. There was no substance left of her to call her own. And after burning like a torch in his hands, she knew she could be nothing more than shapeless, lifeless ashes in any other embrace.

He held her gently now; his kisses were not urgent as he tasted, savored her mouth with his tongue. She became aware that the sheet at her back had parted, and Rolf's knowing hands were massaging her spine, easing the tenseness from her body. Her legs trembled in their continued effort to support her. In another moment she would be lifted into his arms, totally lost in her desire for him. He could do with her as he pleased, as he had done with her before. . .when he had taken her off her guard. But this time it was different. This time she was awake and sober. And even now she was losing herself to his seductive touch. . .and in just another moment she would be his completely of her own free will. But. . . would he be hers? What was she to him? The question was easily answered, chilling her soul.

She was his *friend*. Obviously his definition of friend was a bit broader than her own. She had thought he didn't want her in this way. But she had been wrong. He wanted her. . .as he had no doubt wanted many women before and would want many others after. Women to him were a convenience. And so was she, a two-week fluffy diversion. What he didn't want of her was permanence!

"No!" she sobbed wretchedly, her mind forcing her to pull away from the magnetic spell he exerted on her body. She pushed against him with a strength born of desperation, for she knew if she gave in now, she could never hold herself away from him again. And he would only drive his memory deeper into her before he finally walked away. She could not weaken now and allow him this chance to inflict more profound pain on an already badly trampled heart.

"I'm not going to make it that easy for you! I—I won't. . ." she choked. "Let me go! Haven't you done enough to me already?"

She stumbled away.

Not expecting her sudden protest, Rolf released her easily. "Drew? What's wrong?" He sounded strangely stricken.

Through tears, she sobbed, "Wrong? We're wrong... you're wrong! This whole thing is wrong! I—I won't believe you about last night! You interpreted my condition the way you wanted to. I'm not used to drinking, that's all."

He reached toward her, his expression perplexed. "Listen to me, Drew—"

"No!" She avoided the contact. "I was terribly wrong in thinking you would protect me from Jim! You are no better than he is!"

He straightened, speaking slowly and distinctly, but there was no harshness in his voice: "Do you equate being made love to with a beating?"

Her stomach constricted with uncertainty, but there was no backing down now. She had to fight back, to put a chasm between them that could not be bridged. She had to make him want to keep his distance, to hate her if necessary.

It was cruel, and it was a lie, but she blurted, "Maybe... yes! In some ways I do! At least I didn't invite the *handling* I received in either case!"

"Handling." He repeated her word in a low breath. And she noted with some anguish that a muscle had begun a frantic kicking in his taut jaw as he stepped unevenly away, looking as though he had been physically struck. His face darkened beneath the already tan skin as he replied evenly, "Then I will make you a promise, Drew." His deep voice had gone flat. "I will not *handle* you again. However"—his dark eyes flicked quickly over her and then back up; Drew inhaled sharply to see how hard they had become as he finished—"*I* have no doubts about my interpretation of last night. And I do not regret what we shared." His lips twisted. "At least, I have the memory of the woman you were... in this bed. A person I much prefer to the quailing little girl I see now.''

Thunderstruck by his ungracious comparison, she retorted sharply, ''I don't have to stay here and listen to this!''

Whirling toward the door, she brushed quickly past him, feeling for the briefest instant the strength of his body against hers.

Grasping the door knob, she pulled. It stuck, and for a frustrating moment she struggled angrily to open it, handicapped in no small way by the fact that she could not use both hands while one preserved her modesty by clutching the sheet about her.

Embarrassed at her inability to make a sweeping, disdainful exit, she shot a glance over her shoulder, eyeing Rolf grimly. He stood motionless, his legs spread. One dark brow went up as he quietly observed her struggles. Shrugging his hands into his jeans pockets, he made it clear that he did not intend to help her. He was no longer on her side, and oddly, this knowledge hurt her much more than anything that had gone before.

Letting out a low moan of dismay, she dropped the sheet. It fell quickly to the floor, and Drew transferred some of her anger to it, damning it silently, somehow feeling that it, like the door, had taken Rolf's side, conspiring against her.

Finally, the stubborn portal creaked loudly, protesting its opening, and she dashed out in a flash of rosy skin. The rapid padding of her bare feet was the only sound that broke the stillness. And she knew in her aching heart, that Rolf had not moved.

Chapter Ten

The sun shone warmly down on the noontime bustle of Oberammergau. Comfortable in her bouclé tweed wrap jacket and cocoa flannel pants, Drew ambled along gazing in shop windows, wishing her spirits were as bright as the warm sunshine.

But they weren't. She raised her eyes to scan the painted building before her. It was a woodcarving shop. The second story held a painting of Christ being lifted on the cross by a people costumed in the style of the sixteen hundreds.

Drew knew, from an explanation by Dr. Hartmut, that this was the pictorial story of the promise made by the small German town in 1632, when a plague that had been sweeping across the country miraculously stopped short of Oberammergau.

The people of the village vowed because of the miracle, to give a presentation of the Passion of Christ every ten years, the first of which took place in 1634.

For over three hundred years they had kept their promise. *The Passion Play,* after brief interruptions during times of war, evolved to its present-day schedule of being presented on the first year of every new decade. The next celebration of the Resurrection of Christ would be in 1990.

Her eyes moved on up, past the beauty of the building, and rested finally on the dominant Amergau peak, Kofel, rising above the Oberammergau valley. Drew could see a cross at its highest point, barely visible in the bright blue of the sky, lovely and inspiring, and for a moment, she smiled, breathing in the fresh spring air.

"Mrs. Erhardt!"

The businesslike bite of the words startled Drew back to reality and she turned to see a bullish-shaped reporter, a young female photographer, and Jim.

Having successfully got her attention, the square-faced young man went on, "Mrs. Erhardt, we've been here nearly a week now, and I for one would like a little pace change to send home."

He pulled a toothy grin, flipped on a tape-recorder that was strapped to his shoulder, and lifted a microphone to his lips.

Clearing his throat he went on, "What we'd like, Mrs. Erhardt, is your version of the story. What I mean is"—his smile turned knowing, somehow skeptical—"some of us find it a little hard to swallow, a little too pat, that you and Dr. Erhardt are really planning to make a go of this marriage."

Drew felt herself go stiff and her heart rose to block her throat as he went purposefully on.

"I mean it's perfectly understandable why you married the man—to help him get out of the East and all. But after one week together under the noses of the Reds, when you were a hostage? It's pretty hard to believe true love blossomed. So what's the real tale?"

Drew's eyes moved from the short speaker to the mannishly clad girl who was taking pictures at his side, no doubt getting very revealing expressions of confusion and unease, and then to Jim, taller than the two animated ones before him.

He stood solemnly, green eyes narrowly surveying her, mouth turned down in a frown. She noted that the discoloration on his forehead was now only a dirty yellow, and that the cut was healing nicely. But the festering hatred in his eyes made her shudder.

She tried her voice. "I—I don't understand quite what you're asking."

It was a quiet evasion. She shifted her purse to her shoulder and clasped her suddenly moist palms together.

"What's not to understand?" His question held a

note of irritation. "I just want to know why you're still together now. I mean, Doctor Erhardt is out of the East. What's the real story here? There's more to this than you're letting on."

Squaring her shoulders, Drew was determined not to give Jim the satisfaction of knowing the truth. She began, hoping that at least outwardly, she appeared calm, "I can't really see—"

"Mein Kindchen." Gentle hands on her arms accompanied the familiar endearment. "I have found you again. Are you about ready for lunch?"

She turned to see Rolf's smiling face, the first smile in the four days since their lovemaking; four days of silent, painful passings in the chalet.

The generous gladness of his greeting warmed her to her toes with a rare revitalizing heat that was more welcome than the new spring sun above.

The reporter with the rolling tape would not be put off. "How about it, Doctor? What's going on here? This fairy story about love at first sight—it just doesn't wash with a lot of us. What's the real dope?"

Rolf moved closer to Drew, sliding an arm about her waist, an air of authority surrounding his words as he spoke.

"It's Max Dalton, am I right?" He addressed the smaller man. "Well, Max, have you got a girl friend?"

The little man shifted with the turn of attention. "Me? Sure—sure I've got a girl friend. Why?"

"Were you attracted to her the first time you saw her? Or, perhaps, did you think she was a—how do you Americans say it?—a dog?"

"Well, I—I sure didn't think she was a dog, for gosh sakes." He lowered the mike. "Can't we get back to you?"

"But that's where we are. I'm just suggesting that it is possible to fall in love with someone you've just met."

"Okay, okay, it's possible. Anything's possible, I guess. But this is not probable!" He shrugged his brawny shoulders and continued with a sheepish smile. "I admit I *liked* my gal when I first saw her. I never said I loved her."

Rolf chuckled deep in his throat. "Better turn off the tape then, Max. She might not understand some of this conversation."

Drew relaxed slightly against him as he eased the situation that had so stymied her just moments before.

Max was frowning now, peering down at the tape, but his eyes shot back up as Rolf used his name. "Max"— he paused turning toward the slight, pixie-faced girl— "and Suzy, right?"

The young woman pinkened and nodded, momentarily pausing in her kneeling position for getting the best angle for her next shot.

". . . and Jim Pollard?" Rolf went on to acknowledge the silent, scowling man in back. "All right, I'll tell you the truth, once and for all, and that will be all we need to say on the subject. Agreed?"

There was a vague nodding before the silence became palpable. And Drew felt sure that they could hear the rush of blood through her constricted veins. The truth!

What was Rolf doing! What was he going to say. . . or possibly admit? Had he decided that he didn't care to go through the two weeks protecting a woman he couldn't stand, a woman who would not "pay" him for the service by sleeping with him?

She bit her lip, waiting with the rest of them. Unable to bear to watch his face, she dropped her gaze to a stone in the cobbled walk at her feet and stared at it.

His hand dropped from her waist and her heart plummeted with it.

From the corner of her eye Drew could see Max move his mike closer to Rolf's face to catch his words when they came.

His voice was oddly quiet when he began, "The truth is, that it really doesn't matter what I say here. The romantics of the world will believe that we married for love...and the cynics will think I married this lady only to gain my U.S. citizenship.''

He put a finger to her chin, lifting her eyes. Looking down at her, he locked his eyes with her own, speaking in a hushed tone, ''What really does matter is''—he took her violently shaking hand into his larger, steady one; his smile was tender, almost loving—''what does my wife believe?''

There was a momentary pause before Drew heard the young photographer's breathless, ''Cheeze!''

Rolf heard it too and his finely sculptured lips twitched with humor. ''It appears we have at least one romantic in the crowd.''

Pink-cheeked at the softness of his words, Drew lowered her eyes only to lift them again in silent thanks for yet another rescue. She expressed that thanks in a shy smile which he returned. Yet his was a smile so dazzling that it sent an intense shaft of feeling through her that stole her breath away.

The rest of the world ceased to exist. There was only she, only Rolf. She knew that his performance for Jim and the others was just that—a performance. But she couldn't help but be affected by his gentle nearness.

''And now, love, what about that lunch?''

She nodded as he took her arm.

Max spoke up, ''Hey, Doc. Thanks for the quote.''

Rolf turned back to them and threw a quick wave as he led Drew off down the sunny walk.

She felt a buoyancy she had not experienced in days as they walked past the window of Langs, the largest woodcarver's shop in Oberammergau.

She scanned the displays in the windows. There were several styles of the popular Madonna and Child, from placid to windswept, some stained and some gilded. There were carvings of country folk in native costumes, playful animals and plaques with sayings in German.

In a corner, one carving in particular caught Drew's

eyes. She stopped and let out a laugh. "Look, Rolf." She pointed. "Doesn't that look like Daddy?"

It was a carving of a lanky, bespectacled man poring over a large volume, an intent expression carved on his narrow face. His shoulders were stooped, and his long spindly legs were bent, knees locked tight with two volumes pressed between his legs.

She giggled. "I've seen Dad that way. How perfect! I knew Oberammergau was famous for its wood carvings, but I never expected to find my father!"

Rolf offered, "I'll get it for you if you'd like. You really shouldn't leave Oberammergau without a souvenir to remember your stay."

She sobered instantly. She would need no souvenir to recall her stay here. For that matter, it would be better to concentrate her efforts on forgetting it!

She shook her head. "No, Rolf. I'm sure you understand that I couldn't accept it." Hurriedly she added, "I'll show it to Dad. If he likes it I'll get it for him for his birthday or something."

He set his shoulders in reluctant dismissal and shook his head. "No, Drew, I don't understand why you can't accept at least a small gift from me. I owe you my freedom."

She opened her mouth to protest, but he held up a discouraging hand and finished, "But if you do not want anything from me, I won't force the issue."

He turned to survey the street at her back. "It looks as though Jim and his friends are gone."

Resuming eye contact he went on, "Actually, I've already had lunch. And Doctor Porter is expecting me at one o'clock. He is anxious for my impression of his work on the Tokamak. So, if you will excuse me?"

His offhandedness punctured her balloon of buoyancy and she felt deflated at his obvious eagerness to be away now that they were alone.

Fighting a hot stinging in her eyes she lifted her chin. "Of course, Rolf. You don't owe me lunch...or anything."

"Are you going to be at the meeting later?" he asked as she turned to walk away. "I'll save you a seat."

"No, thanks. I'll sneak in the back; that way my scribbling won't disturb the speaker."

At that she turned, trying for light-heartedness in her wave good-bye.

DREW marked her cassette with the identifying title and dropped it into its case. Her work done for the day, she stood, pressing her hand to the small of her back. Stretching, she tried to relieve a tense ache that had begun during the long hours of sitting taking notes and recording the presentations.

As usual, Rolf had been detained by numerous questions, and as usual, Drew took a cab to the house they shared, alone, ate a sandwich alone, and returned to her room to soak in a tub and then file away the materials for the speeches, which she would compile into a series of articles for the *Los Alamos Scientific Monthly*.

Walking to the glass door that led to the balcony, Drew gazed up at the clear black sky twinkling with stars.

She opened the door and stepped outside, inhaling the crispness of the night and pulling her fleecy robe close about her.

It was unearthly still, and except for the light of her room and Rolf's there was nothing this far out of town to illuminate the darkness.

Rolf's room? Lights?

She turned quickly and stopped, voicing a surprised, "Oh!"

"Hello, *Kindchen.*"

Rolf was there! His door was open, and he was leaning casually against its jamb, arms folded loosely across his chest. He must have come in while she was reviewing the tapes and she hadn't heard his entry.

He wore the coffee-colored flannel trousers, turtle-neck sweater and corduroy Norfolk jacket he had been wearing that afternoon. *Always the casually well-dressed scientist,* she mused.

"Hello, Rolf. I didn't hear you come in."

"I just got back." Straightening he went on, "Aren't you cold out here? It's barely above freezing."

"I guess. . .a bit. But it's so lovely." She moved her hands to her arms, rubbing slowly as the chill began to penetrate.

He did not respond, merely watched her in a totally disconcerting way. Uneasy, she decided not to linger under that disturbing look. "Well, I think I'll go on in to bed."

She turned toward her door.

"At eight-thirty?" His question halted her and she shrugged her answer. "Drew, why don't we call a truce. It's early and I thought we might talk."

"No. . .I. . ."

"Just talk." He finished quietly.

She looked around. His face was serious. He seemed tired, somehow vulnerable, and her heart melted against her will.

"Well, I suppose it couldn't hurt to talk."

"Good." A flicker of satisfaction raced across his eyes as he stepped back out of the door and offered, "You may have the chair."

A bit hesitantly, she followed him into his room and seated herself stiffly in a tall rocker that sat beside the door.

Rolf lowered his big frame to rest on the edge of the room's largest piece of furniture. The bed. They faced each other for a moment as Rolf moved his elbows to his knees and laced his hands beneath his chin.

Feeling an awkwardness in the quiet, Drew spoke first. "Rolf? Whose house is this?"

His lips lifted in a brief smile. "Vacationing friends of Gieslbert Hartmut. It was a fortunate chance, since the conference had everything else in town reserved."

She nodded. "It is a lovely home."

Pursing his lips he agreed with a slow movement of his head.

"Rolf? I was thinking. In the beginning in the East, why didn't you just ask me for my help like you told the press?"

The pleasant expression vanished and he raked a hand through his brown curls, ruffling them further. "That, *Kindchen,* was a mistake. I admit it, and I apologize." Fleetingly a bitter smile twisted his lips before he spoke again. "But you will remember I originally believed I had only hours. I didn't know you, and most importantly, I was used to using totalitarian tactics. In the East people are told, not asked, to do something."

He lifted dark eyes to meet hers. "Do you understand what it is to be desperate?"

Lowering her gaze, she exhaled her sad answer, "Yes, Rolf, I think I do."

As if her few words spoke volumes, Rolf moved in the obvious direction.

"Tell me how it was with Jim."

She hedged. "It's not worth discussing."

He coaxed. "Some men in my position would believe they had a right to know."

Drew's eyes shot up to meet his, an electric storm of emotion flashed in their gray depths. "You have no right to pry. No one does!"

He did not appear affected by her anger as his voice nudged kindly, "Perhaps as a fellow human being I could exercise my right to help. Sometimes just talking to someone can be healing." He was watching her squarely now. "Don't you think it's about time you rid yourself of the pain?"

She stared at him wordlessly for a long moment. Yes, he was right. She did need to talk about it. Yes, she was in pain, and yes, maybe it would be healing to tell him. After all, he of all people already knew her better than anyone, now—possibly even herself!

She sighed and began in a rush of words, "Jim was

handsome, charming and glib. He literally swept me off my feet. It was a whirlwind romance and I thought he was everything a girl could want in a man until. . . until—''

She stopped and closed her eyes, feeling once again the anguish twist her insides.

"Until?" Rolf urged.

She studied him through the dark fringe of her lashes, unable to look directly at him in her embarrassment, "Until the abuses started. . . . First verbal. . . then mental. . . and finally. . . ''

"What do you mean verbal?" His voice was barely above a whisper.

Drew shifted uncomfortably in her chair and lay her head back against the soft lambswool draped across its back, closing her eyes. "He called me 'cold'. . . 'unresponsive'. . . " She couldn't go on.

Opening her eyes she looked at him to appraise his reaction. He was frowning, leaning forward a bit. His eyes were steady, nonjudgmental.

"Go on."

She swallowed. "Then it was mental abuse. He flaunted his little affairs at me saying he couldn't get satisfaction from an 'ice queen.' He said—" Her voice caught and she paused to regain her composure, curling her fingers about the chair arms. "He said I was his, and I'd learn. . . but in the meantime I wasn't enough. . . . ''

She pulled her hand loose and moved it to her mouth to stifle a sob. "Oh, Rolf. Please, I don't want to talk about it."

His eyes narrowed reflectively. "Why did you stay with him?"

She shook her head. "Looking back, I really don't know exactly. I guess it was because I was brought up to believe a marriage was forever. . . and you had to work at making it good." Sighing heavily, she let out a shaky laugh. "And I guess after a couple of years of working at it all by myself, I began to believe that 'love' was only a romantic notion for schoolgirls."

Moving her shoulders in a helpless gesture she finished, "Once the honeymoon was over, I imagined that all marriages must be pretty much the same as ours was—hollow."

He shook his curly head and slowly unfolded himself from the bed, reaching her in one long stride.

"There are two things you must realize, Drew." Taking her cold hand, he firmly pulled her to her feet. "First, between the two of you, you were not the fool."

Pulling her to him in a gentle embrace, he cradled her face against the softness of his sweater, his lips grazing her forehead. "And you must know by now, you can be a very passionate woman."

At his touch, her wits flew into chaotic, directionless flight like a sky full of startled butterflies. Frightened by her reaction, she tried to push him away, but his arms would not allow them to be parted. "Rolf, please—"

"No, just listen. I'm very sorry that my manner when we first met reminded you of Jim's type."

She was drowning in his masculine fragrance and warmth. Her voice became thready and weak. "His type?"

"Surely you don't believe all men are like Jim." It was an urgent whisper.

"No. . . not exactly." She shook her head in the confines of his hand, feeling the soft cashmere move against her cheek.

But inwardly she saw little difference. Both Rolf and Jim were dominant men, prowling animals not content with one mate. It was not in their nature.

She cursed herself silently, stiffening in his arms, wanting to cry out from the depths of her tortured heart—*Damn! Why did I have to fall in love with you! It was hard with Jim. . . it would be unbearable to know you were seeing other women!*

In her anguish she blurted, "No, you're not exactly like Jim. I don't believe you would beat me."

His warm embrace turned cold and stony about her,

and he stepped slowly away. His voice echoed her words in a low tone of disbelief, "You don't believe I would beat you? Is that the only difference you see?"

"Please, Rolf—I'd better go," she stammered, casting a quick glance toward the balcony door and then back up to his brooding face.

"Then go." It was a hoarse groan through tight, frowning lips.

There had been no apparent challenge in those two words, yet an unfathomable paralysis passed over her body as barren brown eyes reached somewhere deep inside the area of her brain that controlled movement, short-circuiting that mechanism.

As she stared into the abyss beyond his eyes, she saw something that might have been described as sorrow. Flinching at the face that suddenly held no peace, she could not draw her eyes away, but could only stand and look at him.... No...no, it was more than just looking at him. Somehow, Drew had the feeling that he was allowing her a glimpse inside him; a look beneath the broad-shouldered aloof maleness; beneath the muscle and sinew that in its very manly package hid from the world any hint of human vulnerability. But suddenly it was there, tearing at her heart.

What she saw seemed like the despair a caged jungle cat might display who, having lost his freedom, has given up hope and care for life itself.

The notion, she knew, must be a travesty on the truth, a crazy flight of her own fantasy...to compare this powerful, brilliant man, who had just *gained* his freedom, with an imprisoned animal. But she couldn't shake the devastating image, or the power of his gaze as his eyes held hers at mute, subdued bay.

The power to move clicked back on, and Drew became aware that Rolf was turning away. Every line of his body was taut, as if he were removing himself from her with rigid control. Staring after his retreating form, a sob welled up in her throat and she jammed a fist to her lips to strangle a betraying cry.

It would be intolerable to have him know she died a little more inside with every step that he took away from her.

A flat click as the heavy door closed behind him echoed loudly in the room which had suddenly grown cold and cavernous. She bit the knuckles of her hand, tasting blood.

She loved Rolf Erhardt so much that at this moment she was positive that a beating from Jim would have been less painful than the crushing her heart had to endure sharing time and space with a man who thought no more of her than he had any other of his temporary playthings.

Running a trembling hand through freshly brushed hair that fell in natural softness about her shoulders, her eyes, shimmering now with tears, were drawn to the bed. The breath caught in her throat with memories of that night almost a week ago, of the man. . . the tender lover he had been.

Tears spilled helplessly as a wave of raw hunger and longing swept through her, and she spun away, running onto the balcony toward the sanctuary of her own room.

Even in her state of bleak emotional agitation, a corner of Drew's mind caught a quick concealing movement in the darkness below.

Was someone down there?

In her shattered state, she dismissed something that would otherwise have caused her concern.

Who could be watching the house? Why?

These questions poised only for a split second on the edge of her consciousness and slid into oblivion before they were even recognized as ever having existed.

Flinging herself through the door, she slammed it as though she were warding off demons and fell dejectedly to her bed, where hours passed before she drifted into an exhausted, fitful sleep.

Chapter Eleven

The note was as clipped and concise as the handwriting. It read:

> Drew,
> I had planned to tell you last night of Dr. Hartmut's invitation for me to visit and speak at the university in Munich. Of course, he expected you to accompany me. But knowing how you feel, I have declined for you, explaining that you felt that you must stay and assist your father. I will be back before the conference ends.

It was signed, plainly, "Rolf."

"Before the conference ends...." That could mean that he would be gone for as long as a week...in Munich. A picture of the sleek Ilka Markus flashed through her mind, constricting her stomach.

She crumpled the note. *A week.*

The thought of Rolf spending that many days—and nights—in Munich with Ilka Markus was the poorest way Drew could imagine to begin a day.

The balled note was aimed at the small kitchen wastebasket. But at the last moment, she couldn't throw it away.

It was something of Rolf's.

Instead, she pushed it into her purse, not really wanting it, but unable to part with anything that held his mark.

"Fool!" She spat at herself blinking back threatening tears as she headed for the door and the morning meetings.

DAYS passed in a dull blur. More than once, her father coaxed her to go on to Munich, saying that he could punch a tape-recorder button as well as she could. He insisted with maddening regularity that her place was with her new husband, not tagging about after a doddering old man.

She had only shrugged his insistence off with forced nonchalance saying that Madder McKenna's daughter was no less capable of doing her job, whatever the complications, than the next scientific journalist.

To her great relief, he took her devotion to duty at face value and finally let the subject drop.

Too, it appeared that a number of the visiting reporters, including Jim, had followed Rolf to Munich. Obviously, it was their feeling that the story was with the recently freed German rather than at the waning days of the conference.

At least this way, Drew had to admit, she was not continually having to confront either the man she most feared, or the man she desperately loved.

But there was one nagging worry.

Why had Jim left her alone? Surely he had not given up trying to get her back just when she was finally unprotected—almost at his mercy. It didn't make sense. But Rolf had been gone four days now, and there had been no sign of Jim in all that time.

She shook off the negative thought with the logical explanation that Jim was, after all, working for a living, and must get the story for his magazine.

She sighed, pulling on a wool sweater-jacket. Determined not to let late afternoon loneliness at the chalet bear down on her another moment, she decided to take a walk along a nearby stream.

Dressed comfortably in walking shoes, navy chino pants and blue striped oxford-cloth shirt, her white sweater-jacket opened to the season's briskness, she ambled destinationless, yet always upward, along the rapidly flowing mountain stream.

After nearly an hour of walking, she was attracted to the rocky edge where a large flat rock protruded over the water. It was, no doubt, an often sought-after resting place above the picturesque town.

Her thoughts, however, were not as peaceful as the placid sight below.

Expelling a long breath, she searched among the pebbles nearby for a flat stone to toss into the stream, to disrupt its flow...a physical parallel to the mental disruption Rolf had made in the flow of her own life.

The first toss was in mid-flight when a familiar voice at her back startled her to her feet.

"Well, well, babe, how do you like spending your honeymoon alone?"

She spun toward the cynical voice, her disquieted mood lurching toward alarm.

"Jim!"

He smiled, a smile that bordered on a leer. "Right on the first guess."

She took a step backward, but, in time, remembered that she was poised precariously over the stream, making that mode of escape require a rough, frigid swim.

She stopped. "I thought—I— Weren't you in Munich?"

He lifted thick shoulders. "Was. But the brilliant Dr. Erhardt began to bore me."

He moved toward her; the crunch of gravel beneath his feet was magnified thunderously in her ears.

"Besides, job or no, I said we'd get together later." Impatience gleamed in the brightness of his cool green eyes. "And since we pack up tomorrow, I figured to-day'd have to be that 'later.'"

Nausea rose in her throat as he took another step toward her. "What do you want, Jim."

"What do I want?" He laughed harshly. "Don't be stupid, Drew. I want you."

Her skin crawled at the very idea. Gulping at the bile

that was rising in her throat, she was unable to trust opening her mouth to speak.

"I want answers, straight answers!" His voice had become razor sharp.

Though she was quailing wretchedly inside, she managed to lift her chin with bravado. "I don't owe you any explanations."

It was impossible to imagine the ugly sneer becoming more obscene, but it did as he closed the gap between them, taking her sweatered arms with rough authority.

"Why didn't you tell me about your marriage when I first saw you?"

She twisted in his painful grasp, grimacing. "Take your hands off of me!"

"You get what you deserve, babe." It was a growl. "Now answer my question!"

She raised cold bright eyes to meet his, offensive, the greenish tint of tornadolike foreboding making her cringe with terror.

He spat, "Why were you registered at the hotel alone...and as Mrs. Pollard?"

She gasped, "Jim—I—we..." Her thoughts tumbled quickly towards the obvious story. "We didn't know when or...if he would get out. To protect him, I had to act as though nothing had changed. You must see that!"

His jaw worked angrily, watching her before he ventured further, "Yes, that's possible. But you can't make be believe you two really planned to make this thing work. I'm no fool. Either you've been hiding behind his name to keep me away or"—he lowered his face toward hers and finished in a guttural whisper—"or you've really fallen for the guy." He snorted without humor. "He just used you to get out of the East. You know it and I know it."

His breath was harsh against her face. "In fact, from what I saw in Munich between him and that Markus woman."

Those words stabbed deeply into her soul and she felt her lips tremble with the hopeless denying shake of her head. "Nooooo!"

The bite of his fingers increased with the slash of his words. "Hell, every waking minute that slinky woman was draped over his arm." His chuckle was dark, evil. "I'm betting she was with him more than a few sleeping minutes too."

Knowing that what he said was true did not make it any easier to hear. In fact, hearing it, hearing that her fears about Rolf and Ilka were true, made it all that much more horrible to endure.

"Stop it, Jim! Stop it!" she cried desperately, pushing at his chest, feeling the comfortless tears well up and overflow.

Her struggles only increased his determination, and he pulled her into a stifling hold against the rough wool of his jacket-shirt.

"Fight me, Drew. That's a good girl. Go on and fight me."

A terrified scream trembled on her lips, but sound would not come.

"It'll be so much better if you fight me." He taunted in a guttural whisper. And to her horror, Drew could feel his desire being aroused by her struggles.

He prophesied with the assurance of a demented dictator, "You'll come crawling back to me after Erhardt drops you flat in the good old U.S. of A. You know you will."

Pounding her fists against his chest, she sobbed, "No, no! I'll never, never want you back. I won't come back to you! Jim, you're sick. You need help!"

He didn't appear to feel the pounding, and Drew became desperate as she saw his wide lips move to cover hers. She couldn't stand the thought of his repulsive kisses.

Wildly she kicked out at his shin. Once finding it, she scraped downward with the hard leather of her shoe along his ankle to end in a solid stomp on the top of his foot.

"Damn!" The curse was expelled with wrathful surprise. "You little bitch!"

She felt herself being lifted off the ground, her punishing foot now dangling ineffectually in midair.

"You don't kick me and get away with it, not by a long shot!"

She watched the world spin as Jim pivoted away from the stream, still holding her suspended in the viselike grip. He put her down with bone-jarring suddenness.

"This time, Drew, you're not getting away." Grabbing her arm as though it were a chicken neck needing to be wrung, he pulled her roughly after him. "I've been watching you and Erhardt in that gingerbread playhouse you've been sharing." He let go a very impolite snort. "And it'll be a real pleasure to do it to you there."

He yanked on her arm and she cried out in pain, stumbling, almost falling, as he growled on, "You've done it with him there, and now it's my turn."

"Done it?" She let the question trail off. Suddenly knowing that what Jim had in mind was more than a mere beating this time. He meant to rape her, and his sick, jealous mind somehow reasoned that the location of the chalet would make his sexual revenge just that much more sweet.

"God! Jim, you can't do this!" she choked.

He jerked his ruddy face around to meet her wide-eyed stare. "The hell I can't, lover. Don't bet the farm on it!" The corners of his mouth lifted menacingly. "You're finally going to pay the way *I* want to be paid!" His narrow eyes glittered with perverted lust. There was no mercy there, and in the ugly face of his twisted rage, Drew knew again a justifiable fear for her life.

Just then she became aware of laughter—faint laughter—and people singing some distance away.

Casting a cautious look toward Jim, who had resumed his rampaging descent, she could tell he had not yet noticed the approach of people.

Dragging her roughly along after him, his eyes were riveted ahead for the first sign of the chalet, as yet too far down the mountain to see.

With difficulty, trying to keep her balance on the uneven rocky slope, she twisted toward the sound, spotting, off almost parallel to them, a group of about eight young men, clad in gaily colored hiking attire, and backpacks, probably ending a day of hiking.

Hope edged back into her mind.

Could she escape? Could she get to the hikers for help?

If she could, she knew Jim would not dare attack her with so many others present. Even without the ability to ask for help in German, the young men would surely recognize a cry for aid.

She knew she would have to act quickly, for at this foolhardy pace Jim was demanding, they would soon leave the merry hikers behind.

Without another moment's hesitation, she flung her leg out into Jim's path and braced herself for the fall as his foot caught against her calf.

She couldn't stifle the groan of pain as his toe pegged the tensed muscle at the back of her leg.

"What the—" he managed before he realized they were falling.

They landed heavily, his body dropping over her legs.

The breath left her in a "whoof," but she had been ready for the impact, taking away as much of the force of it as she could with her arms.

And then, when Jim released her in a reflex action of self-preservation, she pulled out from under his weight, rolling away. She scrambled on all fours in the direction of the hikers as Jim lay stunned on his face near the stream.

Coming to a skidding stop, she dislodged rocks and gravel that tumbled on down ahead of her in a miniature landslide, making her shudder as she watched the rocks bounce and ricochet into the distance.

Heart racing, she peered over her shoulder at Jim. He had lifted his head slightly, shaking it. A low moan escaped his throat.

Spitting dirt, she ran a fist over a stinging scrape along her dusty cheek. Looking down at the clenched fist, she realized that it was shaking violently. She knew she was not safe yet.

Pulling a deep breath that helped renew her determination, she righted herself, wincing at a bloodied spot on her slacks that stuck painfully to her knee.

"Hey, there!"

Biting her lip, she stopped. What could she say that they would understand?

Please! She knew the word for please!

"*Bitte! Bitte!*" She waved a frantic hand.

A young man turned, stopped, then grasped a fellow's shoulder. Suddenly the noises of comradeship ceased, and eight pairs of eyes were riveted on her.

"*Ja?*" the first hiker called.

She heard another moan at her back and knew she must not tarry. As quickly as her bruised body would let her she limped toward the now stilled group.

She knew as long as Jim was down, they could not see him. And rather than have to answer embarrassing questions she called in English, "I—I was walking...I fell. Could you help me back to my house?"

She stopped for a gasp of air and plucked at the sticky knee. "It isn't very far."

Most of the faces stared blankly, but one young man, about twenty years old, stepped forward. "Of course, *mein Fräulein.* We will help you. Come." He moved to grasp her arm, firmly, yet cautiously, as if fearful of doing her any additional harm, while explaining what she had said to his companions.

Once they had heard that she was asking for their help, Drew could do nothing for herself, not even walk.

The youths, Drew could now see, ranged in age from about sixteen to twenty. And in their enthusiasm to help a damsel in distress, the young men were almost comical in their fledgling attempts at gallantry, insisting that they carry her two at a time, on their arms, all the way down to the chalet. When they reached it, the young blond that spoke English asked if they might send for a doctor. Drew sweetly refused, saying that she would be fine. She offered them the hospitality of a glass of iced tea, which was all that she had.

With great good humor, they accepted, drinking thirstily. Then, making certain that she was well enough to be left alone, they set off again for Oberammergau with eight friendly waves and a lusty song.

DREW sat down on the edge of her bed after assuring herself one final time that all of the doors and windows were securely locked.

At this point, she wouldn't put anything past Jim, but she hoped that his painful defeat that afternoon might have ended or at least dampened his desire for revenge.

Sliding the white lace of her nightgown above her knee, she checked the scraped area. It was a bit stiff, but not serious. Neither was the bruise on her calf or the small cut along her cheek.

All in all, she had come away from the near-disaster relatively unscathed. And for her rescue, she thanked providence and the German people's love for hiking.

Reaching for the bedside lamp, she scanned the room once more before she lay down.

Two of her bags lay opened, clothes neatly folded in them. Departure time was scheduled for 2:00 P.M. in Munich. The trip there would require over an hour by autobahn. So she decided it would be best to get her things in order now. Besides, there was nothing else to do locked in her self-styled prison.

She could have joined her father and the other dele-gates at an authentic Bavarian beer festival in town. It was a special festival given by the people of Oberammergau honoring their new friends of the world's scientific community. But she felt far from festive, and declined the invitation, fabricating the tale that Rolf would be calling, and that she didn't want to be away.

Her father accepted the story as delightedly as a child accepts the idea of Santa Claus, leaving her to herself.

In truth, she didn't dare go anywhere that Jim might be able to get his hands on her again. No, it was much safer to remain locked in the chalet until time to fly back to the United States.

Flipping off the lamp, she slipped beneath the cool sheets, and was surprised to realize the degree of tension she was still feeling, even in the security of the locked house.

Unable to close her eyes, she lay there on her side, staring at the glass door of the balcony, back-lit by the bright moon.

Distant music of the oom-pa-pa band wafted up from the festival. She tried to concentrate on a mental picture of the friendly native folk in brightly colored Bavarian dress, the women in fluffy peasant blouses, full petticoated skirts and ruffled aprons; and the men in traditional short leather pants, knee-socks, and small-brimmed hats decorated with a tall feather.

Eventually concentration became less necessary and drowsiness set in. Heavy lids succumbed at last.

INSTANTLY awake, panic flooded Drew's senses as she realized there was a hand over her mouth, stifling her scream.

Grasping a muscled wrist with both hands, she tried to pull the hand away. It wouldn't budge. Attempts to kick out proved fruitless, for a heavy leg, as unmovable as a tree trunk, was thrown across her, pinning her solidly to the bed.

Her mind reeled with hopeless certainty: *Jim!*

He had got in and was making good his promise of rape!

Just then, a harsh whisper penetrated her fright-numbed mind. "Be still, *Kindchen*. It's Rolf."

Rolf? She remained tensed, but stopped struggling, shifting her gaze as best she could with her face held immobile over toward the dark head resting near hers on the pillow.

His eyes were narrowly opened, his expression intent, expectant. But had she been standing at his back, observing him, rather than lying practically beneath him as she was, he would have appeared relaxed in sleep. Only his alert eyes, watching her, and the hand over her mouth gave his wakefulness away.

"There is someone on the balcony. Be still." He breathed the words so softly that she was not absolutely sure he had said anything at all.

But without moving her head, she squinted past him toward the balcony door, and was stunned at what she saw.

A deep shadow moved beyond the paned glass, and the knob rattled softly as the intruder tested its lock.

She swallowed, but her dry throat ached with the effort.

The knob turned again, and this time there was a faint scratching sound, as if someone were tampering with the lock to make a soundless entry.

Drew went cold with dread. What were they to do?

Without warning, Rolf sprang to his feet, and in a loud, deep bark he shouted in German, *"Zum Teufel!"*

Moving toward the door he called in a loud, angry voice, *"Scheren sie sich weg!"*

Drew sat up, clutching the sheet in clenched fists to lips pinched between her teeth.

"Rolf," she squeaked, "please, be careful!"

The shadow at the door bolted at the sound of Rolf's angry shouts, and from the clattering and crashing that followed, it was obvious that the would-be intruder had made a rather uncomfortable exit over the balcony railing.

The immediate danger past, Drew felt herself relax slightly, and she moved her eyes from where she had last seen the shadow back to Rolf. For the first time, she really looked at him.

He stood at the door, the moonlight silvering the boundaries of his massive, silhouetted shoulders.

Her eyes moved down, over the narrow waist, and then on to the sleekly muscled hips and thighs.

Her sharp intake of breath at the realization that he was naked caused him to turn to face her with a quizzical frown. "Are you all right, *Kindchen*?"

She abruptly jerked her eyes away, staring instead into the darkness, suddenly feeling that it was tremendously important that she locate her feet in the rumpled bed covers.

"I. . . yes. . . but Rolf. . ."

She didn't face him, but held a fist toward where she knew him to be, the sheet still clutched tightly in her hand. "Maybe you'd better cover up."

There was a snort of humor and then the sound of his feet padding to the bedside.

"Is that an invitation to join you, love?"

She turned wide eyes up to him, not keeping in mind the problems involved with that soon enough. Then, eyes even wider, she whirled away. "No! No. . ." Licking dry lips, she tried to calm her voice, "No, of course not. . . I—"

He interrupted calmly, "All right, then I'll be going."

The panic rose again, "No!"

Totally forgetting her shyness, she spun around. Rising to her knees, she flung her arms about his wide chest. "No, please, Rolf. Please don't leave me alone."

For a moment she was the only one clinging, holding him, keeping them together. But only for a moment. It was not long before his arms moved to encircle her waist.

He whispered, "You're shaking."

"Don't leave me, Rolf." It was a soft plea that went far deeper than fear. It was a plea from her bursting heart. "Please, please stay."

"I don't think you have to worry. He won't be back."

His voice was as soothing as his hands as they gently caressed her thinly clad back.

"Could it have been Jim?" he asked.

The question was not one she wanted to answer. She hedged. "He went to Munich with you, didn't he?"

His arms tightened about her and his lips moved softly in her hair.

"Yes. But when I noticed he was gone late this afternoon, I came back here immediately."

Drew turned her face up to his and asked in whispered surprise, "You came back here because you thought Jim had left? Why?"

His expression became a curious frown. "Why?" Dark eyes narrowing, he inclined his head, eyeing her closely. "Have you forgotten our bargain? My job is to protect you from him."

She mirrored his frown. "But when you left me and went to Munich, I assumed—" She paused. He was shaking his head sadly.

Loosening his hold on her, he let out an exasperated sigh. "You assumed I was leaving you to him?"

She could only nod.

Motioning toward the edge of the bed, he asked, "May I?"

"Uh...well..." She hadn't said much in the way of permission. But he sat down and was pulling the sheet up to his lap. "Is this better?"

There was an unexpected flash of white teeth. Drew was thankful for the darkness that masked the rosy color that heated her face at the reminder that Rolf was wearing no clothes.

He leaned back against the smooth oak headboard of her small bed, casually bending his outside leg and draping an arm over it to turn more toward her. The sheet now barely covered what it was intended to cover.

Sitting there, he looked all too much like a life-size, silver replica of a languishing Greek god. She found herself staring, fascinated, unable to draw her eyes away from his masculine beauty.

''I'll explain.'' The words brought her head up with a jerk, and he stopped. A crooked grin momentarily flickered across his lips telling her that he knew where her eyes had been resting.

After a painful moment of embarrassed silence, he began quietly, ''I bribed Jim to go to Munich with me by telling him that I would give him an exclusive interview about my marriage and escape. Of course, I knew he couldn't resist following me with that tempting bait.''

Realization struck, and she finished for him, ''And that way he would have to leave me alone.''

He reached out and fingered a curl that had fallen over her moon-lit shoulder. ''It was the only way I could think of, *Kindchen.*''

The small smile was apologetic. ''I imagine he got tired of being put off. And as I said, when I realized he was gone, I was positive he'd come back here.'' He dropped the hand to rest on the bed beside her. ''I'm surprised he didn't.''

She moved her eyes to watch his hand, fingers spread, dark against the white sheet.

A feeling of shame engulfed her for not having told him the truth about Jim's attack. After all, it was only fair to let him know that he had been right in his suspicions.

But she sat silently. She wanted to forget the entire incident.

''Drew?'' He broke the lengthy silence.

''Yes?''

''You know, if that was Jim, he is a very sick man.''

She nodded. ''I know.''

Suddenly the urge to touch him was too strong to ignore. Reaching out, she grazed his hand with her own. "Whoever it was, Rolf, thank you."

Her fingers came to rest lightly on his.

"Bitte sehr. You're welcome, *Kindchen."*

The light contact her hand made with his fingers sent a surge of excitement through her body setting loose wild feelings that she did not care to ignore. Not now. Not tonight.

"Kindchen? Are you still frightened?"

Moving her eyes to his face, she was struck by the fineness of the bones highlighted in the vague moon's glow.

She ventured huskily, "Frightened? No...I guess... I'm fine."

For a moment he just sat, his eyes softly gleaming, moved lazily over her.

"Good." Somehow the word sounded regretful. "I'll leave you to your rest then."

Sliding his legs to the floor, he turned away from her.

"Wait!" She grasped his wrist.

He paused, turning his face toward hers. Now his expression was not sympathetic as she expected it to be. Neither was it as quizzical as it could have been. The look his face held was totally unexpected. His features were grave, his eyes bleak.

"What is it, *Kindchen*?" He spoke in a hoarse whisper, as though his throat had gone suddenly as parched as her own.

"I—I don't want you to go."

"Do you want me to sleep here?" He sounded doubtful.

She chewed hard on her lower lip. "Is the thought that distasteful?"

Her hand at his wrist was now covered by his distinctly unsteady hand. "No, of course not. But"—he paused and a shudder seemed to pass across his broad shoulders—"I can't spend the night beside you just sleeping. I'm no saint, Drew."

Her heart was pounding deafeningly in her ears. She had never asked a man to make love to her before. In fact she had spent her first marriage avoiding the prospect with all her energies. And now she was at a loss at what to do.

"Rolf?"

He regarded her with disquieting eyes. But she kept her courage and slid closer, allowing a hip to rest lightly against his exposed thigh.

She shyly touched his shoulder. At the contact, she realized her hand was ice cold and trembling.

Sensing a tensing in him at her touch, she pulled away, mortified that now that she needed him so, he would be the one to resist.

There was no help for it, though. She could not stop the words that were straining at her heart.

They came out in a long breath. "I don't want you to be a saint, Rolf."

The words, whispered through the shadows, were barely spoken when, in one fluid movement, she found herself drawn into his arms.

His sigh held her name as tenderly as his arms took her into his embrace, and he slowly lowered her to the softness of the bed.

Her lips parted, pliantly accepting moist kisses, kisses that were right, natural...made for only them to share.

For her, this was what love should be—two contrasting elements of nature coming together, making each better, more valuable because of the other.

She had believed, wrongly, that all men were like Jim. And she knew now that without Rolf, she had been drying up, becoming a barren, wasted shell of a woman.

Yet, with his love he had made her new, replenished her, given life to the desert that had been in her heart, and she delighted in his touch.

Rolf had changed, too. No longer harsh, he was often gentle, caring, and she knew, hoped, that he might finally understand, that he, too, needed her, to be complete.

His lips were taking everything she had to give and giving it all back with generous dividends.

Nipping softly at the corners of her mouth, parted in an unconscious smile, he murmured, "At last you come to me, a woman. . . my woman."

His hand moved down, fingers spread, enlivening the skin along her hip.

"My beautiful *stürmisches Fräulein,*" he husked.

"You will never be sorry."

His hand slid beneath the lace of her gown and touched bare thigh as his lips trailed across her cheek, down, stopping to taste the quickening pulse at her throat.

She sighed with contentment as his fingers came to know the woman's body that he brought to life.

A whimper of pleasure escaped her throat as he guided her with knowing gentleness to arouse her desire beyond languishing pleasure toward pulsating need.

The gown she had been wearing disappeared somewhere in the midst of their lovemaking, and Drew became aware of the harnessed strength of his body over hers.

His breath was warm and his breathing rapid as he rested his face between her breasts. Sliding her fingers through his hair, she pressed his face into the soft valley, loving the shudder of heightened intimacy that passed through him.

She knew that Rolf would not satisfy himself until she was ready, until her own desire cried out for release.

He was patient, slow. His hands and lips alone were like many lovers unselfishly giving, giving until she felt she would explode with the fiery hunger they kindled.

Her moan of helpless need, her fingers raking along his back, told him all that he needed to know. His face was above hers, a smile glistened in his fertile eyes.

"A woman with eyes of lightning and hair of flame can only be ice in the hands of a fool."

His reassurance gave her heart wings. Encircling his broad back with her arms, she arched upward to meet him, and joined...one...whole, they escaped the clutching claws of earth together.

Chapter Twelve

Even in her drowsy state, she knew she was being kissed, and being kissed well.

Opening her eyes she let out a throaty laugh as teeth nipped at her shoulder.

"Oh, Rolf. That tickles!"

He lifted his head, smiling. His arms were braced on either side of her on the bed.

"Good morning, wife." The grin widened. "Didn't want to leave without something sweet for breakfast."

She pulled up on her elbows, wide awake now, a feeling of apprehension taking hold. It overflowed into her voice. "Leave?"

He smoothed back a strand of hair from her face. "Believe me, Drew. This is important, or I wouldn't go." He paused, sweeping her with a long, lazy look. "Not with the morning turning your hair to spun sunlight."

She relaxed, smiling shyly. "Don't be long."

Bending down, he placed a light kiss on the tip of her upturned nose, saying huskily, "Don't get up."

His crooked smile was so seductive that it warmed her blood with a rush of urgent desire.

She lifted her hand to stroke his cheek. "Do you have to go. . . now?"

He took her hand in his, squeezing it. "Oh, no you don't, you little temptress. This is really important." Kissing her palm, he straightened. "When I get back, we'll talk."

"Talk?" She teased.

His wink was playful. "Well. . . eventually."

She laughed, glowing from the warmth of his eyes.

Lovingly, she watched the way he moved across the room.

Then he was gone.

She smiled at the memory of him, of his voice, his kiss. . . then, contentedly, she turned over to wait for his return.

THE phone ringing startled her awake. As she fumbled for it, she squinted at her watch, laying on the bedside table.

Ten o'clock! Rolf had been gone over an hour.

"Hello." She fought a yawn.

"Hi, baby. It's Dad."

"Oh, Daddy. Good morning." She turned to her back, cradling her head in one hand. Speaking more to herself than to her father she sighed, "Very good."

"What, dear?"

She giggled. "Oh, nothing. Did you need anything special, or is this a wake-up call?"

There was a pause.

"Dad? You there?"

"Yes." His voice was subdued. "Listen, honey. Rolf asked me to call."

She had the distinct feeling that somewhere a shoe had just dropped, and she tensed for the second one to fall.

"Oh?" It was all she could think of to say.

"Yes." He cleared his throat. "Well, here it is, dear. It seems that Secretary Standish—I believe you met him in Washington? He sends his regards."

He was waiting.

"Secretary Standish? Yes. What about him, Dad?"

She realized she was sitting up now.

"Well, the secretary arrived this morning with some security people. Seems they waited until the end of the conference before taking over. But, now, well"—he exhaled heavily—"well, they took him home. . . Rolf, that is. He's on his way to the United States right now. It appears he is in for some extensive debriefing before he can work on the Tokamak fusion reactor with us.''

It had dropped, the other shoe, and her world as well. The room blurred before her, and she felt dampness along her cheek.

"Drew, baby?"

She nodded, lips trembling. "Yes, Daddy." Her voice cracked. "I—I heard you. He's...gone."

"Yes." His voice brightened slightly. "But he wanted me to tell you he was sorry about it."

She licked at a salty tear. "Sorry?"

She could only trust herself to whisper.

"He said...let's see. He said something like, 'Tell Drew I'm sorry I couldn't kiss her goodbye.' "

Silence.

She took a deep steadying breath. "That was all?"

"All? Why, uh, yes—he did say something about missing breakfast." Coughing nervously, he went on, "Rolf really didn't have much time."

"Of course. I see."

Her father was reassuring, "Don't worry, dear. Secretary Standish did say Rolf would be kept incommunicado for a while. But he'll be all right."

She pressed her lips together, trying to keep from making noises that sounded like crying. She knew what Rolf had meant by his message. "Goodbye" was just that.... He hadn't said, "Tell Drew I love her." No. He'd said goodbye...and sorry he missed breakfast! That was still all last night had meant to him: a little something sweet!

She wanted to cut this short.

"Dad?" She concentrated on composing her voice. "I'd better get off the line and finish packing."

Covering the receiver with her hand, she gulped back a sob.

"Fine. I'll send a car around in about an hour, honey. Okay?"

She nodded unsteadily. "Okay."

The phone clicked in her ear. But she didn't place her receiver on its cradle. She just sat, clutching it, white-knuckled, letting the sobs come.

Slumping forward, she wiped at her face with a shaky hand.

"Good-bye." It was a choked moan. "And I thought..."

She looked at the gray receiver being murdered by her strangle-grip and dropped it back where it belonged.

Pack. I must pack. She knew that she had to move, get busy, try as best she could to push thoughts of Rolf out of her mind, and get on with her life.

Closing her eyes, more tears escaped, and she bit her lip hard. It would not be easy. Exhaling a ragged breath, she pushed herself up from the bed and absently pulled a robe over her nakedness. She felt numb, empty.

He was gone, and as far as he was concerned, it was over.... The bargain was done, finished, in one second-hand "good-bye."

Nearly an hour later, she had showered and dressed in a tailored azalea-colored linen blazer and skirt, paired with a mini-print blouse. As she closed the last bag, the doorbell rang. Her car had arrived.

The husky German taxidriver made quick work of removing the bags, while Drew penned a note of thanks to the people whose house she and Rolf had shared.

Beside it, she left a pair of silver candlesticks she had purchased in a gift shop downtown...a gift to people she had never met, for the use of a house she would never forget...no matter how hard she tried.

Sighing, she pivoted away from the table and, without a second glance, walked quickly out the door.

DREW folded the letter from Reverend Peabody after rereading it for the third time.

He was always so cheerful in his letters, full of child-like enthusiasm, so proud of his part in the secret marriage that helped a valuable scientist defect to the United States—to be with the woman he loved.

He'd sent several clippings concerning the conference that had been in his hometown paper. One of them included a picture of herself and Rolf.

She remembered when Suzy Slade had taken that shot outside the wood-carving shop.

Rolf's smile had been trained on her, his arm around her waist. She, too, had been smiling as she looked adoringly up into his face.

"For heaven's sake," she gasped. "If I didn't know better, I'd believe those two people really were in love!"

Stuffing the letter and clippings into a cubbyhole of the antique roll-top desk, she closed the lid. Sitting back, she thought sadly that she really had been in love. It was Rolf who should be nominated for an Academy Award for his acting!

Sighing, she rested her hands on the curved desk top to push herself up.

She wasn't bitter, just. . .empty. The day's work was done, it was loneliness, memories, that brought her down.

Since Rolf's sudden departure in Oberammergau nearly two weeks ago, she had tried to bury herself in work, smothering her thoughts of him with day-to-day business concerns.

But the nights—two weeks of nights—they had become hard to endure.

She moved listlessly to the stone mantel where a wood carving dominated its center.

She had bought the funny little carving she had seen with Rolf for her father and had given it to him on their return. But this one, she had bought for herself.

It was of a stalwart, young German man, dressed in rustic country clothes. With a booted foot resting on a stump, he leaned casually on the handle of an ax.

Gently, she grazed the wood along the prominently carved cheekbone with a finger.

"Rolf..." she whispered.

The moment she had seen the carving, the stern face and intent searching eyes, she had been struck by the likeness it held for Rolf, and she had had to have it.

She dropped her hand to her side, speaking to him... to herself... to no one. "I'm filing the papers tomorrow. So it will soon be over. You will be completely free."

She turned away. Putting off filing the divorce papers had done no good, would do no good. She knew she must have it done before he returned. After all, what excuse did she have to remain Mrs. Rolf Erhardt now? He was in the United States, safe.

She nodded. It must be done. And it must be done tomorrow.

Without much real interest in the time, she looked at the wall clock over the desk. It was hand-made from a slice of pine trunk, the numerals represented in only four places by square-head nails. Nearly ten o'clock.

Lately, ten o'clock had become early evening for Drew. She was rarely able to sleep before one or two in the morning.

Crossing the white-and-green wool area rug, she pushed open the patio doors, allowing the white sheers to billow into the room on a pleasant mid-May evening breeze.

Stepping out onto the uneven stone patio that overlooked a wooded valley, she was reminded, again, of the East German cottage where she and Rolf had been married.

A new puff of breeze swirled the handkerchief hem of the jade silk gown about her legs. Shivering, suddenly cold, she couldn't tell if the reaction was from the quickly cooling evening, or the emotionally stirring memory. Rubbing bare arms, she looked down at the flimsy gown, a recent wedding gift from several young secretaries at the office. "For when he gets back," the card had read. She hadn't wanted to accept it on false pretenses. But how could she tell five giggly girls the sobering truth?

Another gust of cool air swept the gown out, billowing it bell-like, about her. She shivered again, shaking her head with a humorless laugh. "Looks like you lose on all counts, little gown." She touched the softness of the fabric, pressing the air out of it. "You can't keep a girl warm, and you won't be tempting any male eyes either."

Turning to go inside, she was stopped in her tracks by a voice from out of the darkness.

"Not so, not so, little lady. I'm pretty tempted just now—especially with that light behind you there. Nice, very nice."

She froze. "No." It couldn't be! Whirling back around, she watched, horrified as Jim walked into the shaft of light reaching out from the den.

"Oh, yes, lover. What'd you think—I'd just fade into the sunset?" He put out a hand to grasp at hers.

Reacting quickly in her distaste at the idea of his touch, she pulled away, and hurried inside, trying to close the doors on him.

She was unsuccessful. He managed to push through before she could get them latched.

"Oh, no, Drew. You're not locking me out this time!"

She stumbled backward, away from him, but was shortly halted by a pink velvet wing chair. "W-what are you doing here?"

His lips thinned across his teeth in a pseudo-smile. "Fast-talked the boss into letting me do a follow-up on ol' Rolfie-boy." He tugged at his tie, loosening it as he swept his eyes over her. "Boy, you're some great-looker in that green job—and all that wild red hair." The tie was pulled off and thrown to the floor.

She flattened herself against the chair as he took a threatening step.

"Jim—"

"Hell, I don't give a damn about that so-called genius. But since he'll be away for awhile convincing the Feds of his loyalty, I figured now'd be a good time for us to take care of our unfinished business."

Her mouth sagged open as he began to unbutton his shirt.

"Oh, God! No!" It was a tremulous gasp.

She managed to get her shaky legs to move her far enough to circle the chair, putting distance between them.

Jim's shirt was half-opened as he reached the chair back she had just left. He leaned forward, his elbows resting on it, a confident smile splitting his face.

Drew noticed for the first time that his eyes were shining a little too brightly. That familiar glint sent a shudder of renewed fear through her as she realized he had been drinking.

"You know what, Drew? I've got this whole thing figured out now—took me awhile but I got it wrapped up." He winked and tapped his index finger against the side of his nose, missing his temple. "Jus' took a li'l time, a li'l distance—and some real fine rye."

Her legs were shaking so badly now that she could barely stand. She swallowed spasmodically. So at last he *knew*! Her heart sank like a stone.

He made an impolite sound. "The guy's a three-dollar bill, isn't he? That's what the whole deal was about."

Drew was terribly confused now. Puzzlement pulled her brows down. "I—I'm not following—"

"*Hell,* Drew." He interrupted, waving a hand broadly. "The whole damn time I thought you were using him to hide from me. That's a laugh now, when you think about it." He clasped his hands over the chair back, baring his teeth. "When all the time he was using you to protect his own filthy secret—acting married, even for two weeks, nobody'd ever guess. Why I bet"—he laughed loudly, shaking his head—"I bet the Reds unloaded him on us just to get rid of him!"

Drew's head was pounding and she pressed shaking palms to her temples.

"Jim, if you think Rolf was—" She shook her head, feeling ill. "That's the most ri—"

He cut across her words. "I should have known it for sure when he kept putting off that gorgeous Markus dame."

Her breath caught. "What? But you said—"

He quickly circled the chair, taking advantage of her surprise.

"I said she was hanging all over him." He pulled a hand from her temple as he went on. "That Ilka Markus made herself as hard to lose as trying to throw a cat off a cliff." He scratched his chin, a smirk curling his lips. "But the *Doctor* didn't want any part of her action." He shook his head, clucking his tongue. "What a jerk."

He went back to unbuttoning his shirt, this time one-handed. "And soft-hearted li'l Drew was gonna help him keep his bad old secret."

He jeered. "You two sure must have been some pair—the ice queen and the closet queen!"

His eyes bored into hers. "I should have had it figured out...seeing the lights in both of your bedrooms...I should have had it figured."

Drew pulled at his painful hold on her wrist, blurting angrily, "Jim, I've never heard such—such a ridiculously—twisted—" She groaned, unable to go on with the senseless argument. "Oh, why can't you leave me alone!"

She stopped, drawing a deep breath in an effort to control the tremor of hysteria in her voice.

When she spoke again, it was barely above a whisper. "How could I have ever, ever seen anything attractive about you? You couldn't be half the man Rolf Erhardt is if you had a thousand years to practice."

He eyed her skeptically. "You saying he's not—?" He paused, screwing up his face in a frown.

She stared at him wordlessly for a long moment before a bitter smile lifted her lips. "Far from it."

The frown tightened in rage, and so did the grip on her arm, making Drew wince at the pain in her swelling hand.

"And I suppose now you're gonna tell me you love the bastard."

There was a sudden shallowness to her breathing, and a tight ache began in the pit of her stomach that had nothing to do with her fear of Jim.

Lowering her eyes she fought back tears.

He jerked her arm so savagely that she thought he would pull it from its socket.

Her head snapped jarringly back up to meet his searing eyes.

"Tell me! Damn it! Do you love that bastard?"

Her breathing was ragged and uneven, and she held out a placating hand, pleading, "Jim—"

He grasped her shoulders with the force of wolf's jaws. "Spit it out! You do love him, don't you!"

The truth was torn from her heart with a mournful sob. Shaking her head, she cried hopelessly, "*Yes!* Yes, I love him. . .God help me. I love Rolf Erhardt!"

She grasped his arms, dropping her head forward. Her strength nearly gone, she curled her fingers around his tense arms to keep from dropping to her knees as the sobs racked her body.

His voice was part snarl, part laugh. "You little fool! You let him use you to get his freedom, and then you let him sweet-talk you into the sack!"

He took her chin between punishing fingers, pulling her face back up to his. She was almost thankful that she could not see him clearly through the shimmer of her tears.

"He got it all, you stupid fool. And just what have you got?" He jerked her chin, making her cry out. "Come on now! What have you got—besides *me?*"

Shaking with reaction, fear and pain, she couldn't speak. Striking out in pure, blind emotion, she slapped his face.

"Why you cold-blooded harpy!" An explosion near her ear sent her sprawling to the floor.

Lifting her head, she watched horrified as he shook the fist that had just laid her out, ranting on, "He may have had a sample, but I'm taking what's mine!"

She put up a weak, defensive hand as he squatted over her, his hands moving to loosen his belt.

Suddenly, he rose into the air, still in a squat, feet and all, and slammed into the entry wall, nearly four feet away from Drew's head. Looking up, her eyes focused on a miracle. Standing above her, like a sun-bronzed, Bavarian mountain was Rolf. She breathed his name.

Raking long fingers through his hair, his face and body taut with emotion, he asked gently, "Are you all right, *mein Kindchen*?"

Still in awe, hardly believing he was really there, she could only nod.

"Good." His lips lifted in what appeared to be a relieved smile. "Call the police, love." Stepping by her, he reached the still stunned Jim and jerked him up to lean limply against the entry wall.

Drew's mouth dropped open in surprise at Rolf's request. "What? But—Rolf," she stammered, sitting up, feeling pain in her jaw as she tried to form her words, "is—is that really necessary?"

"Very necessary, Drew. Call them, now." His tensed body shook in the effort to control his anger as his eyes drilled into Jim's—dulled and glazed by the surprise attack.

"Jim!" Rolf's tone grew as cold and flat as a dagger. "You are through harassing my wife. I am pressing charges against you for attempted rape. Do you understand me?"

Jim's face had gone bloodred with Rolf's tight grip on the shirt at his neck. He could not talk, but his mouth worked spasmodically. Finally, his eyes bulging fearfully, he jerked his head in a nod to let Rolf know that he understood.

"Fine." A smile that would have made the devil cringe bared his teeth. "What do you say we wait for the police outside."

Mistakenly believing that he had been asked a question, Jim, dreading the message in Rolf's smile, shook his head pleadingly before being propelled bodily out of the open front door. A painful yelp could be heard as he tumbled down the front steps before Rolf followed him out.

AFTER Drew called the police, she sat, stunned, alone, on the couch for what seemed like a very long time, her mind hard-pressed to accept what had just happened. She heard sirens, voices, and then silence. It was the silence that made her look up. Rolf was standing in the doorway, watching her. Her eyes touching his brought him to action. Two swift strides had him kneeling by her side. His dark features mirrored his concern.

"I am sorry to have left you. But I wanted to get him out of here." He went on, his eyes never leaving hers, "Will you be up to going to the police station tomorrow? They'll have to ask you some questions."

Terribly demoralized by what had happened, she was unable to trust her voice. Moving her shoulders in a small shrug, she avoided his searching eyes.

"It won't be too bad, Drew. Believe me, it's for the best." Cool fingers tested her cheek gingerly. "We'd better get some ice on that."

In seconds he had gone to the kitchen, located ice and a small towel, and was back, sitting beside her.

"Here." He placed the bundle in her hand. His eyes sought hers. But she couldn't bring herself to look directly at him, moving her gaze to her lap.

"I'm so sorry, Drew." He offered quietly.

She put the cold cloth to her burning face. "It wasn't your fault."

He was quiet for a moment before she felt his hand on her chin, turning her head so that she had to meet his gaze.

"I'm talking about having to leave you so suddenly in Oberammergau. We never had that talk."

Eyes the color of brown velvet touched her softly wherever they rested.

"And I'm also sorry I didn't get in to help sooner. I'm afraid I had to break the door to get in."

She swung her eyes back to the door, and for the first time she saw the splintered wood that used to secure the bolt. The mental image of Rolf crashing into the room loomed before her, and she gasped, "I—I didn't hear anything."

His face took on a brooding scowl. "I came through just in time to see you fall." His jaw worked angrily, and his nostrils flared at the memory of his entrance. His voice was strained. "I'll never forgive myself for that."

She touched the tensed fist resting on his thigh, shaking her head in disbelief. "That was a wonderful, crazy thing to do, Rolf. I'll always be grateful." She felt his hand begin to relax beneath her own. "Jim was my problem long before I met you. Please, try to forget it."

Chewing on the inside of her lip, she ventured hopefully, "How—how did you happen to come here?"

He moved his broad shoulders easily, and she saw his dark features begin to soften.

"This is where John Standish's men brought me. They assumed I'd want to come home to my wife."

"Oh...I see."

She pressed her lips together, wishing he had come back to her because he had wanted to.

"You are still my wife, aren't you?"

She shifted uncomfortably, not prepared to answer the why's or admit yes to that question. Why, oh, why had she waited to file the papers! Why couldn't she say "No, Rolf, I'm not your wife," and be able to walk proudly away from him now?

Unable to bear his watchful nearness another moment, she pushed up from the couch, the ice-packed towel spilling to the floor.

Gritting her teeth in agitation, she walked quickly to the curved railing of the staircase, leaning on it for support.

"How much did you hear?" It was a breathless question.

"Enough." His voice was close. She had forgotten his ability to move without making a sound.

Gently, he pulled her against his chest, his hands resting warmly on her hips.

"I know that you love me."

Racked with torment, she denied, "No! No, I don't. I—I lied to—to get Jim to leave me alone!"

Slowly he moved to face her, his eyes branding her with his ownership as he lowered his face to hers.

Feather-light kisses traced the reddened skin along her injured cheek.

Her balled fists began to open against his chest. Her fingers spread over the hard expanse as she sobbed out a weak denial, her body wanting him, her brain attempting to remain rational.

With his lips now close to hers, he murmured, "Tell me you are lying now."

"Please!" she cried, pushing hard at his chest.

"Jim was right! You just used me! You've been using me all along—getting everything, leaving me with nothing. And now you want me to give up my pride, too!"

Pushing with all her flagging strength, she begged, "Please, leave me alone. Just go!"

Slowly, reluctantly he released her, stepping away.

Taking advantage of her freedom, she moved out of his reach. Breasts heaving with emotion, she whirled away, presenting her stiffened back to him.

His voice was soft and contrite. "I'll go, Drew, but not before I give you something that I've carried around with me for the last two weeks."

Silence followed his words. There was no sound, no explanation.

She had played this waiting game with him before, and she knew that he was better at it than she.

Lifting her chin with resolve, she turned back to face him.

"Well?" Her voice sounded strangely calm in her ears.

Thoughtful and dark, his eyes never left hers as he reached inside his coat and drew out a small black box.

Holding it in the palm of his hand, he offered it to her.

"This is the reason I left you that last morning in Oberammergau. You might as well have it, no one else ever will."

She lost her determined calm. Staring at the small box, her heart began to thud wildly in her chest and throat.

She couldn't speak, or even lift her hand to take it from him.

He opened it for her, moving to stand beside her as he did.

She felt dizzy at what she saw and found herself leaning against him to keep from collapsing.

"A—a ring?"

It was a wide gold band, and glittering from it was a trail of twelve perfect, multifaceted diamonds, mounted in the shape of an "eight" resting on its side—the same symbol of infinity that still dangled from a chain about her neck.

His voice was a ragged whisper near her ear. "I had it commissioned in Oberammergau. It wasn't completed until the day the conference ended."

Lifting the ring from its box, he turned her to face him, sliding his arm possessively about her waist.

His lips moved against her hair. "I ask again, Drew, are you still my wife?"

"I—I plan to file the papers tomorrow—" she stammered out the prepared speech as a small shuddery feeling tingled through her at his intimate touch, making her extremely light-headed.

"Don't," he whispered, taking her trembling hand and slipping the ring on her finger.

"Drew"—his voice held a steady, truthful ring—"to have my freedom without you would be to attempt to live without my heart."

He touched a finger to her chin, lifting her gaze from the sparkling symbol of married love to his eyes, now filled with honest passion.

"I love you.... I think I always have," he said huskily. "And I know I always will."

Lifting her fingers to his mouth, he breathed one word, "Infinitely."

Strong male lips moved against her fingers as he added in equally hushed tones, "I was sure that morning on the train."

She breathed in awe, "But why didn't you—"

"Tell you?" He paused, brown eyes glistening. "Would you have believed me?"

She watched his handsome, somber face for a moment, thinking. Then she shook her head.

"I—I suppose not. I would have thought it was a cheap line."

Rolf's smile was understanding. "I knew I had a lot of bridges to mend before you would trust or believe in me."

Lowering his head, he brushed his lips across her temple. "Do you believe me now?"

Drained of every emotion but the wonder of being a woman—Rolf's woman—Drew slid her arms about his neck.

"Yes, my love, I do."

The taste of his lips filled her with a hungry need, and she clung desperately to him.

His lips moved lovingly against hers as his teasing,

tormenting tongue sent a wave of delightful longing through every fiber of her being.

Scorching kisses left a trail of flame from her throbbing lips to the rise of her aching breasts.

Shuddering, he groaned against the rounded softness above the confining gown.

She sighed, pulling him closer. "Darling, you make me so happy."

That last word triggered another thought, and her mind veered wildly away. She laughed gaily, in love with the world.

"I'm so glad we don't have to disappoint Reverend Peabody by divorcing. He's such a sweet man—a true romantic."

Straightening, he shook his head in bemusement, sweeping her into his arms. "At a time like this you think of Reverend Peabody?"

She mirrored the wide grin he gave her, "Oh, yes. And the girls at the office are terrible romantics, too. They'd love to know you like my gown. It was a wedding gift."

She peered up at him, an impish gleam in her eyes.

"You do like it, don't you? You haven't said."

He cocked his head, giving what appeared to be serious and extensive thought to the subject. His eyes moved lazily over her slender form, not very cleverly disguised beneath the green mist of fabric.

Brown eyes sparkled with devilry as he offered his evaluation.

"Well, since you're such a dyed-in-the-wool cynic, yourself, I'll give it to you straight."

His lips twitched with humor, though he was trying to appear stern. "To you it was a gift. To me, it's just the wrapping."

She pursed her lips in mock contemplation. "I think that's the way they planned it."

Their laughter combined in a tinkling harmony of highs and lows as he turned with her in his arms.

He inclined his head toward the stairs.

"What's up there?"

She smiled innocently, snuggling close to his wide chest.

"My bedroom."

"Any other bedrooms?"

She shook her head, a playful pout on her lips. "Sorry, no . . . and there's only one bed, too."

The grin disappeared, and his face took on the intense, sensuous look of a man in love, and ready to show it.

"Only one bed?" he whispered, his voice slightly hoarse. "What a shame."

Lifting her head, she stole a kiss from his jaw as he started up the steps.

Epilogue

"Hi-ho!" Beverly Atkins breezed into Drew's office, blue smock billowing, a large portfolio under one arm. She took the hefty artist's folder into both hands and rested it lightly on the edge of Drew's desk. "Two things." She smiled, big round eyes sparkling with enthusiasm.

Drew turned toward her friend, shutting off the electric buzzing of her typewriter. "Hi, Bev. I see you've finished the drawings. What's number two?"

Beverly's smile turned into a playful smirk as she laid the folder down, nearly covering Drew's desk top. "There's where you're wrong. *That's* number two." She cocked her short curls to indicate the folder. "Number one is the real biggie!"

She assumed her usual single-hipped perch on one exposed corner of Drew's desk.

Sitting back, Drew folded her arms across the teal plaid bodice of her wool dress. She lifted a quizzical brow. "I'm all ears."

"Well," Bev exhaled breathlessly, "I wanted you to be the first to see my engagement ring!"

Drew started. "Oh, Bev," she breathed, her eyes dropping immediately to her friend's left hand. There was no ring.

Confused, she looked back up into Beverly's face, but did not speak.

Beverly giggled, "Well, actually it's merely *symbolically* there, now." She held out her hand, palm down and fingers spread as though she were actually showing a ring off. "Tom did ask the big question. But I'm having a ring custom-made in Albuquerque."

Drew nodded agreeably. "How nice."

"Yes, it is." Beverly was nodding, too. "Actually it will be twenty or so diamonds in the shape of a number ten. I figure it'll total about three carats, all told."

Drew's lips parted in a silent "Oh." She could never tell if Beverly was serious or not with some of her stories.

Bev lifted her chin challengingly, sitting back and leaning on one hand. "You get the significance of a ten, don't you? Perfection!" she beamed.

Drew shook her head, pursing her lips. "Yes, Bev, I get it. But I'm not swallowing it."

Beverly stood up and began rummaging in one of the large pockets of her smock. Her high-pitched laughter filled the room. "Okay, okay. You're too smart for me." She pulled out a narrow gold band with a modest solitaire sparkling from it. "I just thought I'd give you a real scare. After all, your ring has become pretty famous around here—and it's only an eight!"

Drew's light laugh bubbled from her throat as she pushed herself up from her chair. "Bev, you're incorrigible." She took the ring, admiring it. "I'm so happy for you. It's lovely."

"It's *tiny*!" Bev corrected with a derisive laugh. "But it has sentimental value. Tom says it originally belonged to his favorite grandmother." She narrowed her eyes cynically observing it. "Obviously she couldn't have been the Duchess of Windsor."

Taking the ring from Drew, she slipped it on her left hand where it belonged. "But once I get Tom good and married, we'll take Granny's baby sparkler in and trade it for something really huge and tasteless!"

She held her hand under Drew's desk lamp. "Poor baby. I give you a week after the honeymoon's over before some jeweler gets to put you into a high-school promise ring. Then I'll get my gaudy rock."

Drew walked to her coat rack and took a white sweater from it, remarking casually, "Beverly, you

know you don't mean a word of that. You can't fool
me. I'll bet you that nobody could pry that sweet ring
off of your finger with a crowbar—if only because Tom
gave it to you."

Slipping on the sweater, Drew turned back toward her
friend, who was now looking down at the ring on her
hand, her face suddenly serious. Large dark eyes
flickered up to look into Drew's. They seemed a bit
luminous now—as though swimming in liquid. Beverly
spoke softly, "Okay, Drew, maybe we'll give the little
darling thing six months, a year even." She sniffed a
small self-conscious laugh. "Say, don't give me away as
the sentimental slob I am."

Drew smiled kindly. "Okay. I know it doesn't fit with
your sophisticated image."

They both smiled at each other as close friends do.
There was total quiet for a long moment before Beverly
walked to Drew, taking her hands. "It'll be a small
ceremony in Tom's house a week from Saturday. You'll
be my attendant, won't you?"

Drew grazed her friend's flushed cheek with a sisterly
kiss. "You bet," she whispered, her voice slightly
unsteady. "Now, I've got to go rescue Rolf from Dad or
they'll stay at it all night."

Beverly chuckled, back to her old exuberant self.
"Say, how's it working out for Rolf—this Fellow
thing?" She reached for the door knob.

As they left the office, Drew said, "Wonderfully. As
a Fellow, Rolf is free to do pure research, his real love."

Beverly shrugged her shoulders. "Oh yeah? Well, I
haven't seen any gorgeous rings on that hulking Tokamak. I'd say Rolf holds some tattered remnants of
fondness for you—hag that you are."

They walked down a flight of steps to the main office
level and Drew buttoned her sweater against the September evening chill agreeing with a laugh. "Well, he
does seem to prefer going home with me to *working*
through the night!"

Beverly nodded emphatically. "I should hope so. A man with a build like Rolf should never have been burdened with a brain—a waste, I say, a terrible waste! Why he should be at home where you can keep him bare-foot and pregnant." Her pause was no less full-blossomed than her barely veiled suggestion that Drew should be well on the way to motherhood by now. She tried to broach the subject. "Say, speaking of that—"

Drew took her friend's elbow securely, propelling her away toward her own office. "If you're talking about Rolf's bare feet, they're just as marvelous as the rest of him." Ending the conversation briskly, Drew added dry-ly, "If you're not, then I'll see you tomorrow when you've thought of something else to talk about—like, say, the weather. That's always popular."

"Chicken!" she heard her friend call as the glass door swung shut at her back and she headed toward the tech area and Rolf.

The lights blazed high above in the huge Tokamak lab. Drew blinked in the brightness, finally focusing on Hank, an unobtrusive member of the tech area security force. She answered his recognizing wave and walked toward her husband's office. But voices on the far side of the Tokamak prototype halted her.

She moved toward the familiar sound, recognizing her father's voice, "In addition, Rolf, we're dealing with the problem of injecting cold hydrogen."

She could see them now. Her father, though tall, looked almost frail next to his massive son-in-law. Dr. McKenna was dressed in familiar tweed trousers and a long-sleeved button-front sweater. Rolf wore snug-fitting jeans and a rich maroon plaid flannel shirt, sleeves rolled up to just below the elbows. Fine-tooled cowboy boots were the only addition to the work costume that he had worn even behind the Iron Curtain. Yet the boots were *American,* as Rolf was now *American.* And she knew that he wore those boots with a special pride. He was nodding at her father, his deep voice echoing through the vast openness, "Hydrogen ice pellets accelerated in hypersonic gas jets would be my suggestion."

Dr. McKenna scratched his head, "Maybe. . .it certainly deserves a trial—"

Drew's approach, though quiet, could finally not be kept a secret as her heels on the tile announced her coming. The two men looked up from their huddled conversation.

Rolf's smile was quick and devastating. *"Kindchen."*

"Hi, sweetheart." She returned his smile, noting her father's squinty frown as he pushed his glasses up to his head. "Oh, hello, dear."

"Hello, Daddy." She moved between the men, taking Rolf's hand, "It's six o'clock. Time for the little boys to leave the playground."

Dr. McKenna shook his head. "But we are—"

"Hungry," Rolf interrupted. "Come on, Madder. Have dinner with us."

Dr. McKenna's mouth worked. "But don't you think—"

Rolf laughed. "I promise, Madder, if you have dinner with us, I'll explain my theory to your satisfaction. Agreed?"

"Bribery is a crime, you know." Dr. McKenna appeared irritated. But Drew recognized the small light of good humor in his eyes.

She laughed. "It may be. But allowing a parent to starve is not considered particularly saintly in most circles. I'm afraid we are going to have to insist." She put an arm around her father's thin waist. "You'll love what we're serving tonight—Rolf taught me to make it."

Drew drove home while her father and her husband debated, challenged, and discussed the most advanced techniques of experimentation in their field. She pulled up and parked in their drive, following them toward the small A-frame as Dr. McKenna demanded, "What about the deleterious changes?"

The wooden porch reported their arrival in the darkness with a loud hollow clomping as Rolf unlocked the door, turning on the porch light for Drew. He stood back, motioning Dr. McKenna to precede him into the house.

Mounting the steps, Drew noticed a letter in the mailbox and lifted it out. Glancing absently at it, she stopped short, sucking in a breath. It was from Jim! There was no mistaking his heavy-handed script.

Rolf registered her small sound of shock and looked down at her, a puzzled frown marring his handsome features. "What is it, *Kindchen?*"

Drew motioned rather stiffly for him to go in with her father, whispering only, "Give me a minute." Her voice sounded oddly hoarse to her ears.

He didn't move for a moment, eyeing her narrowly. Then he seemed to make a decision. "A minute," he repeated, his expression one of concern. Turning without another word, he stepped inside the door closing it between them.

Shaky fingers tore open the letter. It had been over three months since she had heard from Jim. After he had received a suspended sentence for his assault on her, he had returned to his job in California without a word. She had not expected to hear from him again. Leaning heavily against the paneled door, she looked down, concentrating on the scrawled words. It read:

Drew,

This is not easy for me. But it is something I have to do. First, I want to apologize for all the harm I have done you. I am seeing a therapist, and I believe I am beginning to come to terms with my problems.

Tell Rolf that I bear him no hard feelings. And I hope that someday he will be able to do the same for me. I can see now that he was right to file charges against me. That experience, painful though it was, prompted me to ask for the help I needed to begin to get myself straightened out. I am grateful to him for that.

And, Drew, please don't worry about my bothering you again. This letter will be my last contact with you. I just want to let you know that I wish you the happiness with Rolf that I did not know how to give you.

It was signed, simply, "Jim."

Drew did not realize that she was crying until a tear splashed against the letter's slick surface. Blinking back other threatening tears, she lifted her head, mechanically folding the page and slipping it into the pocket of her dress. Turning the knob on the door, she gave a quick wipe at her eyes and walked inside. Breathing a long sigh, she squared her shoulders, feeling as though a tremendous burden had just been lifted from them.

When she stepped into the living room, she saw that Rolf and her father had settled themselves on the small white couch. Because Jim's letter had left her feeling almost giddy in her relief, she had to press her lips together struggling with a smile to see her large-framed husband perching on the cramped little couch. He always looked so terribly oversized for the small two-seater. The pink velvet throw pillows that Drew had selected so carefully as accent pieces, were lying discarded on the rug beside the wicker coffee table.

Though it had been Rolf's habit to remove the small pillows every time he sat on the couch in an effort to make himself comfortable, he had never complained about her furniture, or even commented on the singularly feminine surroundings. Drew loved him all the more for his silent suffering—a very masculine man living under the cruel yoke of womanly frills.

Rolf was speaking as she closed the door. "We need to test that structural alloy. I feel it would provide a high level of plasma purity. . . ." His voice trailed away, and he looked over toward the door, his expression questioning.

She smiled reassuringly, waving away his concern. "Good news, Rolf. I'll tell you later." Turning toward the kitchen she finished, "You go on with your work. Dinner won't be long."

His nod was lost to her back. She heard only the excitement in Madder McKenna's high-pitched voice. "My boy! I believe you've hit on something there. We must get started on that hypothesis tomorrow!"

Pushing through the door, she felt herself smile. Her father hadn't even noticed she had come in.

"Soup's on, fellows," she called ten minutes later.

"Good." Rolf stood and stretched. "It smells... different."

Drew laughed. He'd reminded her that morning as they made the soup that that had been what she had said when he had first prepared *Kohlsuppe* for her in East Germany.

"I assure you, the taste will not disappoint you." She batted her lashes teasingly, repeating what he had answered, so long ago.

Missing their play, Drew's father stood. "My goodness, Drew, what is that smell?"

She was ladling the thick soup from a steaming tureen into three bowls. "It's cabbage soup with smoked sausage, Daddy. Believe me, it's good for what ails you. Once this soup nursed me back from death's very door."

Dr. McKenna took a seat, speaking matter-of-factly, "Your mother always did that with chicken soup."

Rolf helped Drew into her chair as he answered, "It never hurts to have two life-support soups in a family, Madder."

Dr. McKenna took up his spoon, tasting. "Now, Rolf, about that alloy."

Drew sat back, smiling to herself. She was, once again, thankful that she was a trained physicist. At least she could understand the conversations that would, no doubt, dominate the waking hours of her life from now on.

She felt a light hand on hers pulling her out of her thoughts. "Dear, thank you for your invitation to dinner."

She blinked her eyes up to meet her father's, surprised by the unexpectedness of the remark. He had stopped speaking, appearing thoughtful for a moment as he stared unseeing at the orchid plant that served as the table's centerpiece.

Finally he went on, "You know"—he was vaguely nodding now—"you've grown up to be very like your mother. She was a woman of quality, too."

"Too?" Drew swallowed with difficulty, unable to say more as a flush of happiness warmed her cheeks.

THE last Saturday in September, at two o'clock in the afternoon, Drew served as matron of honor for her friend Beverly Atkins at a small but lovely ceremony at Tom Groverton's home. Now, in the late afternoon, Rolf and Drew decided to take the short drive out to their newly purchased property. After thirty minutes of roaming, Drew walked back up the gently sloping wood inhaling deeply of the pine and pungent earth. Her moccasin oxfords sounded a subdued crackle as they pressed dry needles and leaves deeper into nature's fertile mix.

Ducking under a stunted pine bough, she looked up to see Rolf coming toward her. He was smiling, and the beauty of it immobilized her. She straightened, breathing deeply to slow her heart. The low moan near the tree tops momentarily covered the crunching sound his boots made as a northern gust of wind carried to Los Alamos autumn's first brisk weather.

The same gust that sang above, tugged playfully at Rolf's khaki chamois jacket and ruffled his dark hair, laying a thick lock across his tanned forehead. She watched him, mesmerized as he moved toward her. His long strides, maneuvering him through the dense growth of trees, were as graceful and supple as the movements of a magnificent stag.

She leaned back against the rough pine bark and waited as he approached. Putting his arms out he drew her away from the support of the rough trunk into his musky embrace. The cotton turtleneck felt soft and inviting against her cheek. "Fine country." His warm breath feathered her forehead.

Nodding, she slipped her arms beneath his jacket, circling his back, enjoying the increasing rhythm of his heartbeat with her nearness.

Another whistle above their heads turned into a lonesome moan, and Drew felt a chill through her sweater, shuddering. Winter was coming early to Los Alamos this year.

Feeling her shiver within his arms, Rolf pulled her closer. "Would you like to go home, love?"

She turned her face up to his, and felt her lips lift in a dreamy smile. "I am home, Rolf." She pulled up on tiptoe to brush a light kiss on his jaw. "We're standing in our kitchen, and I am in your arms."

He lowered his face to capture her lips. His kiss—a kiss that had now become as familiar and as welcome as a rescuing hand in the darkness—swept any thoughts of chill away, replacing them with a rush of blood-firing desire. His mouth clung to hers just as urgently as hers to his. Drew pressed herself even closer to him as his hands moved tantalizingly over her back and along the curve of her hip.

A new moan high above them spoke even more clearly of the growing cold. Rolf lifted his head slowly and reluctantly from hers, a sound very like the wind escaping his throat. "My love, I am happy you think of this as our home. But until a structure is built here next spring, we could get very cold making love under the pines." He moved his eyes to a rapidly darkening sky. "Snow is on its way."

She nestled her head against the soft cotton knit that covered his muscled chest, sighing, "Snow..." Squeezing him tightly to her, she admitted almost shyly, "For some reason, Rolf, I have become very fond of snow—especially storms that rage on for days and days.''

She felt his deep chuckle as he stepped away, proving without further need for words how sharply the temperature was dropping. He took her hand, which she realized was very cold, within the larger warmth of his own. ''Come, *Kindchen*.'' They walked up the gentle incline to the narrow road that wound toward Los Alamos.

Back at their new, sleek silver sedan, Drew stopped, reaching into the driver's window and taking out the rolled house-plans.

''Drew, it's too cold—''

In her enthusiasm for the project, she ignored Rolf's doubtful comment as well as the knife-sharp air. ''Oh Rolf, won't it be wonderful!'' She opened the plans, scanning the virgin landscape lovingly before returning her eyes to the architectural drawings.

The elevation they had chosen was well suited to the natural setting—a traditional two-story to be constructed of stone and red cedar, giving the house a rustic country look. It had been inked onto the page, far back among the trees. A drawing of the proposed lower floor pictured a large combined family room, dining area, and kitchen, with an exposed beamed ceiling and tall windows allowing for ample natural light.

The walls were to be made of random-width pine boards, rough cut and lightly stained to achieve a rich, aged look. A huge, open fireplace of Rolf's design, would be built of native stone. Its massive beam mantel would span half the room's length and stand over five feet high, solidly anchoring one end of the family room.

Four spacious bedrooms covered the upper floor. The master suite pictured an expansive redwood deck that would face the distant Sangre de Cristo mountains, allowing Rolf and Drew a never-ending procession of fiery sunsets to enjoy.

Yet, beyond all this, Drew's favorite room was relatively small. To be located on the back, at the south side of the house, was a skylighted sunroom—or as they had already dubbed it, the "Orchid Room." She smiled, fairly sure it had occurred to Rolf, that *it* would be the perfect place for them to locate all of her pink and white furniture.

She curled the plans into their original tube. "You are happy about the house, aren't you, Rolf?"

"Very happy, love." He put a hand to her back and walked with her around the car. "Now, before you turn to ice, please indulge me by getting into the car." Opening the door, he helped her inside.

She looked up at him through a fan of thick lashes, her lips opening in a knowing smile. "You forget, Rolf. No woman married to you has a chance of turning to ice."

He paused, looking down at her, a glint of golden promise sparkled in his eyes. "There is only one thing that could make me happier than I am at this moment."

Her sense of humor bubbled forth. "I know. You can't wait to get my frilly furniture into the Orchid Room so that you can get a giant leather couch, right?"

He let out a hearty laugh. "That too. But, no." He rested a foot on the door frame and reached in to touch her cheek, stroking it softly with his thumb. "I want to start filling those extra bedrooms with little American citizens—to secure my position in this country." His eyes were warm and earnest and Drew felt her heart leap with his surprising revelation. He had never mentioned children to her before. And because he had not, she assumed that he had not wanted any.

She opened her lips to speak, but couldn't trust her voice. Circling her dry lips with her tongue, she tried, "Children? I—you?"

He bent his head toward her, ducking into the door, "Yes. You, I—We." He dropped a soft kiss at the corner of her mouth, and when she turned her face to meet his, he repeated the circling of her lips with his own tongue before whispering, "Does the idea upset you?"

She held her hands up to circle his neck, caressing the

silkiness of his hair. Slowly she shook her head, brushing her lips back and forth across his mouth as she did, "Hardly, darling."

The touch of their lips as she moved from side to side was infinitely light, infinitely pleasing, sensuously so. Finally Rolf halted her motions with a deep kiss, sending a charge of raw longing surging through her body. Strong fingers moved to the nape of her neck, massaging, relaxing her into the total security of his possession as he tempted her lips opened further. The questing of his tongue, exploring, delighted the ultra-sensitive confines within her mouth. He tasted good, and she pressed her hands to his head, holding him closer to her, wanting him more urgently.

With some effort, he lifted his head, groaning her name in a passion-edged whisper. She let her head fall back as he moved his molten kisses to the responsive skin of her throat. Her lips throbbing, Drew realized in some panic that she must stop this quickly, or they would find themselves melting the defenseless snowflakes that were beginning to fall as they made love with oblivious abandon in the open country.

With great difficulty, she dropped her hands to Rolf's chest, feeling his heart hammering as wildly as her own. Pushing him firmly away—but not far away—she inhaled a ragged breath in an effort to bring her voice under control. Opening her eyes, she couldn't help but smile when she saw the confused frown that marred his handsome features.

"What is it, *Kindchen*?" he asked in a decidedly husky voice.

Looking up, she saw the question smoldering in his eyes, and she was struck by the unexplainable power she seemed to have over him—Rolf Erhardt—a man whom she had seen use iron-bound control over his emotions on a number of perilous occasions. She recalled vividly his frightening ability to exhibit exactly the emotion necessary for the parts he had played, be it domineering commander of men, kidnapper and blackmailer, or even devoted husband for a pack of cynical newshounds.

But now he hid his feelings behind no mask, played no part. She could read the vulnerability in those golden-brown eyes. He was as helplessly in love with her as she was with him. He needed her as badly as she needed him, and this knowledge thrilled her to her core. Rolf was her perfect mate—and he would be the father of her children.

A tiny spark of mischief crinkled her eyes as she answered him, "I was just conducting a small experiment." She paused to slide her hands back up to rest on his shoulders allowing her gaze to fall recklessly into the deep golden liquid of his warm eyes.

"What experiment?" A tender smile curved his expressive lips, melting the worried frown.

"It has to do with finding the ignition temperature of a fusion scientist."

He tilted his head, amusement twitching at the corners of his mouth. "And what did you discover?"

Her voice was almost as husky as his as she answered, "I'm not sure. We need to do more...research."

His intense golden gaze traveled lovingly over her face. "By coincidence, research is my area of expertise."

A light laugh escaped her throat as she lifted her eyes up past his face into the dusky darkness of growing night. She could barely see the feathery invasion of winter's first snow as it silently frosted the wooded mesa.

Sliding her arms possessively around to Rolf's broad back, she nuzzled her face against his ear, finding herself hoping that this first of winter's lacy offerings would be one for the record books.

Warming his earlobe with a teasing kiss, she murmured, "That, my love, I know."

Enter a uniquely exciting new world with

Harlequin American Romance T.M.

Harlequin American Romances are the first romances to explore today's new love relationships. These compelling romance novels reach into the hearts and minds of women across North America...probing the most intimate moments of romance, love and desire.

You'll follow romantic heroines and irresistible men as they boldly face confusing choices. Career first, love later? Love without marriage? Long-distance relationships? All the experiences that make love real are captured in the tender, loving pages of the new **Harlequin American Romances.**

What makes North American women so different when it comes to love? Find out in the new **Harlequin American Romance!**

Send for your introductory FREE book now!

Get this book FREE!

Mail to:

Harlequin Reader Service

In the U.S.
2504 West Southern Avenue
Tempe, AZ 85282

In Canada
649 Ontario Street
Stratford, Ontario N5A 6W2

YES! I want to be one of the first to discover **Harlequin American Romance.** Send me FREE and without obligation *Twice in a Lifetime.* If you do not hear from me after I have examined my FREE book, please send me the 4 new **Harlequin American Romances** each month as soon as they come off the presses. I understand that I will be billed only $2.25 for each book (total $9.00). There are no shipping or handling charges. There is no minimum number of books that I have to purchase. In fact, I may cancel this arrangement at any time. *Twice in a Lifetime* is mine to keep as a FREE gift, even if I do not buy any additional books.

Name _____ (please print)

Address _____ Apt. no.

City _____ State/Prov. _____ Zip/Postal Code

Signature (If under 18, parent or guardian must sign.)

154-BPA-NACT

AR-SUB-300

Readers rave about Harlequin American Romance!

" ...the best series of modern romances
I have read...great, exciting, stupendous,
wonderful."
— *S.E.,* *Coweta, Oklahoma*

" ...they are absolutely fantastic...going to be
a smash hit and hard to keep on the
bookshelves."
— *P.D., Easton, Pennsylvania*

"The American line is great. I've enjoyed
every one I've read so far."
— *W.M.K., Lansing, Illinois*

" ...the best stories I have read in a long
time."
— *R.H., Northport, New York*

Names available on request.

ROBERTA LEIGH

Collector's Edition

A specially designed collection of six exciting love stories by one of the world's favorite romance writers—Roberta Leigh, author of more than 60 bestselling novels!

1 **Love in Store**
2 **Night of Love**
3 **Flower of the Desert**

4 **The Savage Aristocrat**
5 **The Facts of Love**
6 **Too Young to Love**

Available in August wherever paperback books are sold, or available through Harlequin Reader Service. Simply complete and mail the coupon below.

Harlequin Reader Service

In the U.S.
P.O. Box 52040
Phoenix, AZ 85072-9988

In Canada
649 Ontario Street
Stratford, Ontario N5A 6W2

Please send me the following editions of the Harlequin Roberta Leigh Collector's Editions. I am enclosing my check or money order for $1.95 for each copy ordered, plus 75¢ to cover postage and handling.

☐ 1   ☐ 2   ☐ 3   ☐ 4   ☐ 5   ☐ 6

Number of books checked_____ @ $1.95 each = $_____

N.Y. state and Ariz. residents add appropriate sales tax $_____

Postage and handling · $_____.75_____

                 TOTAL $_____

I enclose_____

(Please send check or money order. We cannot be responsible for cash sent through the mail.) Price subject to change without notice.

NAME_____
                   (Please Print)

ADDRESS_____ APT. NO._____

CITY_____

STATE/PROV._____ZIP/POSTAL CODE_____

Offer expires December 31, 1983   **30656000000**

RL-A